THE INCREDIBLE HULK™

D0725289

By Peter David

THE INCREDIBLE HULK™

Peter David

BALLANTINE BOOKS • NEW YORK

2008 Del Rey Books Mass Market Edition

Published in the United States by Del Rey Books, an imprint of The Random House Publishing Group, a division of Random House, Inc., New York.

DEL REY is a registered trademark and the Del Rey colophon is a trademark of Random House, Inc.

ISBN 978-0-345-50699-3

Printed in the United States of America

www.delreybooks.com

OPM 9 8 7 6 5 4 3 2 1

To Stan and Jack,
the epitomes of "Incredible"

PROLOGUE

It had been in the Arctic.

The haunted man remembered that that was where the story had climaxed. He even remembered the first time he had heard the story, at the knee of his mother reading him the classic original book *Frankenstein,* because she felt the various movie versions had done a pathetic job of conveying the complexity and majesty of the original tale.

He had seen the climactic confrontation so vividly in his mind when she had read it. The writing style had been old-fashioned and formal, but she had made it come alive to him.

He had not consciously thought about that time for many a year. Now he began to realize that his compulsion to go the Arctic might well have had its roots in the story that his mother had read. That was why it had felt . . . right, somehow. It just seemed the natural place for all of it to be brought to a climax.

The trucker who had given him a lift was a heavyset, grizzled bear of a mountain man, with a craggy weathered face that seemed to have as much mileage upon it as he had logged in his trucking career. His name was Don or Dan or something like that; he'd introduced himself when he'd been kind enough to bring his big rig to a halt along the barren road and pick up the haunted man. He'd asked the haunted man his name and naturally the haunted man had lied. It had become a reflex by this point.

The haunted man's face was narrow and angular, although partly obscured by his brown hair, which had grown long, and the thick beard that he was now sporting.

The battered oil truck that the trucker was driving was moving over a high pass on a frozen road, heading down toward a vast expanse of tundra wilderness spread below. They were traveling through the eastern-most coast of Alaska. Mountains and glaciers were in the distance, and the haunted man spotted the distant lapping waves of the Arctic Ocean, or perhaps the Chukchi Sea.

The haunted man tried to take a greater appreciation of his surroundings. The sun was hanging low in the sky, as it would continue to do for quite some time. The terrain was barren, lifeless. It was perfect.

The trucker looked at him in disbelief when he asked to be let out in what was more or less the middle of nowhere.

But then, deep within his parka, the trucker shrugged. He brought the big rig to a slow halt with a hiss of its brakes. The haunted man shouldered his pack and eased open the door. It offered a creak of protest in response but then grudgingly opened enough for him to emerge. He pulled the hood on his parka up with his gloved hands and closed the Velcro fasteners. The wind stung his face, the bitter cold like needles against his skin. He steeled himself against it as best he could. The trucker called to him one more time, asking if he was sure, but the haunted man simply waved good-bye without both-ering to look behind himself. He didn't hear the engine rev up and knew that the driver was just sitting there, watching him through the windshield, puzzling over where he was going and why. The haunted man prayed that the trucker didn't take it upon himself to follow him and demand to know what was really going on with him. For the first time in quite a while, a prayer of his was answered as the truck shifted into gear and the brakes released. The truck rolled, belching fumes, heading away from the haunted man. Long minutes later the truck was a tiny image against the distant road. It was at that point that the haunted man cast one final glance behind himself. He didn't smile. He had no expressions left, no feelings left.

He was dead inside.

He kept walking, approaching the base of some glaciers. There was a maze of ice and rock between him and the plateau, and he made his way through it slowly and steadily.

He could have accomplished his mission anywhere, really. But the Frankenstein parallel was driving him now. He had nothing left except his sense of drama and the belief that the denouement to his situation had to be executed Just So. In an odd way, he found it comforting. It provided a sort of link to his youth, and to happier times.

Partway through the maze, he shrugged off his pack, rooted around within, and removed something from it. He held it up and examined it for a moment. The blue metal of it glinted off the low-lying sun. He unzipped his parka and put the object he'd withdrawn from the pack into his belt, and then zipped the parka back up again. He continued to walk, leaving the pack behind. Anyone observing would have tried to inform him that he was forgetting something. He was not. He simply didn't care about it. Besides, no one was observing.

At least, that was what he told himself.

He was, as it turned out, wrong.

He continued to walk for so long that he lost track of how long he had been traveling. Finally he stopped and looked around. Behind him were ice mountains, and in front of him a green-black, vast body of water. There was not a human to be seen. No sign of life at all, save for an Arctic fox that he caught a glimpse of before it vanished into hiding.

The sky had taken on an eerie look of green and purple. He wasn't sure why. He wasn't far enough north to be seeing the aurora borealis, and besides, that was typically evident only at night. He couldn't determine whether the sky was really taking on that hue, or if he was just seeing it filtered through the prism of his own imagination.

And then it began to happen and **it's there, a banshee shriek of sound, and the woman, the woman is lying on the ground with other bodies strewn around under smashed equipment, but it is hard to see because the room seems alive with sound that is hammering at him and light that is blinding him, there is too much, too much for him to absorb, and a voice is growling in fury and**

He came out of it.

The haunted man wasn't all that surprised to discover that he was on the ground. When the attacks came, they could literally knock his legs out from under him. And they were coming with greater frequency, as if some part of his mind that he would just as soon suppress was trying to burrow its way into his consciousness. He would see things from another perspective, one that threatened to put him into a state of sensory overload, and he could not be entirely certain that he would ever come out of it.

But that was what it had all come down to. He felt as if he had brain cancer, eating away at him until it threatened to remove everything that he had ever been from existence and leave him no longer himself, but instead someone else.

Something else.

He could not, would not allow that.

With a cry of anguish he yanked off his parka and threw it wide. The wind, which had been blowing moderately, now came up fiercely and yanked it away. He fell to his knees, staring forward at nothing.

Frankenstein . . .

The creature in the book had visited murder, mayhem, and destruction upon its creator's family, and its creator had pursued it to the Arctic. There had occurred their great confrontation as the beleaguered and misled scientist had been forced to face the monstrosity that had been the direct result of his wrongheadedness. In the end, Frankenstein had ended up sickened and dead, and the monster—aggrieved that its actions had been responsible for its creator's demise—resolved to take its own life and fled into the icy wilderness, never to be seen again.

So here, now, was the haunted man, in the Arctic, with murder, mayhem, and destruction visited upon his family and friends, on those who had trusted him and loved him.

But there's no convenient separation of man and monster, is there? A choked sob emerged from his throat as his thoughts staggered to their inevitable conclusion and the chill wind stabbed into him like a thousand long knives. *Creator and creation, man and monster, inextricably intertwined. But the result will be the same, has to be the same. Both must die for the blood on their hands: the creation for having performed the crime, and the creator for having enabled it.*

He pulled free from his waistband the object that he had removed from his pack. He was holding it limply so that it pointed down into the snow, but he stared straight ahead. He closed his eyes as if doing so would somehow erase the inner picture from his mind. That would not do it, of course. But the gun would, oh yes, it would.

He had purchased the gun at a pawnshop, where the pawnbroker was perfectly happy to look the other way where gun laws were concerned. It had taken most of the meager cash that the haunted man had on him. The pawnbroker hadn't had any bullets to sell beyond the single bullet that was in the chamber. That was okay. With any luck it wouldn't require more than one bullet.

Frankenstein died of pneumonia. The creature killed itself, most likely drowning. I could just stay out here and let the inevitable exposure to the elements do the job, but the creature had the better idea. Make it quick. Make it final. Let the punishment fit the crime.

His thumb pulled the hammer back. The gun was cocked.

They would never find his body. That was the way he wanted it. Death was so undignified, wasn't it? He didn't want anyone to see him that way. And besides, there were considerations beyond mere dignity. If they did find his body, they would dissect it. They would try to see what made him tick; what made *it* tick. He couldn't allow that. They couldn't get too close because his greatest nightmare was that they would be blind to the dangers they might unleash, despite all the living hell that had already occurred, and would eagerly try to duplicate what had happened to him. Poetic justice aside, connections to Frankenstein aside, a link to the simple pleasures of his childhood when anything seemed possible and life was a vast, unknown, and exciting stretch of empty road ahead of him aside, all of that aside . . . the simple truth was that the monster had to die here, now, with no possible chance of resurrection.

His heartbeat started to race.

He pulled the trigger.

Or tried to.

At first he thought his inability to do so was due to some sort of last-minute decline of nerves. But when he increased his efforts, struggled to pull the trigger and couldn't, he realized it was far more than that. His own hand was fighting him for control of the gun . . . or, more accurately, he realized, something was fighting him for control of his own hand.

He felt a dull thudding in the base of his skull that rapidly spread throughout his entire head until he felt as if his brain were frying. His eyes began to sting.

Standing a few feet away, the snow fox watched with fascination as the new arrival in its territory struggled to depart as unexpectedly as it had come. The gun the human was holding jerked wide, and the snow fox didn't move because it had never seen a gun. Thus it did not perceive any danger to itself. But when the gun went off, the explosion shattering the quiet, the fox jumped three feet in the air from the sound alone. The fox needed no further hints or invitations to depart the area as fast as its four feet would allow it to do.

The haunted man, on his knees, fell forward, and his arm shot out to break his fall. Except it was not his arm any longer. It was huge and massively muscled and green. The hand had a single bullet in its palm, smashed flat from where it had caught the bullet fired from the gun. The other arm was likewise insanely distorted, and the gun itself looked like a child's toy rather than a real firearm. The only evidence of its legitimacy was the faint trail of smoke, wafting from the barrel end, that the wind was carrying away. The green hand folded around the gun. Then the hand opened and the destroyed gun fell away, clunking to the frozen ground, a small lump of metal no longer recognizable as a weapon.

He crouched there on the cliff edge of the glacier shelf.

He had come to the end of the line, to the literal end of the world. But unlike the protagonist created by a long-dead English writer, he had accomplished nothing. Not even his own death.

A roar of fury erupted from him, and it was impossible to tell if it was his own voice decrying his frustration and humiliation, or the primal howl of something else venting its rage over his attempt to destroy it. Either way, the fury manifested itself in a very physical demonstration of violence as the two massive fists slammed down on the ground beneath his feet.

And then the haunted man's consciousness, or at least what was left of it, howled in frustration, because the unfettered anger of the creature had proven its undoing. A huge reverberation spread out from beneath the contact point of his/its gargantuan fists, and the entire section of the glacier upon which he/it was kneeling—a chunk about the size of an aircraft carrier—broke off from the rest. It slid away from the shelf, bobbed in the water for half a heartbeat, and then tumbled roaring into the sea.

Yes! Yes! The haunted man's voice cried out in exultation. The inky green black of the frozen sea enveloped him, massive chunks of greenish white ice surrounding him, and the powerful suction created by the sudden water displacement sucked him down. *I did it! I got you, you son of a bitch, I got you—*

Except he hadn't. He realized that at the last moment before his consciousness departed entirely, to be replaced by that of something else. There was a last, brief flash of *her,* lying there unconscious, later dead, and he longed to join her, but the creature, the monstrosity, the hulking semblance of a man that lurked within him and was now coming to the fore, had other plans. It was something linked to the most primal urges that were hardwired into the survival instinct of humanity. Fight or flight. And the creature didn't know how to flee; instead it fought, and fought well, and this was a fight that it had no intention of losing.

So it was that the haunted man's mind and body vanished entirely. It was a man who had been upon the ice floe as it dislodged, but it was something very different that landed with both feet at the bottom of the ocean, and

the freezing water that would have killed anything remotely human within seconds from the temperature alone merely provides a mild irritation, and everything else about this situation is better, yes, so much better, soothing even, no pain from lights or sounds or people screaming or things crashing down, this is much much MUCH better, but cannot stay here forever, because sooner or later the puny human will find a way back and if that happens down here, it's the end, must walk, one foot in front of the other, and we do not know where we will wind up, but that doesn't matter, only one thing matters, and that one thing is this:

We are the strongest one there is.

THREE
YEARS
LATER

ONE

Bruce Banner ran through the streets of Porto Verde, Brazil, as if the devil himself were trying to catch up with him. For all he knew, the devil indeed was endeavoring to do precisely that. No harm in making that assumption: It kept him prepared for the day when that inevitably did happen.

He was sprinting up the hill through the favela, a shantytown that was perched on hillsides on the outer edges of Porto Verde. There were any number of such ramshackle affairs in Brazil, consisting of mostly one-story buildings thrown together with everything from bricks to garbage, accompanied by the smells that one could naturally expect from such living conditions. Most of the homes were illegal in their construction, unlicensed, unsafe. But the authorities had no stomach for dealing with the favelas and typically chose to ignore them. The inhabitants, endeavoring to scratch out livings in the marketplace or beg money off whoever came near, were effectively nonpeople. That suited Banner just fine.

Banner descended toward the chaos of houses and streets of the city, sprawled like a living organism, teeming with people. He checked something on his wrist. It was a pulse monitor, and it told him that his pulse was currently clocking in at ninety beats per minute. For someone running as hard as he had been, with sweat causing his shirt to cleave to his body like a second skin, that was low indeed. Anyone else working that hard would have been frustrated that his metabolism was responding so lethargically to the amount of effort he was expending.

Banner could not have been happier.

Banner slowed to a walk and made his way through the streets, as anonymous and nondescript as the slum around him. That likewise made him happy.

He stopped at a market stall, a place that sold inexpensive bags at prices that exceeded their value. It was run by a man named Bezerra, a fast-talker who was always eager to earn a few *reais* whenever possible. One of his many means of doing so was providing a drop point for any packages that Banner needed sent to him. When Banner walked past him, Bezerra merely nodded to indicate that he had something for him. Banner pretended to study the assortment of bags Bezerra provided, and then Bezerra produced one from underneath the counter, a small backpack, and proceeded to extol the virtues of its fundamentally shoddy quality. Banner naturally didn't give a damn about the bag's quality, but merely what was inside it. Nevertheless he pretended to listen, nodded, then pulled out a handful of coins—ten *reais*, the standard terms of their deal—and handed them to Bezerra. Bezerra was wearing a floppy white hat and he tipped it to Banner in appreciation of their transaction. Banner felt the weight of the bag, indicating that it did indeed contain something, nodded silently in response, and went on his way.

Banner's apartment building was a rough-and-tumble four-story affair, one of the few block apartment buildings in the tin-roof sprawl of the favela. He entered his shabby, run-down apartment, although it took a minute to navigate the lock that he had installed in the door. Most of the apartments didn't have locks, on the basis that most of the people living there didn't have anything worth stealing.

Banner entered his apartment and slung the bag onto the pathetic excuse for a bed that served him as well as a pathetic excuse for a bed could be expected to. He awoke routinely with a backache, but was hardly in a position to call up a mattress store and have something nice and comfortable delivered. The only other things in the apartment were a tiny refrigerator in which he kept his meager food, a hot plate that was the only means he had of cooking anything, a small black-and-white television on the floor, and a desk that was held together with electrical tape. The desk was positioned in front of the one luxurious item in the apartment: an electrical outlet. Electricity in favelas was always a dicey affair at best. Typically it was being distributed illegally through the enterprising efforts of a building owner who was siphoning it off a legitimate source. Consequently, every so often all the power would go out in Banner's apartment building when the legit source discovered it was being tapped into and shut down the siphon. It would invariably take a couple of days for the owner to find a new source from which to steal. During those times Banner had to be extremely judicious with the use of his computer, since it wasn't possible to recharge the battery.

There was also one other resident of Banner's apartment: a friendly black-and-white mutt that had followed Banner around during one of his excursions looking for junked material that he could cannibalize for his laboratory. The dog had followed him home and had been so nakedly eager for affection that Banner—despite the fact that he really should have—just couldn't bring himself to toss the poor thing out into the street. So whatever meager food supplies Banner had around the house, he shared with the dumb animal.

He crouched and put out his palm. The dog obediently trotted up to him and licked it.

"It's good to see you too, Rick," he said to the dog.

Today the electricity appeared to be flowing just fine. Banner pulled his laptop computer out from its minimalist hiding place under the lumpy mattress. He set it down upon the desk and booted it up. His Internet access was as sketchy as his electricity, very much hit-or-miss depending upon whether his satellite hookup was interested in cooperating. A good day: He was on-line.

He typed: *Mr. Green. Knock knock.* "Mr. Green," of course, referred to himself.

There was a long pause, so long that he was about to shut down his computer to conserve power on the assumption that there would be no response. Then abruptly there came the soft "ping" of acknowledgment and, seconds later, a response came from the respondent who signed himself "Mr. Blue."

Hang on. In laundry hell.

Banner sighed in relief. There were days where he felt as if "Mr. Blue" were his one connection to sanity, and perhaps even salvation. He typed back, *Received your package. Many thanks. The search continues.*

Happy hunting, responded Mr. Blue.

Banner leaned back and ran his fingers through his hair. It felt ratty. He was going to have to grab a shower in the bathroom down the hall. It wasn't one of his favorite things, since the water had a nasty habit of coming out brown, but he didn't really see a choice.

Then his gaze fell upon a photograph that was lying on the desktop. It had been printed off the Web with the aid of a bad color printer, and the edges were curling up from the crappy quality of the paper and the infernal humidity of Brazil. But at least it was something.

He smiled at the picture of Betty Ross. She smiled

back, as she always did, locked into that permanent expression. He tried to tell himself that she had been thinking about him when she had posed for the picture. He was lying to himself, of course, but hey . . . whatever got him through the day. It was a necessary philosophy for someone who was forced to live one day at a time.

He spent the rest of the afternoon and evening as he always did on a Sunday: watching television, eating alone, studying Portuguese, meditating, scratching Rick behind the ears, and doing his damnedest to keep a low profile and remain off everyone's radar.

The ungainly bulk of the bottling factory in which Bruce Banner worked loomed before him. He trudged into the main entrance, indistinguishable on the line from dozens of other laborers. Looking neither right nor left, keeping his vision focused resolutely on the floor in front of him, Banner filed into the men's locker room where he would change into his gray, nondescript work clothes, as well as gloves and goggles. The changing-room walls were filthy, the floor cracked, and illumination was provided by naked bulbs dangling from frayed wires. The place was a fire hazard waiting to happen, and Banner could only pray that he wasn't around when it did.

Four young toughs in particular were being extremely loud this morning, which was not unusual for them . . . especially on a Monday when they had "played" hard over the weekend. Banner hadn't caught all their names, although there was one, Silva, who appeared to be their leader. It was Silva who, in this particular session of horseplay, shoved one of his associates playfully, who in turn bumped into Banner. Banner staggered back and almost fell over before righting himself at the last second. They didn't apologize, but it didn't matter, because he literally didn't react. His face remained utterly impassive. One would have been hard-pressed to determine if, aside from having to recapture his balance, he had even been aware of someone colliding with him.

Banner said nothing as the four swaggered out of the locker room. He pulled on his gloves and noticed that one or two men were looking at him with what seemed like vague contempt . . . undoubtedly because he had not said something to Silva and his pals. Demanded an apology, perhaps, or even tried to start a fight to teach them a lesson. Banner didn't care. He had far bigger problems to worry about. Well . . . one far bigger problem.

He moved out onto the factory floor, an enormous sprawling forest of machinery, festooned with steam pipes and conveyor belts, the former hissing, the latter grinding, all in a huge open floor with a high tin-roof ceiling. A catwalk ran around the perimeter up above and across to the tops of certain of the largest machines.

Officially, Banner spent his days working in the soda bottling plant. His job was rudimentary: carrying supplies of bottle caps or bottles to the workers who manned the massive conveyor belts of bottles moving through the bottling process. The gunk they bottled was called "Amazona." The taste was nothing special—somewhat fruity, really—and the main thing it had going for it was that it was made with guarana, a plant that flowered in the Amazon and provided berries that were said to have three times more caffeine punch than coffee. In fact, the labels on the bottles advertised "With Guarana Kick!" Banner had never tasted it himself. The last thing he needed was obscene amounts of caffeine in his system. For the past five years the only coffee he'd had was decaf; he certainly didn't need something with more power than coffee coursing through his veins. Granted, supposedly guarana didn't cause jitters the way that coffee did, but he wasn't interested in taking the chance . . . even if Brazil was the third-largest consumer of soda in the world, and he was probably the only guy in town who wasn't drinking it.

A pretty young woman smiled at Banner as he delivered to her and he smiled back but kept moving. Her name was Martina, and as it so happened she lived in the same apartment building as Banner. She had been sending out so many signals she might as well have been a telegraph operator. He ignored them all, remaining politely distant. Some days it was more difficult than others, but in such instances, he would always draw upon his training. Both martial arts and yoga stressed balance in all things. As long as he maintained that sense of balance, he would be able to retain his equanimity and never allow himself to make a potentially fatal mistake. He lived a life with no margin for error.

Later that day, his duties took him to the delivery bays. A supply driver whom he knew named Alves was there, getting ready to go on a run. Alves was a man of the same general temperament as Bezerra, willing to do tasks for Banner if the right arrangements could be reached. Banner crooked his finger toward him and Alves, eyebrow raised in curiosity, came over to him.

Banner pulled out a small book from his shirt pocket. It was a book of flowers and Banner flipped it open. "You tend to wander far afield, don't you, Alves?"

Alves shrugged noncommittally. "I go where the routes take me."

"Through the jungles?"

"It's been known to happen."

"And when it happens, do you ever pass bushes that have this particular bud flowering on them?"

He tapped a page in the book. Alves leaned forward, squinting. "I've seen things like them," he said slowly.

Banner shook his head. "They can't be 'like them.' I'm looking for an exact match."

"Can I borrow this?"

Banner carefully tore out the page and handed it to Alves. Alves looked it over, then folded it carefully and placed it in his wallet. He took a moment to tilt the billfold toward Banner. "Kind of empty at the moment."

"Find me the flower and I'll fill it."

Alves grinned lopsidedly, displaying a row of teeth that showed the effects of drinking as much soda as he evidently did. He put out a hand and Banner shook it firmly.

Things were starting to come together.

He was beginning to feel something that he had not felt in three years: optimism. It was frightening that he was feeling it. More than that, the feeling wasn't leaving him. It stayed with him during his self-defense classes. He was training in a discipline called Capoeira—a combination of athletic movements, martial-arts techniques, and combat theory that had its roots in Portuguese slaves. Music pounded through the studio, essential for the practice of Capoeira. In olden times, slaves had hidden their practice of self-defense techniques as mere dance training, and the use of music had remained vital to this day. Banner found that the music in particular helped him to relax while he worked out, and for someone like Bruce Banner, relaxation was of paramount importance. At the moment he was practicing a series of defensive ducking motions called *esquivas,* but he had also become rather proficient at the technique's assorted kicking maneuvers.

At one point his instructor, the Mestre, accidentally scratched Banner's cheek with his fingernail. Banner immediately pulled away and sought out his bag. He extracted from it a small container of Krazy Glue and immediately applied it to his face. It was hardly anything the American Medical Association would approve of, but it was remarkably serviceable. The Mestre just shook his head, used to Banner's odd behavior by now when it came to even the minutest scratch. Banner had explained to him some time ago that it was a psychological compulsion over which he had no control, and the Mestre had been forced to accept that. It was nonsense, of course. Banner was just being careful. He treated his blood with as much caution as anyone would treat any potential nuclear waste.

After his class, he spent the rest of the early evening poking through the favela's alleyways, sorting through trash and discarded junk, searching for the objects required to build the device that thus far existed only in his head. This particular evening he had found a bicycle wheel that was only slightly bent at the rim; he was relatively certain that he could straighten it out so that it would be usable for his purposes. In the dim light, he nearly missed a superb find: an old record player. He had desperately been hoping to find one. Even in a poor favela, CD players had largely taken over, so stumbling upon a classic phonograph in even remotely usable condition had seemed unlikely.

Maybe things were finally starting to fall his way.

Once having returned to his apartment, he began to assemble the junk into the shape that he was carrying within his head. The sun had set by that point and darkness enveloped the room, fought back only by the single bare bulb overhead. It didn't matter; Banner was operating with something far more than sight. No one in the favela would have recognized the device he was fashioning for what it was: an extremely crude, but perfectly serviceable, centrifuge. It joined the other elements of a homemade lab that he was keeping secreted under his bed. He doubted that, even if someone broke into his apartment and stole it, it would be of much use to them. Then again, it had been his experience that some people would steal anything that was not nailed down.

Right before bed, when he had worked so hard and so long that he was nearly exhausted, he always took the time to engage in meditation. He found that it lessened the chances of bad dreams. Nightmares were among his greatest concerns, because he was terrified at the prospect of losing control while he was asleep and unable to do anything about it.

And in this self-induced trance,

there are bright lights, accelerating right toward us, and a horn honking, so loud and so infuriating, it's almost more than we can take, and

Bruce Banner's pulse began to climb, up to eighty-five.

He used his breathing techniques and forced his pulse to slow. *Steady . . . steady . . .* he told himself. *It was long ago . . . far away . . . it cannot hurt you . . . there is no past . . . no future . . . you cannot change the past, you cannot control the future . . . there is only the present, and that you can control . . .*

It took long minutes, but his pulse eventually dropped to a slow, steady thirty-seven. He drifted in his meditation, and felt content, and the sense of optimism stayed with him.

It told him that anything was possible, and that all might well end happily.

It lied.

But he did not know that yet.

TWO

The manager at the bottling plant was named Marcos de Souza, and it was moments such as this one that the man who simply went by "David" was a complete mystery to him.

Marcos had had a problem with the machine that poured the soda directly into the bottles. The one damned mechanic in the whole damned factory had decided to call in sick, which meant that he was out gambling in some section of the slum and couldn't be bothered to come into work. He'd return soon enough, when he was out of money, but in the meantime production was going to fall behind, and it was going to be Marcos de Souza's head on the block for it.

So he had gone to the one man that he knew might be able to help him out in this situation, and David had been happy to oblige. Marcos watched in fascination as David removed the back from the control box and reworked the wiring. His long fingers moved with practiced dexterity, interweaving the fraying wires with the same confidence that a woman would perform knitting. He paused only once to wipe away sweat from his forehead, and then he reached around and pushed the On button. The conveyor belt, which had ground to a halt, shuddered once and then started to roll forward, slowly at first and then with its customary speed. Several workers applauded sarcastically: they got paid whether the belt moved or not, and had enjoyed the break that the broken conveyor was providing them until the annoying American had fixed it. De Souza, however, made no attempt to hide his pleasure.

As David closed the back of the control box, de Souza sauntered over to him. He spoke slowly, because he knew that David was still only learning Portuguese, and if he spoke up to full speed David would understand maybe one word in four. "Five months you've been helping me out like this. Cut this day-labor crap and let me put you on payroll as my mechanic. I can pay you what you're worth."

David, as always, smiled and shook his head. He started to turn the key in the back of the control box to seal it and, as he did so, de Souza clapped him on the back. It was intended to be merely a friendly gesture, but since it was unexpected, David's hand slid forward. The edge of the control box was sharp and his thumb slid across it, slicing it open.

De Souza didn't see the minor accident, and even if he had, he wouldn't have understood what the big deal was. But David was instantly galvanized into action. His gaze fixed on the bottles below, he started shouting, "Stop the belt! Stop the conveyor belt!" even as he clambered down toward it.

For some God-unknown reason, the freaking moron who had designed the conveyor belt had placed the emergency shutoff button at the opposite end of the catwalk from the on button. So as David quickly made his way down to the factory floor, de Souza sprinted down the catwalk as fast as his short legs would take him.

De Souza got to the emergency shutoff button, flipped open the cover, and punched it. The conveyor belt, which had only just started up, slowly ground to a halt. Then de Souza ran back down the catwalk, trying to find where in the world David had gotten off to. He finally found him about thirty feet down the conveyor belt with a look of relief on his face. "What the hell happened?" shouted de Souza.

"Just some of my blood," David called up to him. He had a cloth out and he was meticulously wiping down a small section of the conveyor belt onto which his blood had apparently dripped. "Got to clean it up."

"What? Why? What's the problem?"

"It's just . . . I figure you can't be too sanitary, you know?"

"Okay. Sure," said de Souza, who wasn't all that sure. The only thing he knew with any certainty was that David was definitely an odd one. But as long as he continued to be as useful around the plant as he was, de Souza was content to overlook those oddities.

As it happened, de Souza also overlooked something else: a bottle with drops of blood dripping just inside the glass lip, down into the soda. Since the soda was already tinted green because of the lime content, it was easy to miss. David didn't notice it either, and so gave de Souza the "okay" signal. Marcos de Souza nodded, message received, and he started up the belt once more. David applied Krazy Glue to the cut as he customarily did, while a polluted bottle of Amazona soda glided away on the belt.

Banner returned to his apartment with mounting enthusiasm. His homemade laboratory had been taking shape very nicely. He had recently salvaged a discarded table during one of his rummaging runs and had transformed it into a makeshift lab table. Eager to get to work, he placed the recently acquired bundle on the lab table. Then he brought his computer online and prayed that his satellite link would be functional today, especially considering that the past two days had been frustrating sessions with insufferably slow or nonexistent feeds. However, the Internet gods chose to be generous, as the linkup was not only immediate, but instant messages promptly began to come through.

Mr. Green . . . hello.

Bruce sat down and promptly typed in, *Success.*

Hallelujah. It's a lovely little plant, isn't it?

Yes.

And you have my notes on derivation of the inhibitor?

Yes.

For most cellular exposures a concentration of 50-80 parts per million will suffice. Keep me posted. And good luck. For good measure he added a ":)" emoticon.

Banner had to smile. Here was an individual of Mr. Blue's obvious brilliance, and the message ended with a sideways smile as might be displayed by the average teenage girl. Banner continued to chuckle even as he threw himself into his work.

Over the succeeding hours Banner worked to extract the necessary compound from the flowers. He quite literally lost track of time. By the time he was finished, he mentally patted himself on the back, because he had originally estimated that the job would take at least five hours, and here he had accomplished it in a mere two. Then he glanced at his watch and his jaw dropped upon his discovering that he had, in fact, worked for five hours as originally estimated; it just seemed like two. Dawn was only a few hours away. Then he smiled grimly: Dawn would be coming up on a brand-new day for him.

Preparing for the final step in the process, he took a small needle and pricked his finger. Because of his perpetual paranoia about his blood being spilled, he practically had to fight his own body's instinct in order to jab the needle into his outstretched finger, and he held his breath the entire time. A single drop of blood welled up on his fingertip and he carefully placed the drop on a glass microscope slide. He slid it under his microscope and adjusted the lens to study it. For half a moment he allowed himself to hope that he would discover that his blood had magically, miraculously transformed to normal by itself. Why not? Stranger things had happened that medical science had no explanation for. Cancer had been known to inexplicably reverse itself. Hell, even fervent prayer was accorded considerable power in some circles. He hadn't been praying especially hard, but perhaps God had decided to cut him a break as sort of an incentive.

Nope. No such luck.

Even after all this time, it was still an unsettling image to gaze upon: his red blood cells fringed with a subtle glowing green energy, like residual radiation.

"Okay. We do it the hard way," he muttered as he pulled the slide out from under the microscope. He took a deep breath and let it out slowly. This was it.

It had taken him nearly the entire night to extract enough purplish liquid from the flowers to fill the bottom of a very small glass. Now he used an eyedropper to extract a minuscule amount in the glass, carefully brought it over to the blood sample, and then squeezed out one, two, three drops onto it. Then he let out a slow breath, abruptly realizing that he'd been holding it. He picked up the slide, trying not to let his hand tremble, and placed it under the microscope. He made a slight adjustment in the lens and looked through once more, knowing that he was going to be seeing the shape of the future when he peered through.

His heart sank.

The purple liquid seemed to be boiling away around the cells. Frying. *Fight back. Fight back, dammit,* he silently begged the flower extract, but his pleadings were in vain. It took thirty-five seconds for the purple liquid to burn away completely, leaving the green tinge firmly in place.

He moaned. His dog, Rick, sensing his master's upset, whimpered sympathetically and rubbed his head against Banner's leg. The sentiment was appreciated but wasn't especially useful.

In his demented imaginings, he could swear he heard his own blood laughing at him. Saying, *Is that all you've got? A flower? A freaking flower? Figures the pansy would use a flower.* And then it laughed loud and long, the winner and still champion, before it faded away into the outer reaches of his subconscious.

Banner pulled back from the scope and put his forehead against the heel of his hand. He tried not to allow himself to succumb to total despair, but it wasn't easy. He wanted to crawl into a corner. He wanted to curl up into a ball. He wanted to die . . .

Don't bother. You know how that will turn out. Been there . . . done that . . . bought the attempted-suicide T-shirt . . .

No. The only path that he could pursue was to treat this as nothing different from any other scientific setback. He had to depersonalize it rather than consider it some overwhelming personal catastrophe. Otherwise he would, quite simply, go out of his mind.

With a herculean effort of will, he pushed himself back from his desk, shifted his attention over to his computer, and began to type. *No mitigation,* he wrote. He sat back and waited, unsure of whether Mr. Blue would be at or nearby the computer at this time considering the hour.

He should have known better.

None? Mr. Blue's reply came. *Your tissue exposure must be relatively high.*

Banner refrained from typing "No shit," and instead settled for the more restrained, *Very high.*

Try a higher concentration. Slightly. 100 parts per million = lethal toxicity.

Banner glanced over at the pathetically wilted flowers. There was no point even thinking about it. He had milked them for all they had.

Impossible at present. Supply is limited.

Not here. We're making pure synthetic by the gallon. There was a pause. Rather than immediately respond, something compelled Banner to wait. He had a feeling that Mr. Blue was thinking. He turned out to be correct, as, after a few moments, more words appeared on his screen: *Why are we doing this backward? Chasing flowers in the jungle = silly. Send me a blood sample.*

Not prudent.

Living with gamma poisoning not prudent. Most people not alive long enough to be helped. Intrigued by your case.

Banner considered it, but ultimately couldn't shake off the security concerns. What was the old line? Just because you're paranoid doesn't mean they're not out to get you.

Not safe for either of us, Banner typed.

You need help. Gamma not something to mess with.

"You can say that again," said Banner.

He needed to get some sleep, but he was incredibly agitated, his mind racing a mile a minute. Banner decided the only option he had at this point was to engage in meditation. It might enable him to settle down for at least a few hours.

Banner lay down on his bed and crisscrossed his arms across his chest. He slowed his breathing, finding his focus . . .

His mind started to drift . . .

Betty . . .

Betty, seated at a lab table and smiling, and she is lying on the campus lawn and

smiling and her lips are pressed against ours, they taste so sweet, the taste of them still lingers, and now she is lying in a hospital bed, bruised and scarred, and there is a military man, a general, Banner knows his face, knows this man, and he is saying things to us, and we recoil in fury, and it is all we can do not to lash out at him, and instead we run, but we do not want to run, we want to lash out and smash him, smash them all . . .

Banner's pulse was climbing. It hit eighty-five, kept on going to ninety. Somewhere deep within his tortured mind, he sensed it, and tried to fight it. He needed to find his calm center, and he ran the images backward through his mind as if reversing a DVD at high speed.

Betty smiles up from the lawn . . .

If he were Peter Pan, he would refer to it as his Happy Thought. Except it didn't enable him to fly; instead it served to ground him. Slowly, gradually, his pulse rate dropped to thirty-seven.

Bruce came out of his self-induced trance, blinking feverishly in the darkness. Only a few stray beams of moonlight were filtering through the window, and they fell upon the dead flowers that he had left piled on his work area. He stared at them long and hard, out of options.

He realized that Mr. Blue was right. He could not assume that he would be able to remain in Brazil forever. If he was going to have any prayer at all of obtaining a cure, he was going to have to take a chance or two. And more important, it was the only hope he would ever have of putting his life together again. Of putting his life *with her* back together again.

He went over to his lab table and, within a few minutes, had used a hypodermic to extract a vial of his own blood. He inserted the stopper, making certain that it was in securely, and then labeled the vial "Mr. Green."

He packed it up as well as he could. It was, after all, fragile, and it was going to have to be able to survive the occasionally less-than-gentle package handling that the locals were going to subject it to. He would bring it to his friend, Bezerra, who would in turn make certain that it went on its way. It wasn't something he was doing lightly, but Banner really didn't see much choice anymore.

No choice at all.

THREE

Eight-year-old James Ferguson, aka Jimmy, aka Jimbo (a nickname he despised), knew his way around the kitchen of his Milwaukee, Wisconsin, home with an expertise that rivaled his mother's. Indeed, anytime she couldn't locate something, she would ask Jimmy, who in turn would be able to find it in short order.

He moved back and forth from the counter and fridge to the table, using a step stool to get what he needed, arranging a little setting with napkin and silverware and plate. His mother worked nights and tried her level best to be available for Jimmy and his brother during the week, and weekends were the only time she had the opportunity to catch up on her sleep. So Jimmy had become accustomed to being self-reliant when it came to making lunch for himself on Saturdays. He felt it was the least he could do, and as his rarely seen father was fond of saying, "I always try to do the least I can do."

He had made a peanut butter and jelly sandwich for himself just the way he liked it, with the peanut butter smeared on thick and the jelly oozing out the sides. He deftly bisected it with a butter knife, and then added a piece of cheese and a few carrot sticks. A small green apple and a handful of potato chips completed the remaining two essential food groups, at least insofar as Jimmy was concerned.

For the crowning touch, he withdrew a bottle of lime-green Amazona soda from the fridge. He took his seat, popped the top, and set it by his glass.

Jimmy took a bite of his sandwich, sighed with satisfaction, and then poured himself some of the green soda in his glass. He took another bite of his sandwich and then moved to wash it down with a mouthful of the soda.

That was the moment that his older brother chose to burst in along with two of his idiot pals. His brother's name was Timothy. "Timothy" and "James" of course sounded nothing alike, but thanks to the vagaries of nicknames, they were forever referred to as Timmy and Jimmy, a reality about which Jimmy felt indifference but which seemed to piss off Timmy no end.

Timmy never failed to find a reason to torment his brother, partly because he felt resentment over the fact that they were "joined at the name," but mostly because he simply could. Timmy zeroed in on Jimmy's lunch, grabbing the sandwich off the plate and snatching the soda right out of his hand. He slugged back the soda and smacked his lips. "Ahhh. Thanks, Jimbo," said Timmy, using the despised nickname because, again, he could.

"Timmy, don't!" said Jimmy in protest.

He grabbed for his sandwich but his brother yanked it just out of his reach and chomped into it. Meantime his pals swiped the cheese and veggies off Jimmy's plate, leaving only the apple and chips. He looked down at his decimated lunch and then one of them grabbed the remainder of the food off the plate.

Jimmy felt tears welling up in his eyes, and he wanted to do anything except let the older boys see him start sobbing like a baby. Nevertheless, despite his best efforts, his eyes stung with frustration over his stolen food and his humiliating sense of helplessness.

All of this welled up in protest within him. His eyes

narrowing, his face flushed with the sort of pure hatred that only an outraged younger brother can summon, Jimmy snarled, "I hope you choke on it!"

Timmy started to laugh, and then suddenly his body began to tremble uncontrollably. At first Jimmy thought that his brother was just messing around. But then his eyes rolled up into his head, which had to be the single most terrifying thing Jimmy had ever seen, expelling from his mind any notion that Timmy was trying to pull yet another joke on him. Timmy's hands, rather than going loose, gripped tightly onto the glass even as Timmy's legs collapsed beneath him. Timmy hit the ground, making an awful sound like a sack of wet cement.

"Timmy?" said his younger brother tentatively.

Timmy never stopped moving. Not only was his body racked with spasms, but also the most chilling thing was that it was happening in total silence. He wasn't crying out, wasn't calling for help. It was as if his mind had completely shut down and something awful, something evil had invaded his body.

The older boys merely stared in stunned horror. The faster-thinking Jimmy was the one who ran to the kitchen door and screamed at the top of his lungs, *"Mommmmmm!"*

"And here's something a little more interesting. Possible gamma sickness. Milwaukee. A kid drank one of those guarana sodas. Had more kick than he was looking for."

General Thaddeus "Thunderbolt" Ross wasn't feeling particularly optimistic about the report. Nevertheless he took the two-page fax from the hand of his aide, Major Kathleen Sparr. Sparr was tall and wiry, with an angular, intelligent-looking face and straight brown hair. In point of fact, she was rather attractive . . . not that Ross ever noticed.

He had been lost in thought when Sparr had entered, so much so that initially he hadn't even heard her. His mind had traveled to a day three years ago, when an unconscious young woman was lying in a room in a hospital bed and he had been trying to talk sense into a shaken, recalcitrant, and ultimately cowardly scientist.

Ross could still see, as if it were yesterday, the scientist pulling away from him, sprinting down the hospital corridor, out the double doors at the end. It had been Ross's original sin to fail to secure the exits. In his stupidity and blindness, it had simply never occurred to him that the scientist would flee. By the time Ross had pulled his wits about him and ordered pursuit, the scientist had vanished and had yet to stop running.

Sparr had jolted Ross from his reverie, placing an assortment of staggeringly dull forms in front of him that required his signature. He had affixed his name to each one, displaying very little interest as he signed them. Then Sparr had brought the Milwaukee incident to his attention.

"Last three were irradiated fruit, not gamma . . ." he started to say.

"Look at the spectrograph in that path report," she said, tapping the fax. "Even the FDA didn't approve that. Whatever it was, it was concentrated. Got less than a tenth of a milliliter and it almost killed him."

His eyes narrowed and he drummed his fingers thoughtfully on the desk. Then he handed her back the fax pages. "Get it confirmed."

"Already put calls in."

She started out but he called out to her, his mind truly coming alive for the first time in weeks. "Where was it bottled?"

"Porto Verde, Brazil . . ."

The wheels were turning faster now as Ross started to make associations, pulling threads together. He could tell that Sparr was doing the exact same thing. "Remember that package we tracked to the girl that just had seeds in it?" said Ross. "Year and a half ago maybe . . . ?"

"Orchid seeds," she nodded. "It came from São Paolo."

Ross snapped alive. São Paolo was the capital of Brazil. It could be a coincidence, a wild coincidence. But every instinct told him that it was far from that. "Get our Agency people looking for a white man at the bottling plant. Tell them no contact, if he even sees them he's gone." She nodded and hurried for the door, and just before she departed, Ross shouted, "And get me Joe Greller!"

Kirtland Air Force Base was situated in Albuquerque, New Mexico, nestled between the Sandia and Manzano mountain ranges. It was home to, among other things, the 109th Special Operations wing. As the sun settled into the horizon, a transport van pulled up, discharging two Special Forces soldiers armed with light gear. They joined three other commandos gathered by the tarmac. A couple of them had worked together, and the rest had a passing acquaintance with one another. They greeted each other, exchanging introductions in a cursory, straightforward fashion. If they had been hanging about the PX or in a bar, they would have been as relaxed and gregarious as anyone else. Here, at the beginning of a mission, they were all business: polite but formal.

"Who's our sixth?" said Craig Saunders, tall and powerfully built with cold eyes that had earned him the nickname of "Shark" in some quarters.

"Blonsky," said Samuel LaRoquette, the oldest and most experienced of the immediate group.

Saunders looked at Armand Martel, with whom he had arrived. Martel tended to speak very little, and had been known to smile only when he was in a firefight. "Never worked with him," said Saunders. "Rookie?"

Martel glanced toward the others. No one wanted to respond immediately, perhaps uncertain of just what, or how much, they should say. LaRoquette took it upon himself to respond: "When Blonsky was a rookie you were still pooping your pants. You seen him since Tora Bora?" The question had been addressed to the rest of the squad. There was silent negative shaking of heads all around. "Right." As if that lack of knowledge said it all, LaRoquette told Saunders, "You haven't worked with him 'cause there's no room in the cave he operates out of for you or anybody else."

Anything else LaRoquette might have had to say on the matter was cut short by the approach of a helicopter. They stood and watched its descent. None of them flinched from the rotors as the chopper settled onto the tarmac. The side door slid open and a commanding presence emerged from the helicopter, bounding to the tarmac before the chopper had even fully settled in.

He moved to join the others. There were greetings exchanged among them that were even more curt than they had been before. The atmosphere had changed with Emil Blonsky's arrival. The rest of them knew it, and if Blonsky was aware, he simply chose not to give any sign.

He wasn't particularly tall, nor did he look especially muscular. His face was long and not all that memorable, which was just the way he liked it. A Special Forces operative didn't need to be someone who made an impression, unless it was in the way they moved and fought and killed. In that regard, Blonsky was first among equals.

"So," said LaRoquette, "do you know what the deal is, Blonsky?"

Blonsky didn't even bother to shake his head. All he said was "Doesn't matter to me. Long as someone tells me where to go and who to shoot, it's all good."

He smiled. It was not a pleasant thing to see.

Ross strode out of the operations building alongside his old friend General Joseph Greller. Greller and Ross were a study in contrast. Ross was built like a walking bulldog, with a bristling mustache and a very much nonregulation cigar perpetually being chomped between his teeth. Greller, several years Ross's senior, was tall and lanky, and walked with a fluid motion that betrayed his long history of martial-arts training. They were also opposites in terms of temperament: Greller quiet, reserved, and thoughtful, Ross blustering and with a short, stormy temper that had earned him the nickname "Thunderbolt," a moniker he had readily and happily embraced. He liked the Zeus-like connotations of it.

"I would try to talk you out of risking yourself in the field, but I know I'd just be wasting my breath. So I got who I could to serve under you," said Greller. "Short notice but they're all quality." He handed Ross the personnel files. "I pulled you one ace. You'll figure out who."

"I know you cashed some chips for this, Joe. I'm grateful."

"Glad to do it. Just make it good."

They shook hands and then Ross turned and headed for the waiting C-103 transport plane. Ross, Sparr, a medical officer, and the team mustered into the plane as the engines wound up. Ross liked what he saw initially in the deployment and operation: There was no delay, no looseness. The team was tight and frosty; he could see that immediately. In less than a minute of their boarding the transport, the C-103 was lumbering down the runway. Then it picked up speed, the engines roaring with power, and soon it was airborne and hurtling into the twilight sky.

Seated in the rear of the plane, the commandos watched the two senior officers huddled toward the front. The general was on the phone, talking to God-knew-who, and the major was taking notes based upon things that he was muttering to her.

"Since when do they fob us off to logistics officers?" said Saunders.

LaRoquette snorted derisively. "Ain't exactly feeling A-Team, is it?"

Blonsky said nothing. He simply sat there, unreadable. If one weren't looking right at him, one might not even realize that he was there. LaRoquette wondered mirthlessly if Blonsky didn't have some sort of ninja training or something.

Major Sparr came toward them then, a manila folder in her hand. She took a seat opposite them and distributed photographs. LaRoquette stared at the image of the man on the photo. Didn't look like much. Probably some spy or weasel with spook information rattling around in his head that the government wanted to make certain didn't get sold to the wrong hands. There were other photos of a building that LaRoquette took to be his apartment building and the surrounding area.

"This is the target and the location," said Sparr. "Snatch-and-grab only, live capture. You'll have dart clips and suppression ordnance. Live fire for backup only. We've got help from local but we want it tight and quiet."

Saunders needled gently, "Little excitement, huh, Major?"

Sparr stared at him. She seemed not to understand what he was referring to, but it was clear to LaRoquette that she, in fact, did comprehend even as she said, "How's that?"

"Good to get out from behind that desk?"

She nodded and, in so doing, confirmed to LaRoquette that she was not only unsurprised by the question but, in fact, ready for it. "I worked intel for Third ID on the way in to Baghdad my first tour. I got bumped to you Rangers in time for Falluja." She glanced at papers in her files as if she needed to check something that she obviously already knew to be a fact. "Says here me and Blonsky got our Purple Hearts same week." She looked back at Saunders, her gaze boring into him. "So no, I'd very much like to get back to my office, thanks. Only way this'll get exciting," she continued, raising her voice to take in the lot of them, "is if you guys screw it up. Any more questions?" she concluded with a tone that suggested questions would not, in fact, be welcome.

"No more stupid ones," said LaRoquette under his breath.

General Ross had come over and stepped in behind Sparr. LaRoquette didn't know if he'd heard the tail end of the conversation, and found himself hoping that he hadn't. This was a hell of a thing: a group of seasoned commandos, and they'd just lost their opening skirmish without a shot being fired, and to a paper-pushing major no less.

Blonsky didn't appear to care about the exchange that had just transpired. "Is he a fighter?" he said, tapping the subject's photograph.

"Your target," said Ross, "is a fugitive from the U.S. government who stole military secrets. Don't wait to see if he's a fighter. Put him to sleep."

Blonsky nodded noncommittally. LaRoquette hoped that Blonsky understood what "Don't wait to see" meant. It had been LaRoquette's experience that Blonsky not only didn't shy away from fights, but in fact welcomed them. He was a walking, talking loose cannon. The brass adored him because he got the job done, but he tended to make his teammates nervous. He certainly made LaRoquette nervous.

"Each team will be issued a radiation sensor that we will monitor remotely as well," said Ross. "First blip, I want to know about it."

Radiation? LaRoquette did not love the sound of that. "This guy steal plutonium?"

"Something like that," said Ross. They waited for further clarification. None was forthcoming. Instead the general said briskly, "That's all," and returned to the front of the plane. Sparr trailed behind him, although she tossed a glance over her shoulder at the commandos.

"Why'd Greller stick us with this guy?" said Saunders in a low voice, eyeing Ross to make sure he wasn't hearing.

Blonsky shrugged, studying Banner.

LaRoquette wasn't really big on trading tidbits of gossip, but in this instance he didn't see any way around it . . . or any harm, for that matter. "Ross was his CO in 'Nam," said LaRoquette. "Green Berets."

"No shit," said Saunders.

"I heard he ran R&D, real black-box stuff," said LaRoquette, lowering his voice further even though he had no reason to think that either Sparr or Ross was listening in. "One of his experiments blew up in his face, literally. They gave him a desk to run."

As one, the commandos looked at Ross and Sparr. They were deep in discussion over the coming mission, going over the personnel files, and Sparr's words floated back to them: "Blonsky's your point man."

All eyes swiveled back to Blonsky. He didn't react, but LaRoquette could tell the bastard was smiling inwardly.

A routine snatch-and-grab. LaRoquette couldn't help but notice that the routine missions were the ones that tended to go haywire, typically because the powers that be had some particularly important piece of information that they declined to share for any one of a hundred stupid reasons.

He wondered what the salient piece of information Ross and Sparr were withholding might be, and hoped that whatever it was, it didn't get him killed in this supposedly routine outing.

FOUR

The bottling company worked hard to keep its workers happy, since happy workers were by definition more productive. This didn't extend to providing them such perks as, for instance, coffee breaks. That did not mean, however, that they couldn't afford to show some meager degree of generosity. At that particular moment, the generosity consisted of Bruce Banner pushing a cart loaded with little bags of snacks—pretzels, nuts, and so on. He went from station to station, fulfilling one of his daily chores. The workers were always happy to see him. Here was a white-skinned American—considered by many of them to be the most privileged creatures in the world—pushing around a snack cart for their convenience. Initially they had needled him about it, but he had accepted their gibes with such good humor that, for the most part, they had warmed up to him. There were a few who still treated Banner with open contempt. Banner tended to keep his distance from them. He wasn't looking for trouble, and he very much suspected that they were definitely not looking for the type of trouble they would find from him.

Unfortunately, on this particular day, Banner's knack for keeping out of situations involving some of his detractors wasn't quite possible to maintain.

As he came around a bottling machine, he saw that a group of toughs—the same ones who had a tendency to "accidentally" collide with him in the locker room—

were hassling young Martina, his downstairs neighbor. Typically they worked on the loading dock, hauling crates, but obviously they had decided to take a break and this was their idea of recreation. They were teasing her, blocking her from sitting back down at her station while Silva showed a distinct inability to take "no" for an answer.

"Why do you act so shy? C'mon, it's Friday night. It's not a sin to have some fun in life."

Her eyes met Banner's; she needed help. He hesitated, torn. He really couldn't risk getting involved. But then Silva tried to stroke her cheek while continuing to mutter what he no doubt thought were clever, even seductive come-ons. She shoved his hand away and told him in no uncertain terms to get the hell away from her. Silva's face darkened, and his forced smile vanished. Banner saw the beast within Silva bubbling to the surface, even as Silva grabbed her arm. "What are you, too good for us?" he said with a snarl.

Every single day was a challenge for Bruce Banner to live a normal, quiet life. He realized at that moment, though, that there was more than just trying to live. There was the issue of being able to live with oneself.

He stepped around the cart, a pleasant smile fixed upon his face as if it had been plastered there. "Everything good?"

They all turned. Martina's eyes silently pleaded for his intervention. Silva was anything but silent. He barely afforded Banner a contemptuous glance. "Dump your load and get lost, mule. We're talking."

You're talking. She's not listening. Figuring that his intent was to defuse the situation rather than exacerbate it, he said in as neutral a voice as he could, "You want some coffee, Martina? With me?" He spoke in Portuguese, slowly and haltingly, but understandable.

She nodded immediately, but Silva wasn't even looking at her. Instead he started to advance on Banner as his three pals stepped in behind him to display unity. "I said beat it. You want a problem?"

Banner backed up. If he was going to wind up in a fight, it wasn't going to be because he didn't make every effort to avoid it. "No problem."

"Too late."

He shoved Banner in the chest, hard. Banner moved with it, bending like a willow tree in the breeze, so that it didn't come close to knocking him over. But the situation was quickly deteriorating as Silva's friends moved to surround him. Martina was screaming at them, telling them to back off. She didn't realize, as Banner did, that matters had moved on without her. This was no longer about her. It was about Banner daring to tell Silva and his pals that they couldn't do whatever they wanted to whomever they wanted.

Banner glanced at his pulse monitor. It had jumped to seventy-five. *Wonderful. This day was going so well. How did it go downhill this quickly?*

He held up his hands and said slowly, still in Portuguese, "Okay, listen. Don't make me angry. You wouldn't like me when . . ."

Then he stopped, because they were frowning at him in confusion. He hadn't been certain what sort of reaction he was expecting when issuing the threat, but it certainly wasn't bewilderment. Then he reviewed the words that he had spoken in Portuguese through his head: *Não me faça com fome. Don't make me hungry.* "No, wait. That's not right . . . ah, shit . . ."

The profanity came not only from his being flustered over his bilingual gaffe, but also from the fact that Silva was taking a swing at him. It was slow and ponderous and probably could have been lethal if Silva was going up against what Banner imagined to be his typical opponent, namely some drunk in a bar. Banner, however, was stone-cold sober, and so he had no problem dodging it. As it happened, he did more than that. He twisted in such a way that Silva overbalanced himself, stumbled, and fell.

Silva was clearly astonished. Banner was only slightly less so. It was one thing taking lessons in a class, in a controlled situation. In the back of his mind, he had always wondered if they would actually work in real-life situations. Apparently it seemed the answer was yes.

Getting to his feet, obviously aware of the surprised looks on his friends' faces and believing that his very masculinity was at stake, the thoroughly pissed Silva wiped his hands and then clenched them into fists. Not screwing around, he came at Banner fast, taking a different, more boxing-oriented approach. Unfortunately for Silva, he didn't have any more luck with a more focused approach than he'd had moments earlier. Banner effortlessly dodged, ducked, weaved, not having to lay so much as a finger on Silva while causing him to flail about helplessly. Silva looked more and more foolish with every thrust that came nowhere near to connecting.

"Stand still, dammit!"

Banner was disinclined to accommodate him. Silva's shouts continued, rebounding through the factory and carrying to the upper catwalks, where they attracted de Souza's attention. The manager bellowed down to Silva and his buddies, "Hey! Cut it out! I got supplies sitting here collecting bugs! You want me to hire somebody else to move it? *Now!*"

Silva looked as if he was seriously considering whether it would be worth losing his job just so that he could continue to have a go at Banner. His friends muttered to him in Portuguese so rapid that Banner couldn't determine what they'd said. The specifics didn't matter, though; the general sense of it was clear enough. Silva placed a finger under each of his eyes and then pointed them at Banner in the universal gesture that conveyed that Banner was now firmly on his radar. The show was not over. It had only taken a brief intermission. They walked away then, with Silva's friends patting him on the shoulder, laughing, and congratulating him on showing the puny American who was in charge. In a few short sentences they rewrote the events of the past seconds so that Silva had Banner on the ropes. Only the intervention of de Souza had prevented Silva from completing the beating that the American so richly deserved.

Banner never failed to be staggered by the capacity that humans had for denial. He had seen it firsthand any number of times. He was moved to wonder whether he was any more above it than any of his fellow mortals. *After all, you keep telling yourself that a cure is possible. Maybe you're kidding yourself as much as Silva and his pals are. The fight you're in isn't all that much different. You keep swinging away at your enemy, taking your best shot, and you have yet to land a single real blow. It might be that Silva and you have far more in common than you'd care to admit.*

Martina was untroubled with the deep musings that plagued Banner. She was busy thanking him profusely. She also seemed to think, if Banner was any judge by the looks that she was giving him, that his acting so gallantly on her behalf was the beginning of something. Banner knew otherwise. He was quite certain that the only thing it was the beginning of was the end: the end of the life that he had created there. After five years of running, hiding, running again, he had developed a fairly reliable instinct for that sort of thing.

That evening he lay on the rough bed in his apartment, staring up at the ceiling. Martina downstairs had run into him by "accident" in front of the building and invited him to her place for a nightcap. He had politely declined. The disappointment in her face was clear, but a dalliance with Martina was simply not something he could afford. It would not be fair to her, or even safe for her. He needed to keep, at the very least, an emotional distance from her for both their sakes.

The neighbor's dog was barking as usual. Banner ignored it, which was not an easy endeavor, but he had forced himself to become used to it. Then he heard a sound that, in contrast to the dog's incessant barking, was simple, short, and clear: a chiming from his open computer that informed him someone was trying to instant-message him. There was only one person that could be.

He rolled off the bed and dropped into the seat at the desk. Rick the dog was roused briefly from its slumber and looked with mild irritation at Banner before settling back down to sleep. Banner tapped the Accept button and stared in disbelief at the word that appeared on the screen.

Success.

He wanted to jump up and scream in exultation. He wanted to pump his fist in the air like some triumphant sports fan whose team had just won a championship. But he reined in his impulse to celebrate, because there had simply been too many disappointments in his life for him to allow himself to feel anything short of controlled scientific interest. He brought his fingers over the keypad and realized they were trembling. He took a long breath, let it out, and typed as neutral a response as he could manage.

Please elaborate.

Mr. Blue promptly did so. *Concentration of 150ppm mitigates the gamma saturation in your sample. Incredible toxicity but it works.*

He had been dreaming of hearing this news for five

years, but still he did not allow himself to feel any enthusiasm for it. Even more confounding, he thought he sensed, just for a moment, something angry stirring within him. He had been sensitive to it ever since that time on a frozen wasteland when he had endeavored to end his life, and *it* had prevented him from doing so. It had never left him since. It remained there, rooting around at the base of his brain, peering out at the world every so often through Banner's own eyes. He could sense it there now, urging him to shut the computer, or—even better—smash it to pieces so that its own existence would not be threatened. He realized in glancing at his monitor that his pulse had been speeding up because of excitement over the news that he was unable to contain. That, in turn, was giving traction to that aspect of him that he desperately needed to suppress. He took a few necessary moments to slow his breathing and obtain his equanimity. Then he resumed typing.

Encouraging. But sample is baseline. I have . . . How best to say it? A creature hiding within me that could be unleashed if I relax my vigilance or allow myself to become too upset? He boiled it down to a simple word that he typed in: *spikes.*

Mr. Blue did not respond immediately. But Banner was reasonably sure the connection hadn't been lost, so obviously Blue was thinking it over. Banner's supposition proved to be correct when, after a few moments, Mr. Blue replied.

Tricky. Can you extract sample during next spike?

That was certainly a no-brainer: No.

Spike can't exceed exposure. What was your original exposure?

Data no longer available.

Another pause to consider. Then: *Toxicity at this level too risky without precision.*

Banner hesitated before typing in the million-dollar question: *Will it cure me?*

It seemed an eternity before the answer came back, although it was in fact only seconds. *Barring new gamma exposure . . . good chance.*

Banner felt woozy and didn't understand why. Then he realized that he had stopped breathing. He consciously forced his lungs to take in air, and even as he did so, his mind was racing. He reached for a pad of paper and scribbled the words "Data from Maynard" on it. There were so many thoughts tumbling around in his head that he had to make sure to jot down the one that was more important than all the others.

Then he typed, *Will get back to you. Thank you.*

Pleasure. Hope you walk through the door one day. You must be a very unique individual.

Banner refrained from typing back that "unique" was an absolute and therefore didn't require the modifier of "very." Mr. Blue represented his salvation; this was no time to turn into the grammar police. Instead Banner closed the computer and leaned back in his chair. He needed to focus his thoughts, and instinctively he knew the way to do that: He stared at the picture of Betty that was never far from him or his thoughts. It was much too soon to start getting excited, but at least he could allow himself to acknowledge that he might be a step closer.

As he always did, he packed up his equipment into his knapsack. Old habits died hard, and he had long become accustomed to being prepared to leave at a moment's notice. If an emergency exit presented itself, he wouldn't be able to spend time getting himself packed up. Then he remembered the note on the pad. He tore it off and shoved it into his pocket.

He knew that he should try to grab some sleep now, but he was too keyed up over the prospect of a possible cure. Banner being keyed up was never a good thing, and so he sat cross-legged on the floor, slowed down his breathing, and dropped himself into a meditative state and

Betty is looking worried through the glass shield of the control room as the disk of the gamma gun comes over his face. Banner's face is reflected in it, and in that reflection is a white cross upon his forehead, and suddenly his point of view shifts except it is not his point of view anymore, it's the other's point of view, *his* or *its*, jarring and surreal, and everything seems hyperaccelerated and viewed from much higher, ten feet it seems. And there is Betty on the ground, a horrible gash on her forehead and two other people on the floor pinned beneath broken lab equipment and the sounds of a gunshot and Ross is backing up while an aide fires a sidearm, the muzzle flashing repeatedly, and it means nothing except that it's irritating the hell out of us and we charge and a massive discolored hand reaches in, grabs Ross's arm and jerks him out of view so quickly that it doesn't even seem real but rather like a sequence from an old movie being undercranked to convey comedic speed, and then things speed up like an accelerating juggernaut, plowing through a troop of screaming soldiers who scatter in the face of whatever is approaching them

Banner's eyes snapped open. Immediately he consulted his monitor, which dutifully informed him that his pulse was locking in at ninety-one. That was no good. It was hardly in the red zone, but it wasn't exactly conducive to a state of deep meditation. It was clear he wasn't going to be able to clear his mind tonight, and so he gave up and rose from his seated position. The apartment suddenly felt too small and claustrophobic. Instead he went to his refrigerator and pulled out a single beer that he had in there. Normally he wasn't much for drinking, since he couldn't chance losing control. But he was so wired that he had to hope it might relax him. He wandered up to the roof, where he cracked open the beer and sipped it slowly, feeling intensely isolated. It was as if there was the rest of the world and then, over in a separate corner, him. He looked out at the city spread before him and felt like an outsider looking in.

At least the beer served its purpose of relaxing him. He returned to his apartment, stretched out on his bed, and, with Rick curled up at his feet, fell into a deep and nicely dreamless sleep. The dog from downstairs continued to bark as always. The stupid thing never seemed to sleep except, presumably, during the day, when no one was around.

It was blissful, this not dreaming. No horrific images were assaulting him, and he didn't have to keep awakening and checking his pulse monitor. For once, blessed sleep had enshrouded him, enfolded him, and he might actually feel rested for once in the morning when he woke up . . .

. . . woke up . . .

Wake up.

It was a voice shouting a warning in his head, his own voice. He had no idea why, and he lay there in a state of momentary confusion, his desire to continue sleeping at war with something deep within that was trying to let him know that he should haul himself out of bed right this second.

His mind splitting down the middle, he asked himself

why was this necessary? There was no immediate threat, all was peaceful and quiet, all was—

All was quiet.

He drifted back to sleep, not processing the significance of the fact that the dog downstairs had ceased its barking.

FIVE

Deep in the shadows of the alley behind the building where the target was believed to be residing, Blonsky's squad lined up behind him, waiting for the signal. Blonsky scanned the back entrance with the aid of night-vision goggles that cast the entire area around him in pale green. There was no reason to assume there was any sort of ambush waiting, but Emil Blonsky had lasted as long as he had because he operated on the belief that there was never a reason *not* to assume there was an ambush waiting.

He surveyed the area a few moments more and then said confidently, "Clear."

Two of the shadows along the wall detached themselves and moved into a crouch toward the back door: Saunders, side by side with Carl Curtis, a young hotshot with extensive martial-arts training. Saunders and Curtis had their dart rifles held at ready, with MP5 submachine guns slung and balaclavas covering their faces.

Blonsky, Saunders, and Curtis moved toward the back door. In the meantime, LaRoquette had come in through the front, making certain that Banner didn't try to beat a retreat in that direction. They converged at the bottom of the stairwell that wound up toward the top floor. Blonsky continuing to take point, the four commandos moved silently up the stairs. If one had been looking right at them, one would have thought them insubstantial shadows for all the noise they made.

A dog was waiting for them on the landing. It had been barking constantly since they first entered the building, and even before. Blonsky had quickly had more than enough of the annoying creature and fired off a tranq dart. It thudded into the side of the dog. The animal didn't even give a yip of protest; it simply fell over, the tranq taking instant effect.

The commandos moved past it without giving it a second look.

Going on the assumption that their intel was correct, they moved toward the apartment number that they believed to be Banner's. They covered all doors and corners as they moved, doing it by the numbers just as Blonsky had told them to do. Banner's door was at the top of the stairs. Gesturing with quick hand signals, Blonsky conveyed to his squad what he wanted. Curtis split off from the others, heading up the steps toward the roof just to make sure that Banner didn't somehow manage to escape in that direction. Blonsky and the other two took up positions outside Banner's door. Saunders dropped low and pulled out a fiberscope, or "snake cam" as it was nicknamed. He fed it silently under the door so that they could get a view of the inside of the apartment. LaRoquette, meantime, applied small plastique packs to the hinges and the lock. Common sense said that they could just kick the door in, but Blonsky had no intention of taking any chances. Shock and awe, that's what this was about. If the door had some sort of special locks in place, they would need the plastique to get in. If it didn't, well, scaring the little creep with an earsplitting explosion wasn't necessarily a bad thing. Nothing wrong with having him so startled and confused that he was paralyzed with fear and thus an easy target for the tranq dart. Blonsky faced the door, eyes flicking to the sides, submachine gun held ready.

Saunders was using the camera to scan the room. He

studied it carefully and then looked up and mouthed a word to Blonsky: *Dog*. Apparently Banner had a little canine friend and it was heading toward the camera, investigating it. There was no sound of barking coming from within. Obviously it wasn't quite as loud and obnoxious as the animal they had had to tranq. Blonsky could hear the click of the dog's toenails from the other side of the door now as it approached the camera. There was no other movement from within, or at least none that Blonsky could hear. The dog may have noticed the camera, but apparently Banner remained oblivious of it.

Perfect.

Saunders held up a hand, indicating that Blonsky should be ready to move. He never took his eye away from the viewer. Then he actually smiled in what appeared to be amusement. Blonsky looked quizzically at him and Saunders indicated through gestures that the dog was licking the camera lens. Blonsky rolled his eyes. A million-dollar piece of army ordnance and it was going to be covered with dog slobber. Then the clicking toenails moved away from the door. The dog apparently found the camera of insufficient interest to hold its attention and was returning to bed. LaRoquette held up one finger, pointing right, signaling that Banner was lying down. That meant they had a visual confirmation of Banner in the bed. That was a relief. Everything was as it seemed and Blonsky didn't have to worry about booby traps. That didn't mean such concerns were far from his thoughts, but the chances were that this entire business was going to be concluded inside of a minute.

Blonsky had a direct link up to a black van outside. He tapped a signal into the transmission device that was mounted on the front of his helmet. Blonsky also had a camera mounted on his helmet, which fed into monitors in that same black van. It wasn't the way that Blonsky liked to do things. He preferred to operate without Big

Brother watching him. But this was today's army, so what could you do?

The black van sat at curbside, nearly invisible in the darkened street. Inside the van crouched Sparr, Ross, and a Brazilian liaison officer named Monte. They were watching the monitors intently, able to see and hear the feed from Blonsky's head cam. There were additional monitors that provided them views from the roof courtesy of Curtis, who had positioned himself there, from Martel, who was in front of the building, and from the fifth member of the squad, Carl Parmenter, an experienced strategist who had moved in behind Blonsky's team and was maintaining a view of the back of the building. They had Banner bottled up, all right. Now it was just a matter of shoving a cork into the bottle.

"Geiger?" said Ross.

Blonsky's camera angled down as he checked a unit affixed to his gunstock. There was an LED readout on it that provided a measurement of radiation. If Banner was going to undergo any sort of metamorphosis, the rads would be sufficient to trigger a response on the Geiger counter and give them at least some warning.

The LED remained dark. Nothing.

Major Sparr, all efficiency, checked the readouts of the monitors on the other two team members who had similar units on their gunstocks. There appeared to be no readout on any of them. She shook her head. "Negative."

"Take him," said Ross.

They were the two words that Blonsky had been waiting for. He nodded to LaRoquette, who triggered the charge. The door of Banner's apartment blew off its hinges with a sharp fast crack. Blonsky was in first, the others covering angles behind him. Blonsky spotted

Banner's sleeping form right where it was supposed to be, dropped to his knee, and fired at the target. The tranq dart sank into the body with a soft *thwip*. Just to play it safe, he fired three more into Banner's body and legs. It was enough to paralyze a hippo, much less a single sleeping man. Banner would literally never know what hit him. He would awaken to discover himself trussed like a prize turkey.

Blonsky moved to the bed and yanked the covers back. He discovered nothing there but pillows and a Styrofoam head with a cap and wig on it.

The commando leader wanted to unleash a string of invective directed at the world in general and Banner in specific. But he was far too experienced to allow such unprofessional behavior. Instead, dropping the need for silence, he called out, "Target's on the move."

Banner's window opened out onto a narrow channel of space created through two other buildings that adjoined it, and led down into an adjacent alley. His knapsack on his back, Banner was creeping down it as silently as he could, hanging on to a rope that he had affixed to the handle of the window. Passing a kitchen window, he looked inside and saw Martina. She was in her underwear, busy pouring herself a glass of water from the sink. Apparently she was having a sleepless night. The motion at the window caught her attention and she glanced toward it. She jumped, dropping the glass of water and almost letting out a startled scream. He put a finger to his mouth, indicating that she should remain silent. She barely managed to do so, staring at him goggle-eyed.

In the apartment, Banner's dog was barking at them furiously. It was making it hard for Blonsky to think, even as he methodically took aim with his tranq gun and squeezed off a shot. It thudded into the canine and the dog promptly fell over in midbark. Blonsky was already ignoring it, glancing around to see if there was anything in the meager apartment that he had missed on first glance.

Then he spotted the rope tied to the window. It was swinging slightly, as if some weight was still attached to it.

He dashed to the window and looked out and down into an adjoining alley. If Banner had released it, he had done so mere seconds ago, because the rope was still swinging.

Blonsky was beginning to see why Ross and Sparr had made such a big deal about this guy. This simple snatch-and-grab was becoming less simple with each passing second. At least there was only one exit from the alley, with the other end butting up against a building.

"He's on the ground, going rear," said Blonsky.

"Dammit!" Thunderbolt Ross snapped out even as the van's tires spun and then gripped the pavement. The van shot around toward where the back alley opened out.

Sparr was busy barking orders through the comm links. "Team three, stay on station in case he doubles back," she told Parmenter. "Team four, move around to the side, cut him off." Team four, in the form of Martel, obeyed, as was clear through the motion of his camera unit. Team two was Saunders and LaRoquette, and Blonsky was simply referred to as team leader.

Banner suspected that the soldiers—for such was what he assumed them to be—had by now discerned his window exit and were moving around toward the back of the building. Unfortunately for them, they had leaped to a false conclusion. A dangling rope that led to the bottom of the alley didn't automatically mean that he had landed there.

He didn't allow himself even the slightest feeling of triumph in outwitting them, even as he crouched by the door of Martina's apartment. Instead he focused all his energy on keeping his breathing slow and easy. This was exactly the sort of situation that he had been training for when it came to his yoga and meditative practice. Keeping his pulse down while running was merely a warm-up for staying calm while on the run. He nodded to Martina, who opened the door a crack. She peered out, giving Banner the opportunity to remain out of sight for as long as possible. She looked back to him and mouthed the word *Nothing.* The moment she did he was out the door, not even pausing to thank her. It wasn't out of a lack of gratitude or even haste. He didn't want to take the chance that someone might see him thanking her. If they thought she was merely a terrified woman forced into cooperating with him, the army would have no interest in her. If, on the other hand, she was considered an accomplice, she could wind up in a facility somewhere being grilled for days on end.

So without so much as a word to her or even a backward glance, he sprinted for the steps. He ran so quickly that he almost took a header down them and prevented that catastrophe only at the last second by grabbing the banister to slow himself.

He emerged from the front door, his mind racing. If his little distraction had proven successful, then whoever they had watching the front would have been pulled around to the side. Forcing himself to slow was like tying a couple of anchors to a speeding car, but he managed it, since a running man was going to attract more attention than a nonrunning man. He managed a carefully controlled walk, although it vaguely gave him the air of someone in dire need of a bathroom facility.

* * *

Martel was running down the alley, trailing the black van, which was maneuvering deftly through the constricted space. Then something just barely caught his peripheral vision behind him and he spun to see the intended target walking away as calm as you please.

Banner glanced in Martel's direction. Both men froze, and then Banner was gone before Martel could bring his tranq gun to bear.

"Target acquired!" Martel snapped into his comm unit even as he doubled back and headed for the sidewalk.

"He's getting away!" shouted Ross. "Turn us around! Turn this damned thing around!" and he slammed his fist against the interior wall.

But the alley was too narrow for the van to turn. Instead Monte, the Brazilian officer, jammed the van into reverse and backed up as quickly as he could, keeping an eye in the side-view mirror to avoid hitting the alley walls. He was only moderately successful as the bumper scraped along the walls, sending off sparks, and a couple of trash cans were sent clattering.

"Hurry up!" said Ross.

"He's doing the best he can, sir!" Sparr assured him. Ross just fired her an angry glance and she realized it would be wisest to limit her comments to updates of Banner's movements.

Banner bolted through the favela at a dead run. Despite the lateness of the hour, it was a Friday night and thus the streets and buildings were choked with people having a good time. This served as both an impediment and an advantage: There were plenty of people in Banner's path, which made maneuvering difficult; however, it also made pursuit more difficult for the commandos. He didn't think they would hesitate to shoot through others to get to him, but at least the bodies would be there to serve as obstructions.

He glanced at his pulse monitor. All those jogging excursions where he had worked to keep his pulse rate down were serving him in good stead as, despite the exertion, he was maintaining a pulse that alternated between seventy and seventy-one. He didn't even bother to glance back over his shoulder, simply assuming that they were behind him and acting upon it. The one thing he had going for him was that he knew every turn, every street, every alley of the favela, and they didn't, couldn't. He darted down a back alley and through a courtyard where kids were playing soccer. On the other side of the courtyard, the road dropped off sharply. To be more accurate, it virtually disappeared, opening out onto the hillside upon which ramshackle buildings were perched. There were narrow alleyways that threaded through them, but Banner, sensing the proximity of his pursuers, didn't take the time to get to them. Instead without slowing he hit the roof of one of the low-slung buildings. The tin roof creaked beneath his feet as he ran across it, then dropped down to another building at a lower level, and then another as if he were playing leapfrog. Angry, shouted complaints arose from the inhabitants of the buildings, bellowing that they were trying to get some sleep and who the hell were these stupid kids who were jumping on their roofs?

You think you have problems? I'd trade places with you in a heartbeat, Banner thought grimly as he continued to ricochet from roof to roof, making his way down the hillside.

Blonsky and his team arrived at the crest of the hill and spotted Banner descending ahead of them. He had too much of a lead for them to follow him directly, but Blonsky saw another way. He read the angle of Banner's descent and realized that if he could cut around faster on the ground, he had a shot at cutting him off. He indicated to Saunders and LaRoquette that they should follow Banner along the rooftop path while he broke to the left, looking for a faster way down. Banner was quick-thinking, granted, but Blonsky was certain that he was in better shape and faster on his feet than the fleeing scientist.

The van blasted through the night streets of the slum. Blonsky was keeping them apprised of Banner's trajectory and his own attempts to come around at him from the bottom.

There was a GPS in the van, but it was useless. The buildings and layout of the shantytown changed from month to month, week to week, or even day to day. Monte kept shouting assurances, though, that he knew the town better than anybody and would find a way around on the streets. Ross merely grunted acknowledgment as he watched the video monitors displaying chaotic green images of the chases from the head cams' point of view.

Banner, still on the rooftops, whipped through some laundry that people had drying on a line overhead. He tossed it aside. He was wearing a zippered sweat jacket with a hood; he now pulled the hood back in order to leave him unobstructed vision. It was lucky he did so, because he almost overshot the edge of the roof. Had he done so, he might well have broken his leg. Even a sprained ankle at this point would be all that was required for his pursuers to catch up with him. He jumped down to the next level and kept going.

* * *

LaRoquette wasn't quite as fortunate as Banner.

Running just ahead of Saunders, he ran through the same laundry as Banner just had and was momentarily blinded by a stray sheet. It caused him to miss seeing a drop between the two roofs and he plummeted between the two structures and hit the street. Fortunately it was only a drop of a single story. He landed and came up in a roll. He looked up and saw Saunders looking down at him, making sure he was okay. "Go, go!" shouted LaRoquette, and Saunders vaulted the distance between the two buildings, maintaining the pursuit. LaRoquette bolted to his right, seeking another route in order to catch up while endeavoring to maintain a visual with the fleeing Banner.

Sparr studied the pursuit on the monitors. Each of the commandos was equipped with a unique tracer that enabled her to track where each one was on an overlaying grid. She saw that the dots were beginning to converge: Saunders directly behind Banner, Blonsky coming around from the left, LaRoquette from the right. Parmenter, Curtis, and Martel had also joined the pursuit and, thanks to Sparr keeping them apprised of Banner's path, were at least heading in the right direction. They were too far back, however, to be of immediate use. That could well change, particularly if Banner shifted course or got incredibly lucky. As it was, Sparr was busily feeding information to the pursuit force in order to facilitate the chase.

"Leader, we're at your ten o'clock," said Sparr. "Team two, pushing target at your four. Move right and you've got him boxed." She turned to Ross and, with the air of a chess player sensing an imminent win, said, "Three more moves. Game over."

Ross was not celebrating just yet. Unlike the others, he was fully aware that there was an additional factor at play. Thus far it had yet to transpire. He glanced at the radiation monitors and there continued to be no reading from them. It could well be that Ross was being paranoid. That the additional factor he feared was not going to come into play. It could be that it was merely a distant nightmare, a thing of the past that need never menace anyone again. He prayed that would be the case. He feared that he was wrong, and wondered—not for the first time—if he was setting up his team to fail.

Should he have told them what they might be facing? No. What was the point? The odds were that they would not have believed him. He didn't care if they thought he was a surly old desk jockey. That wasn't going to affect the mission. If on the other hand they thought he was nuts, that indeed might have a negative impact.

No. No, better to keep the additional information he had to himself. After all, even if he had told them, there wasn't a damned thing they could have done to prepare themselves for it.

Banner reached the bottom of the hill and another section of the favela. The roof of a bar was directly in his path. He bounded off it and landed in the streets, right in the midst of a considerable number of people. With any luck it would be easy to lose himself in the crowd of weekend revelers.

He turned to the right and directly in front of him was a commando emerging from an alleyway. The sight of him had barely registered before the commando, with cat-quick reflexes, aimed and fired in one motion. Banner twisted to the right the instant he saw the gun and the instinctive motion saved him; something breezed past him and clanked off the tin wall of the building next to him. The sound spoke volumes to Banner. It hadn't been a bullet. A bullet would have gone right through the wall as if it were tissue paper. The projectile fired at him had rebounded. It was probably some sort of tranq dart.

Idiots. You should be trying to kill me, not take chances. Don't you know what's good for you? Don't you know what I can do?

That was when he realized: They probably didn't. Ross most likely didn't tell them. The general was probably still operating on the delusion that he could somehow capture and harness the power represented by the creature within Banner. Madness. It would be like trying to use paper cups to harness the force of a lava flow.

Shakespeare said it best: What fools these mortals be.

Even as all that ran through Banner's head, he spun to the left and bolted into a thick crowd of revelers.

Sparr had smiled grimly when she saw Banner appear on Blonsky's monitor. *Game, set, and match*, she thought, and then Banner avoided a tranq dart and vanished into the crowd. When Blonsky lost sight of Banner, so did she. *Son of a bitch has more lives than a cat.*

Banner was reminded of the news story he had read involving a man who was determined to prove that he could survive the power of a hurricane. Convinced that he would withstand the force three winds, he tied himself to a sturdy tree outside his home while the rest of the town evacuated. Basically he challenged God to take his best shot, telling his neighbors that it was, in the final analysis, just wind. What kind of pussy couldn't handle a little wind? When the neighbors returned to town the next day, they found the man's remains crushed beneath a tractor trailer that the storm had tossed at him with the ease of a teenager chucking a Frisbee. The moral of the story, aside from that some people are idiots who are best removed from the gene pool sooner rather than later, was that preparation took you only so far.

Bruce Banner was starting to run up against the limits of his preparation.

All the jogging in the world, all the yoga, all the meditation, simply couldn't overcome the stress to which Banner's mind and body were being subjected. His pulse monitor, which he didn't even have the time to look at because he was running so hard, was up to one hundred and ten and climbing steadily. He knew that he was in trouble, and wasn't going to be able to keep this up much longer. One of two things was going to happen: He was going to fall victim to a tranq dart, or his pursuers were going to fall victim to him.

To *it*.

He ran through an alley, around a corner, popped out, and saw a black van skid to a halt directly in his path. The side door was yanked open and there, staring balefully at him as if looking across an expanse of years, was General Ross. They locked eyes for the first time in three years.

Don't be distracted. Don't let the adrenaline overwhelm you. Your instincts will guide you.

He couldn't reverse direction; at least one and maybe more commandos were in hot pursuit. His glance took in Ross's hands. They were empty. He wasn't holding a gun, which meant that if Banner closed the distance between them he wasn't risking himself. That had been Ross's mistake, perhaps thinking that the mere sight of him would paralyze Banner as if Ross were a gorgon or a basilisk.

Sorry, General. Not today.

Instead of turning, Banner dashed across the street right in front of the van. Ross started to clamber out of the van, shouting Banner's name. Banner ignored him and seconds later had reached an alley across the street and vanished into it once more.

Ross had no idea what he expected Banner to do upon seeing him. Realize the futility of continuing to run? Lift his arms over his head in surrender and beg for mercy? It hadn't turned out that way, and only as Banner shot past the van like a rocket did Ross realize he should have had a tranq gun in his hand. If he had, the chase would be over.

Even as Ross cursed himself out for his tactical misstep, Sparr remained all business. "Okay," said Sparr to her teams, "past mobile unit now and heading oh-nine-zero."

Banner was breathing hard, too hard. Although he didn't want to admit it to himself, the sight of Ross had disconcerted him. Nameless, faceless pursuers were one thing. Eye-to-eye with Thunderbolt Ross was something else entirely. There were too many memories and too many emotions tied up in those memories. And right now, emotions could well be the death of—well, not of Banner, certainly, but of just about everyone else around him.

He made a hard right into a wider part of the street. He had to slow, because it was filling up with people, which continued to be both help and a hindrance. There was too tight a throng to his left to get through, so he darted to the right. Then four guys emerged from a bar and wandered directly into Banner's path. Unable to slow his forward motion, Banner slammed into the foremost of the four young guys, and his heart sank when he realized it was Silva, out with his three oafish companions.

It wasn't enough that they were already predisposed to feeling nothing but hostility toward Banner. Their pugnacious attitudes were exacerbated by the fact that they were drunk and spoiling for a fight with just about anyone. Banner's arrival on the scene could not possibly have been more ill timed or unfortunate.

Silva squinted blearily at Banner and for half a heartbeat Bruce thought that he might manage to avoid an altercation. He should have realized that nothing was going to go simply this night.

Even in his inebriated state, Silva immediately recognized who had plowed into him. There was no preamble, no chitchat. Silva spat out a curse and took a wild swing at Banner.

If he hadn't been able to land a finger on Banner while he was sober, certainly the odds of his doing so while drunk dropped precipitously. Banner easily sidestepped, grabbed Silva's sleeve, and sent him hurtling into a pile of trash. Before any of his cronies could react, Banner darted into a side alley. Silva's friends hauled Silva to his feet and took off after Banner.

Banner continued to wend his way through darkened alleys, hoping against hope that he had managed to shake all his pursuers. It felt as if half the damned favela was chasing him. Then he looked up and saw that the bottling plant was directly ahead of him.

He hurried toward it, hoping that the sheer size of the place would give him somewhere to hide in order to elude pursuit. He ran toward the nearest entrance. A security chain was hanging across the door, but that was hardly enough to slow down Bruce Banner. Having made a practice of trying to prepare for any situation, he slid a thin, flexible piece of wire out of a side pouch on the knapsack. He eased it into the padlock. Despite the situation that he was in the midst of, he nevertheless worked calmly and efficiently. Within seconds he was rewarded with the snap of the padlock unlatching. He yanked clear the chain, stepped through the doorway, and then pulled the door closed. He left the chain dangling on it to give the appearance that the door was still secured. It would survive a passing glance, but not close inspection. Still, there were only so many things that he could allow for.

The commandos had come together from all different directions, directed that way by Sparr in the van. Unfortunately, they had all lost visual contact with the target, and he didn't seem to be presenting them the opportunity to reacquire him.

Blonsky had decided to take the high road, literally. He was striding across rooftops, trying to get some idea of where Banner had disappeared to. One skinny scientist with no resources, completely on his own, eluding a trained team of commandos with a combined century's worth of experience among them? It was simply intolerable.

Then, a short distance away, Blonsky thought he saw something moving near what appeared to be a factory. He pulled out his binoculars and scanned the area. It was a quartet of locals, and one of them was pointing toward a metal back door of the factory. Blonsky shifted his binoculars slightly to see what they were pointing at, and realized that the security chain on the back was hanging too loose to be especially effective. He zoomed in on the padlock. It was hanging open.

Kudos to the locals, who had clearly had too much to drink. They had just performed a service for the United States government. In exchange, Blonsky would try not to shoot them through the heart if any of them got between him and his prey.

He spoke firmly into his microphone. "Target acquired."

*　*　*

Banner passed through the changing room. It was dimly lit and smelled of mildew. There was a steady drip from one of the showers. He slowed for a moment to check his monitor and the results were encouraging: His pulse had dropped from one hundred and three to one hundred and one. If he could just remain here a few minutes, he could manage to bring himself to his baseline. Even better, perhaps they wouldn't pursue him into the factory at all. It was entirely possible that—

Then he heard a clanking noise from behind him. He knew instantly what it was: The door had been pulled open. He hadn't managed to fool them. Silva and his pals, or the commandos, or both, were coming after him. His pulse promptly rose back up to one hundred and three.

He made his way out onto the factory floor. It was odd to see the place, normally teeming with activity, now so silent and dark. He crept through the darkness, keeping an ear out for pursuit behind him. "Pursuit" might have been far too strong a word, because yes, as it turned out, it was indeed the Brazilian bullyboys who had found their way in. It gave Banner a moment of relief; at least it wasn't the commandos. He was reasonably sure that he could handle these guys, particularly since it was clear from the way they were loudly whispering and stumbling into things that they were seriously hammered.

There was an exit on the far side of the building. It was constructed differently from the door through which Banner had entered, with a powerful security lock built right into the door so that it didn't require a chain and padlock. However, it also meant that a simple push bar on the inside would open the door from within. The exit sign glowed dim green, salvation summoning him in the darkness. He moved to it, glanced left and right to see if he was unobserved, and then as quietly as he could depressed the bar and pushed on the door.

Silva was standing right outside, waiting for him.

Banner was caught completely flatfooted, paralyzed not only with surprise, but with personal chagrin. Here he was one of the smartest individuals on the planet—not his own assessment, but that of others whose opinion he was willing to trust—and he had just been outmaneuvered by a Neanderthal who at the moment couldn't pass a blood alcohol test. This was beyond dangerous; this was downright embarrassing. Silva barked out a loud laugh and shoved Banner backward even as he pushed his way inside. Banner stumbled, recovered, and turned to run, only to discover that Silva's pals were right behind him. He tried to back up, get some distance so that he could prepare himself for hand-to-hand combat again, but there was too much happening and he couldn't focus his energies. One of them got a lucky punch in that clocked Banner on the side of the head, causing the world to spin around him, and then another swept his legs out from under him. Banner went down, hitting the floor heavily. He tried to bring his mind back to a place where he could mount a defense, but then he felt something stirring within him. Something dangerous, something terrible. It swiveled his attention away from self-defense and entirely on trying to push down the creature inside. As a flurry of kicks pummeled him, he was barely aware of it. He was busy fighting a two-front war and he was losing both of them.

Silva strode forward, grabbed Banner by the back of his shirt, yanked him to his feet, and slammed him up against a piece of machinery. The world was splintering before Banner's eyes, and he tried to reassemble it piece by piece. There was blood foaming between his teeth. He spit out a mouthful and managed to say, "Please don't do this," mangling the Portuguese . . . not that it would have mattered to his assailants if he'd spoken with perfect fluency. His monitor was racing beyond a hundred and ten. He didn't see it.

One of them yanked his backpack off him, muttering something about trying to sell the contents. As insane as it sounded, he was more concerned about the backpack and what was in it than he was about his own life. If he lost the computer and the unique contents on its hard drive, he might as well be dead. He tried to lunge toward it, but two of them were holding him by either arm. Silva lightly slapped him across the face. Banner tried to pull free, but he had no leverage, no room to maneuver.

"What? I can't understand you," said Silva in response to Banner's plea. "No fight? Not so tough now, huh? Try those fancy moves again. Come on, we all want to see."

He shoved Banner back and the other two released their hold. Banner was propelled into a large lever extending from a machine. It drove hard into his back and Banner cried out in pain.

The commandos moved through the locker and office area in two-by-two formation with Blonsky once again taking point. Then they heard the sounds of laughter combined with a moan that was very likely coming from the target. Blonsky gestured and the commandos behind him fanned out.

Blonsky studied the terrain in front of him through his night-vision goggles. The entire area was transformed into a surreal world of black. Through the forest of pipes and metal, he was able to make out a few green illuminated patches. The patches consisted of five men, or more accurately, four men who seemed intent on reducing the fifth man into a bloody pulp.

*   *   *

The camera that Blonsky had mounted upon him also contained night-vision capability. It provided Sparr and Ross with a perfect view of everything that was happening in the factory.

Ross didn't like what he was seeing at all. Where the hell had these four goons come from? The best chance they had of taking Banner down lay with the commandos and their tranq weaponry, and even they were on a clock that they didn't know was ticking down. Ross was starting to regret having kept them in the dark, but it was too late to do anything about it now except pray that they got to Banner before these local toughs with a beef got to the creature.

Banner's pulse rocketed to one hundred thirteen as two of Silva's pals spun him and sent him slamming against more machinery. His mind scattered, all he could summon were individual words in Portuguese. "Stop. Please stop. Me. Angry. Very bad."

"You bad angry, son?" said Silva with a chortle. "*I very bad angry.*"

Before Banner could respond, he caught a glimpse of shadows separating from the darkness, converging. All thoughts of even trying to regain his equanimity went right out the window as his pulse slammed up to one hundred and twenty-seven. "Let me go! You don't understand. Something really bad is going to happen here!"

"Yeah," said Silva, who had no idea how much he was understating matters. "Something bad is going to happen."

"Target acquired," Blonsky said softly into his microphone, his voice reaching everyone else in his unit as well as the van. He had a clear vision of Banner's neck through his night scope. "Get ready to move quickly. We don't need these jerks killing him before we can get to him once he goes down."

His finger tightened on the trigger. He took in a breath, let it out slowly and squeezed.

The instant the tranq dart flew, one of the goons belted Banner in the gut, doubling him over. Not only did it cause Blonsky to lose Banner as the target, but also the idiot stepped into the dart's flight path. It thudded into his shoulder. Blonsky muttered a curse as the goon spun, looking confused, and then his legs promptly began to fold.

Even as Blonsky chambered another tranq dart, a sudden green pulse of light cut across his night vision. It blinded him momentarily and so he didn't immediately see that the radiation sensor LEDs were suddenly into the red zone.

Banner heard the *thwip* of a dart and the startled cry of one of his tormentors. He instantly realized what had happened. Then something screamed in his head for release, and he managed, through vision that was hazing over, to see his heart monitor racing toward two hundred.

He tried to push it back, but his mind screamed *Too late, too late,* and another part of his mind responded with a single, satisfied word: *Good.*

And then Banner was gone.

SIX

Darkness, the darkness feels good, hide in the darkness, no light, no light is good, light hurts so much, but there is noise, so much noise, and they are coming, the noise hurts, must make the noise stop, must make them stop . . .

In the van, Ross bolted forward in his chair as he saw the readouts on the monitors. "What the hell?" said Sparr, but Ross made no reply, his attention locked on to the arrays in front of him.

Inwardly, Ross raged against the x factor that had been introduced into the proceedings in the form of these idiots, this band of bozos. They had wandered into the middle of a carefully planned military procedure and buggered the entire works. It was like having the Keystone Cops show up during the Trinity test, unleashing laughs and nuclear holocaust.

Except in this case the nuclear holocaust was on two legs.

Blonsky ripped the night-vision goggles off his head in response to the blinding flash of energy. He blinked furiously, trying to clear his vision, and signaled the rest of his squad to remain where they were.

The Brazilian toughs turned, their attention shifting

to their fallen comrade. One of them, misplacing the blame, kicked the crumpled Banner, demanding to know what he had done. Clearly these guys weren't the brightest bulbs in the box, since Banner wasn't remotely capable of even defending himself by this point, much less mounting an offense that would have taken down one of them. Banner writhed on the floor, groaning, and the groans were escalating in volume. It was odd, because it seemed to Blonsky as if Banner were reacting to some sort of pain being generated from within rather than anything these idiots were doing. It almost looked as if he were having a heart attack of some kind.

"What the hell?" said one of the gang of Brazilians, and Blonsky couldn't determine if he was reacting to discovering a tranq dart buried in his pal or something that was happening with Banner. But Blonsky was unsure what *could* be happening with him other than bleeding profusely.

Sparr's voice came over the comm unit: "Is target neutral? Did we get a shot?"

Blonsky was ready to respond in the affirmative. After all, he had indeed gotten a shot off, even if it did hit the wrong guy. As for being neutral, well, it certainly appeared that Banner wasn't going to be offering up much of a threat.

Sparr studied the monitors, still cast in the green of the camera night vision. Nothing she was seeing was making any sense. There was Banner, all right, on the ground, but the radiation readings were practically off the chart. Was he carrying some sort of nuclear device on him? Was it about to detonate, reducing the entire town to a pulsing crater?

She looked to Ross for explanation, but his face was sallow, his expression stunned. For no reason that she could fathom, she decided he looked like a man who was standing far enough away from Hiroshima to see the burgeoning mushroom cloud, not understanding the full mechanics of what he was witnessing but instinctively knowing nevertheless that the end of the world was nigh.

Blonsky watched as one of the goons shouted "Shut up!" at Banner and tried to kick him. Then he let out a yelp of confusion, unable to pull his foot away.

"Silva, what's wrong?" one of his pals cried out, and suddenly Silva vanished.

Blonsky had no idea what he had just seen. One second the man, Silva, was there, and then he had disappeared into the shadows that had enveloped Banner. Ripped upward by the leg, his terrified scream was joined by the roar of something unlike anything Blonsky had ever heard. At first he thought it was a wild animal, but it made no sense. How could something like that have wandered into the factory?

Nor did the voices of such modern animals begin to capture the sheer ferocity of what Blonsky had just heard. Blonsky was not a man given to fanciful thinking, but to him it sounded like something that was ancient while the distant ancestors of modern animals strode the earth. It was something beyond animal, beyond human.

And, as insane as it sounded, Blonsky felt as if it were calling to him, summoning him, like a siren song.

They are here, they are gnats, they must be smashed, one at a time, all together, no difference, smash them all, and there, crouching over in corner, watching with hungry eyes, one not like others, smash him last . . .

*   *   *

Sparr flinched back, yanking her earphones away from her head in response to the deafening roar that came across it. Tentatively she replaced the earphones and watched the screen, trying to see and hear what was going on and wrap her mind around what she was witnessing.

In the dark of the factory, she heard the sound of bones cracking and the man who had been called Silva screaming. Then he came abruptly back into view, flying out of the shadows as if hurled from a catapult. By Sparr's estimation his arc reached fourteen feet in altitude as he hurtled the length of the factory like a ball tossed by an oversized child. He hit the far wall headfirst with such an audible impact that Sparr found herself hoping he didn't survive, since he wouldn't have much of a life to look forward to if he were still sucking oxygen.

Then the roar faded.

Sparr felt as if she were watching an old horror or science fiction movie, with an alien monster lurking just beyond their ability to see it. Except these were not helpless, weaponless teenagers—the favorite victims of such films—facing the shadows. These were trained, armed commandos who, for all the good that their training and weaponry was going to do them, might as well have been helpless teenagers.

What happened next was chaos.

Blonsky held back and ordered his teams to do likewise. It was clear that they were faced with some new element that had to be assessed, and if the gang of idiots was willing to serve as cannon fodder so the commandos could better understand what they were dealing with, that was fine with him.

Unfortunately the locals didn't seem inclined to cooperate.

Instead, having no desire to tangle with whatever had just dispatched their pal, they turned and tried to bolt. Two were successful; the third was less so as something massive reached from the shadows and grabbed him, like a predator on the savanna dragging down a trailing gazelle.

The remaining two sprinted right past Blonsky, ignoring the terrified screams of their abandoned buddy. Blonsky paid them no mind; if they were leaving, they were of no use to him. Instead he was trying to make out the gigantic arm, the impossible fist that had clamped on to the one thug, thwarting his departure.

Sparr switched her attention to LaRoquette's camera, which seemed to provide the best view. Through a maze of metal, she was able to make out an enormous green figure lifting another, much smaller figure, one of the goons for whom Sparr was feeling no pity whatsoever. She didn't fully comprehend everything that was happening, but she intuited that these clowns had screwed up everything and whatever it was they had unleashed, they had brought it on themselves.

The thug struggled and screamed helplessly, and then abruptly he went limp. The creature that had him appeared to study him for a moment to see if he had any more fight left in him, and then discarded him like a rag doll.

"Where's the target?" shouted Sparr to her team. The response was incomprehensible as everyone chattered at the same time, reports overlapping and none of them making any sense.

That was when Ross silenced all of them with four words that Sparr heard but didn't understand: "That *is* the target."

Dead silence. Sparr looked to Ross, her face a question.

"That is the target, goddammit," said Ross again. Then, addressing his commandos rather than Sparr, he continued, "Put all your tranqs on him. Every one you've got. *Do it now.*"

LaRoquette and Saunders advanced, firing as hard and as fast as they could. Sparr watched as dart after dart penetrated the shadows. Unfortunately that was all they seemed to be penetrating, because she heard a series of thuds as if the darts were striking a concrete wall. They fell into a small patch of light and Sparr zoomed in via the camera lens. The dart points were bent at right angles.

"Body armor?" she said, but it didn't make sense. They would have just rebounded from body armor. The tips wouldn't have bent. Ross didn't even bother to shake his head. He just watched the proceedings with a haunted expression.

A huge foot emerged from the shadows and stepped on the darts. Sparr couldn't make out the color of the skin because of the night vision, but she could see that it looked wrong somehow. It was not normal human flesh tone. It seemed more like something that would be appropriate to a dinosaur.

Then the creature—for that's what it seemed like to Sparr, that's what it had to be, it simply couldn't be human—charged.

A couple of oversized tanks filled with some of the basic ingredients for the crappy soda they manufactured here were between the creature and its attackers. They didn't slow the monster at all; it simply brushed them aside as if they were empty garbage cans. On the monitor, a huge blurry green shape was bearing down on team two. Saunders was heard to scream, *"Holy shit!*

Go live! Go live!" Tranq darts were dispensed with; live ammo was the fallback as the two of them whipped out machine guns.

The monitor in the van showed Sparr a blurred green form advancing on team two with speed that seemed unnatural for something that huge, and suddenly Sparr's view was awash in a blur and static and the sound of roaring rage and soldiers screaming.

Muzzles from MP5s flashed in the darkness, and there was a clatter of weaponry, deafening after all the silence of the tranq darts.

Noise, so much noise, and little lights in the air, like bugs, they are bugs, the puny humans are nothing but bugs, swat them, swat the bugs . . .

Blonsky should not have been shocked by that point, and yet he could not help it. He watched in astonishment as Saunders barely dodged the massive arm grabbing at him, but LaRoquette was hoisted into the air as if he were a puppet on strings and the puppeteer had tired of his antics. He never stopped firing, bullets flying everywhere. Blonsky crouched back behind the machinery as bullets bounded off the metal ceiling and annihilated bottles of some sort of beverage sitting immobile on conveyor belts. The gun muzzle spun, the effect almost like a child in the dark twirling two light sticks.

Then something flew past his field of view. It was LaRoquette, smashing just to the right of the machine that Blonsky was hiding behind. He fell to the ground, unmoving, arms and legs splayed in the manner of a lifeless doll. Apparently he had struck some sort of On button when he'd made contact with the machine, as bottling machinery roared to life. Blonsky did nothing to try to shut it down; the cacophony of clanking metal and engines and spinning lights could serve to provide cover from whatever the hell it was they were dealing with.

Saunders came in behind Blonsky, and even in the darkness Blonsky saw the barely contained terror in Saunders's face. But Saunders was far too much of a professional to succumb to the obvious fear he was feeling. Instead both of them shifted their attention to the problem at hand. Blonsky saw that the shadow was on the move again. Blonsky dropped to his knee and opened fire on the shadow as it moved to the right across his field of vision. Saunders did likewise, standing right behind Blonsky. Neither of them was able to get a clear shot as rounds clanked off the metal of the machinery and storage tanks.

Team three, consisting of Parmenter and Curtis, raced up behind them, adding their own firepower to that of Saunders and Blonsky. In a slightly better position to advance, team three did so, moving farther along the row of machinery and pouring a stream of tracer bullets at the thing in front of them. In the strobe effect created by the steady stream of muzzle flashes, Blonsky could make out the creature's form moving, looking powerful, surreal, unclear but very much in evidence.

Saunders moved in behind Parmenter and Curtis. Blonsky paused in his barrage, knowing they were shooting blind. No point in wasting ammunition. He scanned the area, looking for another means of approach, and spotted a set of stairs leading up. He broke away and headed for them.

Sparr watched from the van, never having felt more helpless or frustrated, as Parmenter and Curtis moved into a more open area, trying for a better angle, with

Saunders moving in right behind them. They brought their weaponry up and opened fire once more. It seemed impossible to her that they could all be missing, but equally impossible that they were all hitting home. Yet what she was hearing seemed to indicate that they most definitely were not missing. Yes, there was the sound of bullets clanking off the jungle of metal pipes and machinery, but there were also the sounds of bullets hitting . . . flesh? Except Sparr knew that sound, knew it all too well. This was different. When the bullets struck home, they made a flat, thick sound as if ricocheting off reinforced rubber.

Then she zoomed in one of the cameras on the ground in front of the advancing teams. She couldn't believe it. Bullets were piled up by the dozen, all of them smashed flat.

She looked wordlessly to Ross. He looked like a man who was living his worst nightmare and was helpless to awaken. And unlike the standard state of dreaming, he wasn't alone. Sparr and the commando squads were trapped in it with him.

Blonsky reached a catwalk that appeared to run the length of the factory. He moved quickly across it, giving no thought to stealth. Instead his boots clanked along the steel grillwork, through which he could see tracer fire streaking from the other commandos' guns.

Several of the bullets must have clipped some sort of heating pipe, because steam was now billowing out, enveloping the shadowed form below. Saunders seized the opportunity by grabbing a stun grenade off his belt and throwing it into the steam as if hurling a ninety-mile-per-hour fastball. The three soldiers ducked for cover. The grenade whooshed through steam, hit something, and exploded, a concussion blast. Just for an instant, the flash of the explosion backlit the massive form that was in front of them. It seemed to be staggered by the impact, and then the steam wiped out their view of it.

Silence.

For a second, the briefest of moments, Blonsky allowed himself to wonder if the grenade had taken out the creature. Yet even as he did, he knew that it couldn't possibly have. Not this creature. It was beyond the ability of something as simple as a grenade to hurt.

He was right.

There was an earsplitting roar, even more furious than before, as if it were angry that the powerless mites sprinting around the factory floor had dared to try and inconvenience it. It occurred to Blonsky that perhaps the sudden brightness of the grenade had flash-blinded it, at least, but that wasn't going to deter it. That was just going to piss it off.

He was right again.

With a sickening pounding of steel, a tank that was ten feet high and must have weighed tons bounded across the floor toward the commandos below. It was so tall that it bumped up against the grillwork directly in front of Blonsky, shoving it upward. He jumped back to avoid it, but was thrown off his feet. He crashed heavily to his chest, jolting violently the camera that had been mounted on him. He heard something crack and suspected that the lens had just shattered. *That should be the least of my problems.*

The soldiers below were not quite so fortunate when it came to getting out of the juggernaut's path. Saunders leaped out of the way, but Parmenter and Curtis, in the forefront, were unable to get clear in time. The heavy tank slammed into them, knocking them to either side. Each of them landed heavily and didn't move. They were still breathing, but in no condition at that point to do anything other than lie there and groan. Saunders did not, however, get away unscathed. He landed wrong, and there was an audible snapping of bone. Saunders screamed, howling that his leg was broken. Blonsky didn't doubt that Saunders was correct, but there wasn't a whole hell of a lot that he could do about it.

Ross stared at the array of monitors, not a single one of which were of any use. They were all still functional, but there were no images being displayed on them. The cameras were dead.

The only thing they were getting were the sounds of moaning coming over the microphones of the few remaining soldiers.

Ross had had enough. His men were paying for his shortsightedness, for his stupidity, while he cowered inside the van? That was simply unacceptable. He threw open the door and leaped out of the van, ignoring Sparr's shout of *"Sir! No!"*

Inside, Blonsky sprinted along the grillwork. Either his men were dead or, if any of them were alive, they were in no condition to contribute to "the festivities," as Blonsky was fond of referring to such operations. He moved as silently as he could on the steel grating, tracking the shadowy figure that was moving under him. Nevertheless he was still making noise, since the catwalk wasn't exactly built for stealth. But the being below didn't appear to be reacting to him. Either it had lousy hearing, or else it was perfectly aware of his presence and simply didn't give a damn.

He tried to get ahead of it so that he could line up for a shot. It had to have a weak spot. Everything, no matter how seemingly impervious, had a weak spot. It was simply a matter of finding it. Perhaps an eye or a shot into an ear that would penetrate the brain. If only he could get the proper angle.

The creature continued to thwart his efforts, although Blonsky couldn't tell if it was by accident or by design. Blonsky's target angled under a stretch of catwalk, blocking Blonsky's shot, heading for the dark of the far corner. Still, Blonsky thought that he could get in position right above where it was heading if he was fast. He clattered at high speed along the catwalk and got there just as the shadow moved under him. He braced his gun on the rail, aimed for a headshot. The shadow stopped and looked up at him. Eyes that were suffused with green glared up at him.

Say good night, you bastard, thought Blonsky as he fired.

The creature twisted slightly and the tracers rebounded harmlessly off its shoulder. It bellowed, but in defiance rather than pain.

More noise, more insects, more little men trying to hurt us, hurt me, hurt us, so much noise, so much light, hard to see, hard to think, don't think, no point, just hurt them back, make them suffer, make them pay . . .

Blonsky continued to fire, going for a broad spray, hoping that one of them lucked into a point of vulnerability. He might as well have been peppering the creature with a barrage of marshmallows. The creature slapped away some of the tracers as if they were mosquitoes. The rest of them continued to ricochet off its hide.

The gun clicked on empty. Without ever once taking his eyes from his target, Blonsky ejected the spent clip and jammed in a fresh one. In the brief respite, the creature dropped the arm it had been using to ward off the bullets and stepped half out of shadow, snarling up at him. For the first time, Blonsky had an unobstructed view of its face.

It was a vision of fury incarnate.

Blonsky was frozen, awestruck, and then he was snapped out of his paralysis as the creature drew back its arm and Blonsky saw it was holding something.

A forklift.

Impossible, impossible was all that Blonsky had time to think before the forklift came hurtling through the air right at him.

He dove. It crushed the catwalk where he had just been standing, causing it to collapse partly, leaving him literally hanging on for his life as he dangled above the factory floor. He was afraid to make a move; if he tried to pull himself up, the sudden shift could cause the catwalk to tear completely loose and send him crashing to the floor. However, if he remained as he was, twisting from his precarious grip, he was an easy target.

The creature below had him; it was as simple as that. There was nothing he could do if it decided to reach up, pluck him down, and give him the same treatment that it had given the other commandos.

Except the creature appeared to have lost interest in him, perhaps because Blonsky no longer represented a threat. Still hidden in shadow, it ripped a huge piece of machinery out of the cement block that anchored it to the factory floor. It hoisted the machinery clear of the floor, balanced it for a moment, and then charged with it like a battering ram toward the nearest wall. It smashed apart the wall effortlessly, sending brick and mortar crashing down and a thin cloud of dust rising from the impact. Blonsky coughed and almost lost his grip.

* * *

Ross was running toward the factory just as one of the walls exploded outward. He jumped back and squinted, trying to make out whether something was moving through the debris and rubble as he was very much expecting. It should have been easy to spot, considering its size, but it wasn't. The shadows and clouds seemed to be working together to hide him, as if they were protecting a creature that was darkness and destruction by nature. Just for an instant, he thought for sure he saw a massive form moving through the inky blackness of the night, and then—impossibly—it was gone.

Ross, his chest heaving, stared after it into the night. It was as if he thought he could summon it back through the sheer power of his will.

Naturally he was unsuccessful. In the final analysis, it was probably better that way. God only knew what he would have done if the creature had returned.

He stepped through the hole in the wall, lifting his feet clear of the piles of debris. For a moment he flashed back to the days of boot camp, when he'd just been a soldier threading his way through an obstacle course. Everything had seemed possible in those days when he had first been embarking on his career. Now, as it turned out, when dealing with Bruce Banner and his rampaging alter ego, it seemed that truly anything *was* possible . . . for Banner, if not for Ross.

He entered the factory and looked around at the debris, the chaos, and the destruction. Then he heard a noise and looked up.

Emil Blonsky was dangling from a half-destroyed catwalk.

"Get down from there," said Ross. "You look like a damned fool."

He turned around and headed back out of the factory

just as Sparr came running up to him. "You abandoned the van?" he said sternly.

"Monte has it under control. What happened, General?"

"Banner got away. That's all that need concern you, Sparr. I want a forensics team on the ground in five minutes, going through Banner's apartment molecule by molecule, if necessary."

"Yes, sir. Don't worry, General. We'll find him."

"You mean we'll find him *again*, don't you, Major?" said Ross coldly. "We found him once. He slipped through our fingers, and now we're going to have to find him yet again, and he may well get away again. Isn't that what you meant?"

Sparr said nothing. From the look she gave him, there was nothing that she really could say, nor that she wanted to say, other than the one thing left open to her: "I'll get the team to his apartment as ordered, sir."

"Good."

He heard a thud and a low string of profanity from within the factory as Blonsky hit the ground, but that didn't slow him as he headed back to the van with a cloud of frustration hanging upon him.

The sun rose relentlessly, signaling the start of another day whether Ross liked it or not. As he stood in Banner's unimpressive apartment, watching the sun's rays creep over the horizon, Ross very much suspected that the day was definitely going to fall into the "did not like it" category.

Sparr had been in intense discussion with a white-coated forensics technician, who was laying out for her what they had discovered thus far. Then she walked away from him over to Ross, who was standing there with his arms draped behind his back, waiting to hear what the bad news was going to be. "The stuff in the bottles was basic lab chemicals," she said. "He was cooking up something but there's no trace of it. He zeroed the place. Not a scrap of paper. Like he knew we were coming."

"He didn't know. He's always ready to leave."

There was the sound of footsteps at the door. *Maybe he's returned to surrender,* Ross thought mirthlessly before turning to see that, no, obviously, Banner hadn't had a change of heart. He was, however, returning in spirit if not actuality, for it was Blonsky who was striding in with what appeared to be Banner's backpack.

"Tell me that's what I'm hoping," said Sparr.

"Knew something was different right before I got the shot off," said Blonsky, handing the backpack to Sparr. "He had it on when he bolted."

Ross hoped the damned thing didn't explode. He wouldn't put it past Banner to find some way of boobytrapping it. Sparr, however, clearly didn't share his concerns, and proceeded to open and empty the backpack before Ross could tell her to be cautious. Fortunately for all concerned there was nothing particularly threatening about the backpack. "Not much in here," said Sparr.

"There wouldn't be. He's learned to travel light."

"Which means that anything of his that is in here is going to be particularly important to him . . . which makes it important to us," said Sparr as she emptied the contents onto the small table that must have served as Banner's desk. There was an antenna device that appeared to be designed to tap into the Internet, and a laptop computer.

And a picture.

Naturally Ross recognized it immediately as Blonsky picked it up and examined it. The admiring look on

Blonsky's face sickened Ross. Blonsky said, "Good-looking for a scientist. Girlfriend? Or she helps him?"

Ross's hand moved so quickly that even Blonsky, for all his training, didn't see it coming. That was reflected in the look of surprise on his face as Ross snatched the picture from his grasp and said brusquely, "She is no longer a factor. We closed that door to him a long time ago. He's alone. He wants to be alone." He tapped the computer and said to Sparr, "But see if he's been talking to anybody."

Blonsky stepped around Sparr, who had been between him and Ross, and something shifted in his expression from mild curiosity about the girl in the photo to whatever it was that Ross had been hiding. And it was clear that Blonsky knew by this point that Ross had been less than forthcoming. How could he *not* know? "Forgive me," he said sarcastically with the air of someone not seeking, nor caring if they receive, forgiveness, "but does somebody want to talk about what the hell went down in there?" and he gestured in the vague direction of the factory. "Because he didn't lose us and he wasn't alone. We *had* him and something hit us. Something *big*."

It was fortunate that Thaddeus Ross wasn't partial to smiling, since it would have been hard not to do so under these circumstances. It was at least mildly amusing that Blonsky still had not fully processed just what it was he had witnessed. Then again, it shouldn't have been all that surprising. How does one comprehend something that is simply completely beyond all previous experience?

"Our colonel here," said Sparr, indicating Monte, "says there are rumors in the street about sightings. A farmer says he saw a gorilla going into the edge of the forest."

For a moment Ross hoped that Blonsky would accept that, but he should have known that the commando was smarter than that. "Bullshit, that was no gorilla. It was ten feet tall and green . . . or gray. I couldn't tell." Blonsky noticed that Sparr was looking at him skeptically. "You didn't see it. I did."

That much was true, and Ross was grateful for it. Things had happened so quickly that the video monitors had never gotten a clear glimpse of the Banner-spawned creature before they went on the blink. "No, I didn't," she admitted. "But it sounded like animal."

"That was no animal. It threw a forklift like it was a football. It was . . . It was the most . . ." He searched for the right word and settled on, ". . . incredible thing I've ever seen."

"It's gone," said Ross flatly, having no desire to continue discussing it.

"Where?" said Blonsky, showing no interest in getting out of Ross's face. "Something like that doesn't disappear."

Ross snorted at that notion. "Two thousand miles of jungle to hide in? Trust me, it's gone."

"*Trust* you?"

There it was, the challenge in the air, thrown there by Blonsky, who was waiting for Ross to respond to it. Blonsky knew that Ross had been holding back; that as far as Blonsky was concerned, Ross had hung his squad out to dry. He didn't consider the general trustworthy, and Ross couldn't blame him. Fortunately, he also didn't give a damn what Blonsky thought of him. Ross simply stared levelly at Blonsky who, upon seeing that Ross wasn't about to take the bait, decided to focus his ire on their original target. "If Banner knows what it was, I'm going to find him and put my foot on his throat and ask him. You can have him after that."

Great. Now Blonsky was about to make it personal, with no true inkling of what it was that he was thinking of embarking upon. Sparr said, "Local PD's on alert, but that's not going to be much help. He must have got out when that thing attacked . . ."

"That was Banner." Ross had spoken the words before realizing that he was going to. Sparr didn't seem to be any more capable than Blonsky of comprehending exactly what it was they had encountered. "You mean he led us into it?" she said.

Ross was never the most patient of men, even on his best days, and this was hardly one of those. He had, however, no one to blame but himself for this. If he'd sat them down ahead of time, walked them through it, at least they would have had time to process the theory of what they had seen, even if the actuality of it had been overwhelming. As it was, they were left trying to play mental catch-up with . . . well, Blonsky had said it best: the incredible. The word meant defying belief, and that was certainly the pass to which they had come. "No," said Ross, forcing himself to remain calm rather than express irritation with her, "I mean it *was* Banner. It wasn't an animal. It was *him*."

Blonsky and Sparr exchanged looks, each wondering if the other had perhaps interpreted what Ross had just said in a manner that made sense. "You're going to have to explain that statement," said Blonsky.

Ironically, Ross had been about to. But the arrogance in Blonsky's tone was enough to push Ross in the opposite direction. He was a general; he didn't take orders from grunts, even grunts as highly trained as Emil Blonsky. "No, I'm not," said Ross. "You did your jobs well, both of you. We were undermanned and that's my fault." His voice softened and he said as much to himself as to them, "I didn't think it would happen again." He knew that was no excuse. It was his job to expect nothing but to anticipate everything, and he had been foolish enough not to allow for the possibility that Banner would transform into the monstrosity. He had deluded himself; he hadn't anticipated it because he didn't want to, and his denial had cost good men their lives. That was knowledge that he was simply going to have to live with, but that didn't mean he had to like it. He turned to Sparr all business and said, "Pack up and get our men on the plane. We're going home."

Blonsky leaned back against a wall, holding his rifle muzzle and looking as if he was trying to process information that was going to change his whole worldview. Sparr looked much the same, although she was looking more thoughtful than stunned. Ross walked out of the room and headed for the roof.

Once he reached it, he stood there and stared toward the black line of trees beyond the city. Although it was morning, the sun was still low enough on the horizon that the jungle was in shadow.

For a moment, Ross felt as if he had something in common with the primeval ancestors of humanity, staring into the jungle with superstitious dread and wondering what sort of demonic, unknowable creatures were lurking within.

How the hell was Ross going to spin this? He tried to figure out some positive aspect, something that he could take back home and say, "At least we accomplished this."

Nothing was coming to mind, probably because there was nothing he could say. He was going to take a hit on this, and he deserved it. Actually, he deserved a lot more than that, and Ross—a devout man who firmly believed in the concepts of heaven and hell—was certain enough that eventually he would be called to account in the only court that truly mattered.

Meantime, a being who seemed to be the living incarnation of hell on earth was wandering the jungles of Brazil, and short of carpet-bombing the jungle and razing it to the ground, there wasn't a damned thing that Thunderbolt Ross could do about it.

SEVEN

The Iguazu Falls, cascading down into the Iguazu River on the border of Brazil and Paraguay, were so impressive that Eleanor Roosevelt, upon seeing them for the first time, had memorably lamented, "Poor Niagara!" since the famed New York waterfalls paled in comparison.

It was the steady thundering of the falls that slowly caused Bruce Banner to awaken. In his slumber, his sleeping mind had mistranslated the sound of falls into the pounding footfalls of a creature beyond imagining. Slowly, Banner's mind fought its way back to consciousness and he managed to raise his head and see the falls in the distance.

He immediately realized where he was. He had seen the falls about two years ago and never forgotten the sight. A guide had told him that, according to legend, there had once been a jealous god who had coveted a beautiful aborigine girl. She had spurned her heavenly suitor, instead attempting to flee with her mortal lover down the river in a canoe. Historically gods did not respond well to rejection, and this particular god had been no exception. Supposedly he had split the river, creating the twin falls and sending both of the lovers tumbling from the canoe, one into each cascade. Thus they would be separated into two eternal plunges, always within sight of each other but always apart.

As the chill morning air cut through Banner's skin, he

realized he could relate to that, particularly if he considered himself to be one fall, Betty to be the other, and that—that monstrosity—to be the godlike being that endeavored to keep the two of them apart.

Oh yeah . . . this is going to be a good day.

The one bright spot was that he had not awoken in captivity. He did not want to dwell on the reasons for that. It was all vague flashes to him, broad impressions at best. It was probably preferable that way; he thought that there were screams of terror lingering at the outermost regions of his memory, the screams of men dying horribly, and he, or it, was doubtless responsible for that. Yes, by all means, the less remembered, the better.

He stood and looked down at himself. There were tatters of his shirt hanging off his shoulders, and his trousers were ripped up and barely decent. Shoes, socks, were long gone. Small loss; the road beneath him was muddy and disgusting, so his shoes would have been ruined anyway.

Bruce Banner trudged down the road, trying to keep himself focused on his current situation and not allow his thoughts to wander. If he did, he would dwell on the fact that he had lost his computer, lost his means of communicating with Mr. Blue, even lost the picture of Betty. Oddly, he found that to be the most disheartening of all. *Where the hell are your priorities,* he wondered, and then thought that maybe they weren't so out of whack after all.

The muddy trail led him to a more mountainous road, with hardened dirt and copious small pebbles that were tearing up the bottoms of his feet. He should have known better than to dislike the muddy trail that he'd been hiking, because this was clearly his reward: worse road.

Then he heard the grinding of an engine behind him. He realized that it might be a military vehicle; that Ross had somehow managed to track him. He tried to find the energy to sprint back to the jungle and realized that he couldn't bring himself to do it. He wasn't physically tired, but mentally he was at the end of his tether. *Nothing left in the tank,* as one of his old lab assistants might have said. If Ross and his people had indeed managed to find him, he was just going to stand there, raise his arms over his head, and say, "Fine." If it meant that he got a warm shower, a shave, and a decent meal out of it, the rest might all be worth it.

As it happened, General Ross was deprived of his victory, because it was not, in fact, a military truck. Instead it was a logging truck rattling up the incline. Banner could see the confused reaction of the man behind the wheel upon spotting Banner on the side of the road, waving his arms desperately. He knew what he must have looked like: some poor devil that had been jumped by thieves, stripped of his possessions, and left to wander the jungle.

Banner half expected the truck to speed up and leave him in its wake. Instead, to his surprise and relief, the truck slowed and then stopped. The trucker rolled down his window.

"Can you help me?" Banner said in Portuguese.

"*No hablo Portugués,*" said the trucker.

Great. Spanish. Damn that tower of Babel anyway.

"Where . . . ?" Banner said automatically in English and then tried to reorient his brain and switch to Spanish. "*Donde . . . donde estoy?*"

He realized after he'd spoken that he'd said the wrong thing. He had wanted to ask the trucker where he was bound; instead he'd asked where he was, which Banner actually knew. Fortunately the result was the same, as the trucker explained that they were on the border of Brazil and Paraguay, and the trucker was bound for the latter, which was some eighty kilometers away. That was fine with Banner, who ditched his attempts at Spanish and instead, with a hopeful expression, chucked his thumb in the universally understood gesture of trying to hitch a ride. The trucker hesitated but then shrugged. Banner was clearly unarmed, and besides, what did the trucker have that was worth stealing? He nodded, and Banner, grateful beyond his ability to express, clambered into the cab.

By late afternoon, Robert Bruce Banner—one of the most formidable intellects in the known world—was bumming money in the streets of a Paraguay slum. Other beggars cast him angry glances as he managed to scrape together a small amount of money, probably owing to the novelty of having a shabbily dressed American looking for handouts. He had discovered that people enjoyed giving meager handouts to Americans; it made them feel superior.

As much as his stomach was growling at him, demanding to be fed, Banner's first priority had to be finding attire. The fact that he was an American was enough to make him stand out; at least clothing would enable him to blend in to some degree.

Fortunately he managed to scrape together enough money before day's end to go to the marketplace. There he found a stall with cast-off clothing, most of which the manufacturers had discarded because they were irregular. Rummaging around, he found a pair of purple pants with a good deal of give to them. Even better, he found a selection of Lycra shorts. An extremely obese woman was standing near him and to the right, sorting through the clothes. He held up the leg of one of the pairs and stretched one leg hole wide. *"Más stretchy,"* he said.

The person running the stall wanted more for the clothes than Banner had on him, but Banner managed to talk down the price. The seller's willingness to be flexible might well have stemmed from a desire to get the shabby-looking Banner the hell away from the merchandise, since Banner's presence was keeping other potential customers away.

In a muddy alley full of raw trash—the type with which Banner had become far too familiar in the past years—he pulled on his new clothes. The words of Mark Twain came back to him: *Clothes make the man. Naked people have little or no influence on society.* With this makeshift ensemble, Banner wasn't going to have much more influence on society, but at least it was something. He started to ball up his shredded pants with the intention of tossing them on a pile of garbage nearby. Then he noticed a piece of paper that had fallen from the pockets. He tossed aside the pants, picked up the paper, and unfolded it. He saw his own handwriting with the reminder *Data from Maynard*.

It was not an endeavor he was looking forward to, but he had no choice. He had no idea how he was going to accomplish it, but at least he still had his freedom. As long as he possessed that, he still had the ability to go where he wished and do what he wanted. It was simply a matter of being ingenious enough to figure out how to go about it. And he was confident enough in that regard. He was sufficiently brilliant to have gotten himself into and out of any number of fixes so far. What was one more impossible task, after all?

On the C-130 transport plane, Saunders was lying unconscious, having been put to sleep through medical means so he wouldn't have to deal with the pain of his splinted leg and his arm in a sling. Still, he was better off than his compatriots, who were strapped down to their respective beds, immobilized in full body casts, doped up to the gills and mercifully out cold. Blonsky, the only one who was relatively unscathed (a sprained ankle didn't count as far as Ross was concerned), was likewise asleep in the back of the plane.

Ross had not yet brought Sparr up to speed on what they were dealing with. He was too busy with the results of their studying the contents of Banner's computer. This thing was a treasure trove of information, a snapshot of Bruce Banner's priorities. Of particular interest was Banner's correspondence with an individual who was nicknamed simply "Mr. Blue."

Since Ross always had trouble reading documents on computer screens—they tended to give him eyestrain—he was busy reading the correspondence on printouts that Sparr had provided him. Sparr, meantime, was studying the results on the computer itself. The machine looked to Ross's admittedly untrained eye as if it were being held together with spit and baling wire; trust Banner to be resourceful in keeping such things functional.

As he flicked through the history of Banner's correspondence, he slowly began to understand what he was reading. "He's trying to get rid of it," said Ross.

"Get rid of what?" Sparr said, looking up.

"*It*. His chemistry. He's trying to neutralize whatever powers the transformation."

He looked to Sparr, expecting her to share his concern. Instead she stared at him, uncomprehending. "And that's *not* a *good* thing?"

Ross supposed he should have expected as much. It was bare hours earlier that Sparr had been informed of the impossible transformational abilities of Bruce Banner. She hadn't had time to process fully the ramifications, so she would not have understood. Even so, he couldn't keep the impatience out of his voice, as he said, "No, it's not a good thing, Major. I'm not after Banner, goddammit, I want what's inside him!"

Sparr's expression said it all: *Are you insane? Have you completely lost your mind?*

But she was far too much of a professional to say any of that. All trace of her astonishment evaporated and she said briskly, "Well, he's tight, this one," and tapped the computer screen. "No names, all authors' names deleted. He was using a randomizer to tap different wireless networks every time he went online. We can't even trace where his e-mail went or where it came from." She sounded apologetic, as if any of this was somehow her fault. She added, "We'll have the agency people down here keep their radar up," but she didn't sound especially hopeful. No reason for her to be; she knew as well as Ross that it was too late.

"It doesn't matter," Ross said, confirming what she had worked out. "He's already on the move."

"We'll find him, General," said Sparr with conviction. "We'll find him before he hurts anyone else."

Ross hoped that she was right. But his greatest concern was that Banner would hurt others . . . *because* they found him.

They're going to find you.

The thought kept flitting through Banner's mind and would not go away.

It followed him as he hitched a ride on the back of a truck with migrant farm workers.

It followed him as he hiked through rugged terrain to avoid border crossings.

It followed him at night as he tried to grab some sleep in a random doorway in an equally random city. He huddled against rain that poured down upon him as if working overtime to make his life as difficult as possible and he tried to put the sense of constant danger from his mind. Finally he drifted to sleep, and as the passing

lights of cars played over him before moving along the
street . . .

**Lights are coming at us, so bright, and the
sounds of a truck horn and a huge crash,
and an explosion, and the noise so overwhelming and**

Banner snapped awake. He shoved the bases of his
palms into his eyes, rubbing the sleep from them.

He felt the anger deep within him, so pure, so un-
diluted, that—not for the first time—it seemed to him
that it had a personality and life all its own. And that
personality was the thing that kept pounding that same
thought of *They're going to find you* through his head.

And still it continued, even after he left the city far behind and found himself crossing the border from Mexico into the United States. He was surrounded by a
group of about thirty people, some of whom were giving
him odd looks since they couldn't fathom what in the
world an American was doing sneaking into his own
country. But nobody asked because, well . . . that wasn't
how it was done. Everyone watched out for themselves
and everyone's business was his or her own.

Even so, when a young child in an overly large family
fell behind in a gully and his parents, dealing with their
large brood, didn't notice at first, Banner stopped while
the child's fellow Mexicans passed him by. He extended
a hand and pulled the child out of the gully, then slung
the youngster up onto his shoulders and hurried his pace
to catch up. The boy's mother had just noticed his ab-
sence when Banner came up behind and handed the boy
off. She smiled gratefully and spoke too rapidly to Banner for him to follow what she'd said. It wasn't necessary, though. The smile said it all.

But still . . .

They're going to find you.

It was there, omnipresent, and Banner finally realized

that it wasn't merely the fact of its existence that he found so disturbing. It was that part of him was actually welcoming it, waiting for it with worrisome anticipation. It wasn't just *They're going to find you*, but *And when they do . . . we'll make them pay.*

He was appalled by the notion that any part of him would welcome the prospect of battle. Yet that was the case here and, when he considered his situation, he couldn't come up with a reason as to why it shouldn't be so. If they had just left him alone, none of this would have happened. Instead he was a perpetual victim, fleeing in the face of an army that just could not get enough of harassing him.

Banner found himself resenting his being perpetually cast in the role of quarry. Wasn't it natural for him to want to strike back? To take the initiative and drive home to them, to General Ross, that enough was enough?

"Shouldn't I just want to smash them?" he muttered, and then he caught himself and heard the words he had just spoken. He stopped as various Mexicans continued to run past him and pushed the notions out of his head as if they were physical things. Then he took a deep breath, let it out slowly, and started running once more, as if he could outrun his own thoughts.

Which, for a while, he was able to do. For several hours, in fact, until the phrase came back to him unbidden as he hitchhiked toward his destination . . .

They're going to find you.

Let them try, Banner thought and, for some odd reason, didn't feel at all disturbed about doing so.

EIGHT

General Joseph Greller sat at the desk in his office, staring at Thunderbolt Ross as if seeing him for the first time. Certainly if he had, in fact, been meeting Ross for the first time, and a total stranger were telling Greller what Ross had just told him, Greller would be halfway to having the man committed. As it was it was all Greller could do not to ask Ross if he was bucking for a psychiatric evaluation.

"You wanna tell me that one more time?" Greller said slowly as if he thought Ross might be joking over this.

Ross picked up on Greller's incredulity, which wasn't all that hard to do. A blind man would have discerned it. "Do I look like I'm not being serious, Joe?"

"T," said Greller, using his old nickname for him, "I've known you a long time and I've never seen a cooler head under fire. I know something bit you in the ass down there." He shook his head. "But that is one hell of a white-whale story. And I am way out on a limb with you on this already."

"Ask Blonsky."

"What, not Sparr?" said Greller.

"No."

"Why not?"

"Because Blonsky had a front-row seat. Besides, Sparr is my aide. You probably think she'll cover for me no matter what."

"Will she?"

Ross shrugged. "Maybe. Maybe not. Doesn't matter what I think, though. What matters is what you think."

"All right, fine." Greller leaned back and rubbed the bridge of his nose as if his eyes hurt. "Get him."

Ross did so, opening the door and gesturing to the outer office. Blonsky strode in, looking sharp in his dress uniform. "Have a seat," said Greller, gesturing toward the chair that Ross had vacated. Once Blonsky sat, Greller continued. "The general here has told me quite a story about what you people encountered in Brazil."

"I wouldn't know about any stories, General Greller," said Blonsky. "I only know about what I saw, and what it did to my men. That was no story, sir, no fairy tale. It was all too real, and good men paid the price for it."

"Paid the price at the hands of a gigantic destructive monster," said Greller, making no effort to keep the skepticism from his voice.

His tone didn't appear to register on Blonsky, or if it did, he ignored it. "Yes, sir, I'd say ten or eleven feet. I'd put it at fifteen hundred pounds easily but it could've been more. And green. Or gray. Greenish gray." When he saw Greller's eyes narrow at the apparent inability to keep his facts straight, Blonsky merely shrugged and said "It was very dark" by way of explanation. He went on to say, "I put three clips in it, sir, and it didn't even flinch. I didn't miss; I'll stake my medals on that."

"That's quite a wager, all things considered, Captain. Is there a medal you haven't won?"

"Medal of Honor, sir. A high percentage are given posthumously, of course."

Greller considered that for a moment and then turned his attention back to Ross. "T, you wanna tell me what the hell you think is really going on here?"

"Banner's work was a tangent of Bio-Tech," said Ross after a moment's hesitation.

Greller didn't make the connection at first. Then, when he started to, he couldn't quite believe what Ross was saying. "You told me you were going to Brazil to nab a scientist. Are you telling me another one of your Super Soldier experiments went haywire?" When Ross nodded, Greller leaned back in his chair, amazed. "And you didn't think it important enough to give me a heads-up?"

"I didn't realize how bad the situation had gotten. It was my miscalculation; I take full responsibility."

"Yes, except you're standing here without a mark on you and I've got two men dead, a third who will likely never walk again, and a fourth who still hasn't regained consciousness. So who's *really* bearing the brunt of your miscalculation?" Ross didn't answer; what was there for him to say? Greller let out a long, annoyed sigh. "Didn't *anything* come out of that program that didn't turn into a mess?"

Sidestepping the question, Ross strode forward and spoke quickly, imploringly. "Joe, we're talking about something that could be an incredibly dangerous weapon in the wrong hands and we have no idea what his intentions are."

"And you're expecting me to provide you with what-ever you need in order to make certain that doesn't happen. What, precisely, are you looking for?"

"Well . . ." Ross cleared his throat and it was obvious that he had some very specific notions in mind to that effect.

Before he could enumerate them, Greller put up a hand, silencing him. "Put together a new list. And," he added, his voice severe, "be prepared to explain *every-thing* on it." The message he was conveying was loud and clear: No more miscalculations. Everyone was to be laid out and judged on its merit without Ross withholding information at his discretion.

Ross nodded and Blonsky saluted, and they walked out of the meeting. Greller sat forward, resting his head on his hands. "Ten foot tall, green and gray. T, what the hell have you landed us in now?"

Blonsky's curiosity was reaching the boiling point. "*Super Soldier* experiments?" said Blonsky as he trailed Ross down the hallway. "Are you telling me he becomes that thing at will?"

"I don't have an answer to that, soldier."

"Greller said it was your program." When Ross didn't respond but instead kept walking, Blonsky persisted, "Well, if we developed it, how'd it end up in some egghead? What the hell happened?"

Ross bridled at Blonsky's tone, stopped, and turned sharply. Blonsky took a step back, startled but not afraid, as Ross said with a snarl, "You're asking questions way above your pay grade, *Captain.*"

If Ross had been under the impression that Blonsky was going to back down when the rank card was played, Blonsky quickly disillusioned him on that score. "Listen, I've run into some bad surprises on crap missions before," said Blonsky. "And I've seen good guys go down because someone failed to let us know what we were walking into. And I've moved to the next one 'cause that's the job. But *this*?" He shook his head. "This is a whole new level of weird and I don't feel very inclined to step away from it. So if you're taking another crack at him, I want in. And with all respect," he added, "you should be looking for a team that's prepped for it and ready to play, because if that thing shows up again, you're going to have a lot of professional tough guys wetting their pants."

Ross studied him hard. He hated to admit it, but Blonsky had hit all the right notes. Blonsky could have been Ross himself thirty, forty years ago.

"Well, all right then."

He said nothing more, but instead turned and walked away. Blonsky followed him, not having to be told to do so. Ross led Blonsky out to a darkened hangar, where the shapes of resting airplanes were barely visible in the shadows. There was a mechanic's table with a work light suspended over it. Ross walked over to the table and leaned against it. He gestured for Blonsky to take a seat and he did so. He sat perfectly still, his hands folded in his lap, and waited attentively for Ross to speak.

"Let me emphasize that what I'm about to share with you is tremendously sensitive to both me personally and the army," said Ross. He waited for Blonsky to acknowledge that, and Blonsky nodded in understanding. "You must be aware that we've got an Infantry Weapons Development program." Blonsky nodded again. "Well, in World War Two, they initiated a subprogram for Bio-Tech Force Enhancement."

"Super Soldier."

"Yes." Ross's expression made it clear that he didn't think much of the term. "An oversimplification, but yes. It got shut down after the war, and then some years back, I stumbled over the records and saw the possibilities." He gestured around them, indicating the operation that was under way around them. "Dusted it off and got serious work going again. Bold work. Across the hall they're trying to arm you better. We were trying to *make* you better, in all the obvious ways and some not so obvious."

"And Banner was part of the project?"

Ross nodded. "Banner's work was a very early phase. It wasn't even a weapons application. His team was combining myostatin with low-dose gamma bursts. *He* thought they could strengthen cellular resistance to radiation. *We* thought it could give our boys built-in insulation against all that depleted uranium nobody likes talking about. It was promising, but politicians don't give a flying F about what *real* soldiers need." Ross made no effort to keep the bitterness from his voice. He had a lengthy history of hostile encounters with politicians and he wasn't the least bit hesitant to let others know exactly what he thought of the weak-willed, spineless fools who held the purse strings for the military. "They like big twin-rotor heliplanes that don't work that they can build in their states. And so our money was running out." He winced at the recollection of what happened next. "Banner was so sure of what he was on to that he tested it on himself. And I . . ." He wanted to deny any knowledge of it. He wanted to state that Banner had proceeded without his approval and that, had he known, naturally he would have prevented it. In short, he wanted to lie. But there was no point. "And I let him," he said. "It was supposed to be very low-exposure and something went very wrong. Or went very right. I still don't know."

Blonsky didn't seem interested in judging Ross on his actions. Instead he was simply curious as to the results. "Why did he rabbit on you?"

Ross had to admit that it was a reasonable question. "Banner was brilliant, one in a generation. But there are people who grasp that peace and freedom derive from power and people who don't. He doesn't. He's a scientist. He's not one of us."

It was obvious from Blonsky's expression that he appreciated the inclusiveness in Ross's phrasing. He nodded in acknowledgment of what he saw as the truth of Ross's words. "So it'd be good to nail him, sure, but why not just take the data to someone else?"

"Because he *is* the data. And he skipped before I could get him on the table and get it out of him. As far as I'm concerned, that man's whole body is property of the U.S. Army."

"You said he wasn't working on weapons. But you were trying other things?"

"One serum we developed was very promising, but it didn't pan out. Or," he said, correcting himself, "it *did* but it was unstable. Made the subjects unstable. I wanted to refine it, but then Al-Haquid happened." He shook his head grimly at the recollection. The entire business had been a total fiasco. A global scandal had ensued when it had been revealed that terrorist suspects were being used for medical experimentation in a detention facility at Al-Haquid. Personally, Ross hadn't had a problem with the concept. Why not press the bodies of America's enemies into service out of medical interest, especially when their best-case scenario was that they were going to blow themselves to bits anyway in service of their terrorist missions? Unfortunately, rather than take a defiant stand and try to explain their reasoning, which might well have gone over with the American public, there had been finger pointing and excuses among the decision makers. The results had been that heads had rolled, especially when photograph evidence had turned up showing the so-called victims splayed naked on tables with doctors leaning over them. "Those pictures at the hearings," Ross grumbled. "The whiners in Congress lost their nerve and they killed it."

"I have real contempt for people like that," said Blonsky.

"You and me both, Captain. You and me both."

This exchange of mutual disdain sat there for a moment, one more step in the unlikely bonding between the two of them. Ross studied him, the wheels turning in his head. "Blonsky, how old are you? Forty-five?"

"Thirty-nine." Blonsky sounded slightly annoyed that Ross had overestimated his age by six years.

Ross laughed it off. "You know, when I came back from Vietnam I was twenty-seven. I looked forty-five. So you're beating the curve." He saw Blonsky smile at that and relaxed slightly. "It takes a toll, doesn't it?"

"Yes, it does."

"So get out of the trenches. You should be a colonel by now, with your record."

"I'm a fighter," Blonsky said firmly. "That's all I ever wanted to be. I'll do it for as long as I can." He leaned back in the chair and looked thoughtful. "It's funny. If I could put what I know now into my body ten years ago, that'd be a guy I wouldn't want to fight."

Ross knew at that point that he had his man. Forcing his voice to remain casual, even disinterested, he said, "I could probably arrange something like that. If you're *really* interested."

Blonsky looked up and stared at him for a long moment before he realized what was being offered. Unconsciously he dropped his voice to a whisper, as if they were being observed. "You said they killed it."

"They killed the program."

"But you kept some of it," he said with growing understanding.

Ross smiled. "You ever hear of saving for a rainy day? Well, I think it's raining."

The research facility was at the far end of the base, in a building so boring and unassuming that Blonsky—who had been on this base any number of times—couldn't recall ever having noticed it before. Ross drove the jeep that transported them over there, and during the entire drive not a word was exchanged between the two of them. Blonsky felt the same way he did when he was on a mission, during which there was no needless chitchat or pointless exchange of niceties. Ross was all business, and Blonsky could respect that. In fact, he was finding a lot about Ross that he could respect.

There was a medical technician waiting for them. Blonsky wondered only briefly how he had known to be there and then gave it no more thought. Obviously Ross had been looking ahead, considering possibilities. It implied to Blonsky that Ross might well have been maneuvering their entire conversation in this direction, looking for a new subject to be experimented upon. If that was the case, it didn't bother Blonsky in the least. He wanted to be better equipped to take on that creature that Bruce Banner could transform into, and if Ross was going to arrange it for his own reasons, who gave a damn as long as it was done?

The technician, a thin black man with the name "Thomas" on a small name plate on his lab coat, led them down into a secured medical storage room. Blonsky watched in silence, as both Thomas and Ross had to punch in codes on keypads, first to get through entrance doors, and then to open one of a line of cold storage lockers. As mist billowed out, courtesy of liquid nitrogen preserving the contents, Ross nodded to Thomas. Thomas, wielding a pair of tongs, carefully removed a metal canister.

It took about forty-five minutes from the time Thomas extracted the Super Soldier serums from the canister to Blonsky finding himself lying on a bed in a lab. As Ross looked on, Thomas was finishing the preparations, inspecting two separate IV bags that were hooked up to stands. The tubes ran down into needles, one into Blonsky's right thigh, and the other into his hip.

"You'll get two separate infusions," said Thomas, "dripped in very slowly. One into the deep muscle," and he pointed to the leg, "and one into bone marrow centers," and he indicated the hip. He looked a bit apologetic as he went on, "The bone ones are going to hurt."

"We're giving you a very low dose only," said Ross. "I need you sharp out there, disciplined. First sign of any side effect and we stop and you're off team until you straighten out. Agreed?"

Blonsky nodded. But he knew that even if he felt as if every muscle in his body was on fire, he'd be damned if he'd let on to Ross or Thomas. He was determined to see this through to the end, whatever it took, and Blonsky excelled at hiding any signs of pain. It was easy. He just disconnected his mind, shut down his pain centers, refused to acknowledge that anything was disturbing them. Pain could be controlled, especially when there was a worthwhile goal to achieve in controlling it.

I'm coming for you, Banner. You and that creature hiding inside you. We're going to have a throw down, you and me, and it's going to turn out very differently than the last one. You probably think you're unbeatable, but you're going to learn otherwise. Oh yes . . . you're going to get schooled, big-time.

NINE

Culver University was a sprawling, semirural campus in southeastern Virginia. In his time there, Bruce Banner had never been happier. It was the perfect place for a scientist: a place of learning that was almost hermetic, with students engaging in lengthy discussions about arcane aspects of research with the ferocity and determination usually accorded matters of life and death.

It made him feel good to be alive.

He stood under a tree, leaning casually against it as if he had every right to be there. Two students walked past and ignored him, which was exactly the nonreaction he'd been seeking. He took the time to scope out his surroundings, not overly intense, but careful. It was a measure of the paranoia that Ross and company had instilled in him that he kept waiting for commandos to come leaping out from behind trees or buildings. But there was nothing. All was still, all was peaceful, just as a campus should be.

He took a slow breath, let it out, and then strolled across the campus, feeling as if he was achingly obvious in trying not to be noticed. Students continued to give him not so much as a first look. So much for the notion of him being loaded with so much charisma that people couldn't take their eyes from him. He approached one building in particular and looked up at the words across the entrance: MAYNARD HALL OF PHYSICAL SCIENCES.

He watched as students and faculty flowed in and out, and waited until the crowd appeared to have thinned. Then he walked up the steps, taking them two at a time, but froze when he got to the door. Through the glass front he saw that a security guard was checking identification while students were being passed through a metal detector. There was far more security than there had been in his day. Apparently his primary plan, namely to stroll into the place and do whatever he wanted, was out of the question. He was going to have to go to plan B . . . whatever the hell that was.

He walked away, head down, thinking, trying to come up with some other angle. He stopped and looked up at another building: the biology faculty building. It was much smaller, barely larger than a brownstone. The building faculty directory was conveniently located on the outside, solving security issues that Banner might have encountered. He ran his fingers down the row of names, wondering if this was a shot in the dark . . .

Nope. There it was:

Cellular Biology—Doctor Elizabeth Ross.

He realized that he was smiling, and figured he probably looked like a fool.

Bruce knew without question that the best possible thing for him to do was be somewhere else. Anywhere else. He endeavored to direct his feet as far away from the biology faculty building as he possibly could. Yet he managed to wind up only about twenty yards away, seated on a bench and once again endeavoring to master the technique of being inconspicuous while in plain sight.

He had managed to acquire a few more accoutrements since crossing the border back into the United States, courtesy of an overflowing Salvation Army bin. He had extracted a couple of deposited bags that hadn't been pushed all the way down, and the bags had yielded a denim jacket that fit him, a new canvas backpack, and a handful of books. He took refuge behind one of those books now, using it to obscure his face so that he could keep an eye on the building without making himself too visible.

The entire time he was chiding himself for the bone-headed maneuver he was attempting. There was every possibility that Ross would have people monitoring his daughter on the assumption that Banner would try to make contact somehow. Of all the people on the planet, Elizabeth Ross was the one from whom Banner should be trying to distance himself as much as possible. Yet here he was like some stalker, hanging around outside her office and waiting for her to emerge so that he could . . . what? Wave to her? Impossible. Speak to her? Unthinkable. Beat himself up emotionally by watching from a distance the woman he dared go nowhere near so that he could stew in his own sense of guilt and frustration and hopelessness? *Yeah . . . that pretty much sounds like it's right up my alley.*

He decided that now was the best time to give up on this misbegotten idea before he got himself in too deep. He was about to close the book, get up, and walk away, and suddenly he froze before he could do any of that.

Betty had emerged from the building. She was chatting animatedly with another woman who was taller and redheaded and, according to the bits of conversation drifting his way, was named Marlo.

Banner thrust the book more directly in front of his face just to make sure that she didn't spot him. It wouldn't have mattered; he could have sat there with a neon sign reading "Hey, Betty, over here!" and she likely wouldn't have noticed him since she seemed so preoccupied. He wondered what they could possibly be discussing that was so interesting.

She was every bit as lovely as he remembered her. The

years between them had done nothing to diminish her radiant beauty. Dark-haired, elegant, almost ethereal, she seemed to glide more than walk, as if she were moving expertly across a frozen lake rather than ground. At least that was how it seemed to Banner, but he would readily admit that he was hardly unbiased in his perceptions of her.

Keep away from her. Wait until she passes, until she's out of view, and then turn and walk in the opposite direction.

She passed by without glancing toward him. He was starting to think that he had missed his calling; judging by the stealth capacities he had displayed thus far, he might have had a promising future as a shadow warrior.

She and Marlo kept going and Banner prepared to turn his back on her and remain exactly where he had been these past three years: safely out of her life. Instead, as soon as she was a safe distance away, he stood and followed her.

You are such an idiot.

He offered his inner voice no argument as he paced Betty Ross, trying to look very much like someone who wasn't pacing Betty Ross. The last thing he needed was to be reported to campus security as some sort of totally out-of-place weirdo who was pursuing a member of the faculty. Every scrap of common sense he possessed told him that he should be doing anything except what he was presently doing. Yet he could not help himself. He was beginning to realize how alcoholics felt. He was addicted to Betty. She was in his blood, in his soul, and he couldn't expunge her no matter how much he desired to. His need for her overwhelmed everything, including common sense.

In a bizarre way, it was liberating, thinking with his emotions for once rather than dispassionately assessing a situation and acting accordingly. He just hoped this reckless indulgence didn't end in disaster, while wondering how it could possibly not turn out that way.

Another indicator of the passage of time: Starbucks had landed a beachhead on campus, just as they had managed to do pretty much everywhere else in the country. That was where Betty and Marlo were clearly headed. Banner, a slave to stupidity, followed. He kept his distance and watched for precisely forty-seven torturous minutes while Betty and Marlo chatted about who-knew-what. He briefly considered strolling in, acting surprised. "Betty! What are you doing here? Crazy coincidence, huh?" But he discarded that notion along with about two dozen other scenarios that were equally ill advised.

Betty appeared to be getting a message on her Black-Berry. He imagined what it might say: *Betty. This is your father. Look to your right and see if Banner is anywhere in the vicinity.* Betty didn't look in his direction, so that was something of a relief. Instead she smiled and typed out a reply to whomever was writing to her. Banner had never quite understood the theory behind text messaging. Technology had finally developed portable phones so that people could speak to each other wherever they were, and the very next development had been a device that enabled people to not have to hear each other's voices anymore. He just didn't see the point. Bringing people together and then distancing them? It was sending mixed messages. Then again, if you were going to send mixed messages, then the best way to do it was with a BlackBerry, so . . .

Marlo had become involved in talking with someone else and Betty, having bid her good-bye, was now walking across the campus. Faced with yet another opportunity to do the right and smart thing, Banner once again didn't hesitate to do the monumentally stupid thing and fall into step behind Betty.

This is ridiculous. She deserves to know you're still alive. She deserves to know that you're trying to cure your condition, that you're here in the States, that and so many other things, but mostly that you still love her. Stop trailing after her like a lovesick schoolboy and go to her.

He started to pick up the pace, knowing that it would take him only a few moments to overtake her. He tried to imagine how she was going to react. Would she leap into his arms? Would she slap him for dropping out of contact for so long? Would she break down and sob, or maybe just pass out, or some combination of all those? It was impossible to know, and yet—now that the moment was at hand—he couldn't wait to find out.

Then he stopped dead in his tracks.

A man had walked up to Betty, smiling with the easy familiarity that only a lover could project. They came together, embracing, and he kissed her on her upturned lips. The man was tall, square-jawed, black-haired, good looking. Clearly he made her happy. Banner had never seen the man before, but the fact that Betty so obviously adored him was all Banner required to despise him instantly.

She called him by name: Leonard.

Banner decided he hated the name "Leonard" as well.

Betty and Leonard linked arms and walked away. Banner watched helplessly as if he were standing on the opposite side of a vast gorge as Betty interlaced her fingers with Leonard's.

It drove home to Banner, as nothing else could have, how different his and Betty's existence had been the past three years. She had moved on, developed new and permanent relationships, followed a career path, and lived a life. Another life that had nothing to do with Bruce Banner. Banner, for his part, had existed in limbo, his life on hold while he tried to stay one step ahead of his pursuers and rid himself of the living time bomb within him. He had wilted while she had blossomed.

He had been deluding himself in thinking that he had any place in Betty's life anymore, or that she would be at all interested in having him in it.

He tried to tell himself that it could have been worse. That he could have yielded to his impulses, approached her, and allowed her to see his world imploding when she told him—as she inevitably would—that he was merely a relic of her past instead of anything resembling a part of her future.

Good for me. I couldn't be happier. My instincts were right. Everything worked out for the best. All I need now is a knife to cut my heart out and we can have a perfect end to this perfect day.

Stanley Lieber was the owner of Stanley's Pizza Parlor, a mainstay of Culver University for as long as anyone could remember. Stan had started there in a part-time capacity back when he'd been a student, just to have some spending money. Back then it had been called Goodman's Pizza, and he'd formed a strong relationship with the then-owner, Marty. When Stan's family had undergone catastrophic financial reversals in the stock market, Stan had found himself without tuition to continue as a student. Marty had kept him on and over time Stan had found his work at the pizza place to be far more satisfying than anything he'd ever experienced as a student. Gregarious by nature, becoming assistant manager at Goodman's Pizza had been a perfect fit for him. When Marty had decided it was time to retire, Stan had been his natural successor. Thus had Goodman's Pizza been rechristened and Stan Lieber had found his niche.

Nationwide pizza chains had tried to open up in competition with Stanley's over the years. One by one they had folded up their ovens and vanished into the night, leaving Stanley's Pizza Parlor winner and still champ, as untouched a part of campus life as the statue of the school's founder that stood in the middle of the quad. More so, in fact, considering that some years earlier a group of students had drilled a gaping hole through the statue's head with an experimental laser. At least Stanley's was still in one piece while birds routinely built nests inside the founder's skull.

Forty years earlier, Stan would never have dreamed that he would be in his sixties and a permanent fixture of the campus that he had initially seen as a mere way station in life. Now he couldn't imagine spending his life anyplace else. His only regret was that he had not groomed any sort of heir for himself, as Marty had done with him. Oh, there'd been this one kid once, some years back. A brilliant mind, great head on his shoulders. Loved pizza. Worked part-time in the parlor, just as Stan had, and displayed the same sort of energy and enthusiasm that Stan remembered he himself had possessed. Somewhat uncharitably, Stan had found himself hoping that the lad would meet with some sort of financial catastrophe so that Stan could take him under his wing as Marty had with him. Then he'd found out the lad was so brilliant that he was there on a scholarship, all his courses and his living expenses covered. The job at the pizza place was just to have some extra walking-around money. Ah well. So much for that plan.

Still, Stan had never forgotten that young lad with the brilliant mind and the promising future; a future that, from what Stan had heard sometime later, had gone completely off the rails. The young lad and his girlfriend . . . oh, she had been a looker. So much his match in every way. They'd been a handsome couple and her mind had been as sharp as his. Stan envisioned a long happy life for the two of them, except, well, that hadn't worked out either. It was like the song said: Life was what happened while you made other plans.

It was late evening and Stan was preparing to lock up. He was standing at the front door, flipping over the OPEN sign to the CLOSED position. He caught a glimpse of himself in the glass of the door and tried to find some sign of the youth he had once been in the lined, careworn face with the mustache and thinning gray hair that gazed back at him.

Suddenly a younger man's face replaced his own, looking in at him with a sense of urgency. The newcomer rapped on the door and Stan was about to inform him in a loud voice that they were closed, sorry, come back tomorrow, special on pepperoni, it'll be worth it. But the intended hucksterish lines died in his throat as he realized who it was that was standing on the other side of the door seeking entrance.

"Oh my God," he whispered and quickly opened up. *"Bruce?"*

Bruce Banner nodded. Stan immediately pulled open the door and gestured for Bruce to enter. Stan was shocked at his appearance as he hustled Banner into the back room. He looked wan and wasted and more desperately in need of three slices of pizza than anyone Stan had ever seen. (Stan tended to measure people in distress by how many slices he thought they required to deal with whatever problems they might have, and this was a three-slicer if ever he'd seen one.)

Bruce offered no protest as Stan shoved a slice into his hand in passing. "I can warm that up if you—" Stan started to say, but he didn't get to finish the sentence as Banner practically shoved the thing down whole. Stan realized he might have underestimated. Good thing he had half a pie left over.

He brought the rest of the pie into the back room as

Bruce sat on a rickety chair. "I can't believe it's you," Stan said. "I thought I was losing my mind."

"I know the feeling," Banner said ruefully. "I have it at least once a day myself."

"What the hell happened to y—" Then Stan put a hand up. "You don't have to tell me if you don't want to. I'm not going to pry."

"I appreciate that, Stan."

"But so many rumors! People say the worst things without any idea what they're saying." He said it wheedlingly, trying to keep to his promise about not prying but at the same time trying to determine what had happened.

Banner smiled at the transparency of Stan's ploy. "Stan, I promise you, whatever you've heard about me isn't true." He'd devoured two slices and was embarking on the third.

"I know it," said Stan, patting his leg. "I know people and I always knew it. But you know how I felt about you two. Have you talked to . . . ?"

Anticipating the question, Banner was already shaking his head. "No. She's with . . ."

"Samson. Yeah, you heard," said Stan.

Bruce frowned. "Well . . . no. Didn't hear, actually. Kind of, well . . . saw."

"Saw? You *saw* her? And she didn't see you? What were you, following her around?"

"No," Banner said far too quickly to be telling the truth. "I just . . . happened to spot her across the quad. On the way here. With some guy. Some . . . big, disgustingly good-looking guy. Named Leonard."

Stan understood. Banner was like a tentative swimmer debating whether to enter the water. It made sense that he would be dipping his toe in experimentally instead of just diving into the deep end. "That would be him, yeah. Leonard Samson. He's a head shrink. They say one of the best. But a good guy. Take my word. Reminds me of you a lit—" Then he saw Banner's face and caught himself. "Sorry, Bruce. What can I do to help?"

"I could use a place to stay for a few nights."

"You'll stay in the spare room upstairs. Use the back, nobody'll see you come or go."

"Great. One other thing . . . can I deliver a few pizzas?"

Stan smiled. It was like old times. "Perfect timing. My regular delivery kid wanted the week off to study for exams. Deliver all you want. But," he added, "someday you gotta tell me what all this was about."

"Stan, if I told you, you'd never believe me."

There was something in Bruce Banner's expression that told Stan he was probably right about that.

TEN

Bruce got to work immediately the next day.

Still feeling the need to keep as low a profile as humanly possible, considering that he was out there in plain sight delivering pies, he wore sunglasses and a "Stanley's Pizza" baseball cap pulled down low on his head as he biked across campus.

How far you've come, Bruce, that you're back to doing your old job from ten years ago.

Of course there was far more involved than just delivering pizzas. Granted, it made him feel like less of a freeloader on Stan if he was doing something to earn his keep, but he had other far more pressing priorities.

His first stop was a dorm room full of kids who were arguing over a physics problem. He couldn't help but smile for two reasons: First, they reminded him of himself at that age; second, every single one of them was dead wrong with their answer. Bruce knew the correct response, but somehow felt that telling them would hardly be the best way to keep a low profile. Word would spread that the pizza delivery guy at Stan's was some sort of genius, and everyone who needed help on just about anything would wind up seeking him out. Not the brightest move.

So he left them to their confusion with great reluctance and continued to his next stop, the sorority house of the Alpha Theta Omega sorority. From what Banner recalled of them, their designation had been well se-

lected because these girls considered themselves the be-
all, end-all of greatness. The moment a laughing blonde
opened the door, took two pies, a bag of garlic knots,
and a bottle of Coke from him without even acknowl-
edging his existence and proceeded to close the door in
his face while uttering a perfunctory "Thanks," he knew
that some things around campus hadn't changed.

He put his hand against the edge of the door and prevented it from shutting. She looked at him oddly, apparently noticing him as a person for the first time.
Astoundingly, it was clear that she had no clue why he
was preventing her from simply taking the food *gratis*.

"Ummm . . . sorry," he said, unsure why he was apol-
ogizing. "That's $46.50."

"Oh. We have an account with Stanley. He knows us.
We're Theta."

"I can see that you are. Do you mind if we call him?"
Bruce didn't have a cell phone, so he gestured toward
the inside of the sorority house, indicating he wanted to
use their phone.

Any last vestiges of pleasantness on her face evaporated, replaced with annoyance. "Yes, I mind. Anyway,
it took forever and now it's cold."

She opened the top pizza box. Steam rose from the os-
tensibly cold pizza. She pulled out a black olive and
flicked it off her finger, and it landed on Banner's hat.

"Ooops. Sorry," she said with as much sincerity as
she had said "thanks" moments earlier.

"You know, you shouldn't make me angry," Banner
warned her. "You wouldn't like me when I'm angry."

"Whatever, psycho," she said dismissively, and slammed
the door on him. Peals of laughter issued from within.
That line about making him angry had sounded so much
better in his head, but it didn't appear to be striking fear
into anyone. At least he'd said it correctly this time instead of massacring it in a foreign tongue, but he had to

think that he might want to consider saying something else when he wanted to warn someone off from annoying him. Perhaps *I'm the best there is at what I do, and what I do isn't very nice.* Or *It's clobbering time.* That sounded good.

He turned to step off the porch and a fat keg delivery kid was coming up the steps. Obviously he'd seen the entire encounter.

"Dude, where are your balls?" demanded the kid. "You can't lay down for that shit! You gotta smash that door in and . . . and tell them . . ."

"It's clobbering time?"

"Yes! Exactly!"

"I'll keep that in mind."

As much as Banner would have loved to go three rounds with the Alpha Theta Omegas, no doubt reducing them to quivering lumps of jelly with his rapier wit and vastly superior intellect, he had more pressing considerations at the moment. To be specific, the target of this entire endeavor: Maynard Hall.

He walked up to the security guard in the main lobby, two pizzas in front of him as if he were carrying a shield. "I got a delivery on five," he said, trying to keep his voice flat and even. There was no reason for him to sound nervous, and if he did, that alone might be enough to alert the guard that something was wrong.

The guard said cautiously, "I don't think anybody's up there."

Banner had expected that, but he tried to make it sound as if it were unwelcome news. "Oh man, everybody's bailing," he said with a moan. "I already got a medium with no takers. You want it?" He indicated the top box.

The guard beamed and reached for it. "God bless, brother." He waved Banner through.

The fifth floor wasn't Banner's destination; it was the

sixth, the site of his old laboratory. He stepped out of the elevator and moved down the corridor, feeling nearly overwhelmed by a sense of nostalgia, of depression, of loss . . . a dozen emotions warring for dominance. He felt as if he had to force himself to feel nothing, lest he be overcome by it all.

The lab itself was not remotely what Banner remembered. It was still a large open space visible through half-glassed walls. But the long worktables were full of computer terminals, and larger supercomputer arrays were along the walls. It had been turned into a computer science lab in the intervening years.

Even more problematic was that it wasn't empty. There was a lone grad student burning the midnight oil at a terminal. He looked brain-fried, his eyes bleary. He looked up at Banner, except Banner's thoughts were a million miles away. He was seeing the lab not as it was now, but as it had been . . .

Betty is standing behind an Asian grad student, while Banner is focusing on the gamma pulse machine. He catches a glimpse of himself in the polished metal of the machine and sees the white cross made of light on his forehead, and then the memories begin to spiral forward and there are horrible sounds of sparks and static and crashing metal, smoke, two of Banner's grad students lying still under a large smashed console driven back into them, Betty still on the ground next to them, a gash in her head, a military aide also dead on the floor with a gun in his hand and between Bruce and the door is General Ross looking up, up, because Bruce Banner, or the thing that was Bruce Banner, is looming over him, and Ross is backing up, clutching

his left arm, his face twisted in agony, and Ross is trying to get to Betty who is

Looking up at Banner, the grad student seemed to be coming out of his study-related stupor as he focused on the pizza. Banner took a moment to compose himself, shunting away the memories that had flooded over him, all unwanted. He forced a smile to his face and entered the lab.

"Those douches in radiation called this in and then split," said Banner. "You want it?"

"Whoever you are, you are my new personal hero," said the student. "Amadeus Cho, at your service, and you couldn't have come at a better time. Gotta feed the brain."

"Feed away." He placed the pizza in front of Cho and then, trying to sound as casual as he could, indicated the nearest computer terminal. "Hey, would you mind if I jumped online for a second?"

"Totally," said Cho, waving him to go ahead.

He got to work accessing the university's mainframe. The screen prompted him for a user name and he typed in "Dr. Elizabeth Ross." The password prompt then came up. It had always amused him in movies when people were depicted trying to crack into someone's computer account and just seemed to magically guess the user's password after one or two false tries. Fortunately enough Banner had a leg up, because Betty had never been hesitant to share her passwords with him back in the day, and she was a creature of habit. So the odds were that she hadn't changed them.

He typed in "BettylovesBruce."

The word "Rejected" came back at him immediately.

Well, it just doesn't get more ironic than that, he thought, but he was not finished yet. He tried another of her old ones: "Cellsunite." The computer seemed to ponder that one for a moment, and Bruce's heart was in his throat; if that one didn't take, he really *was* going to wind up having to throw words at random at it and pray one of them stuck. Fortunately it didn't come to that, because the computer accepted the password and he was in.

That was as far as his luck took him.

He began searching, not Betty's files, but his own. Specifically, he was trying to find records of his own work. But a search under "USMD Research Protocol 456-72378" produced no results. Neither did "Gamma Pulse." He tried everything he could think of, including his own name, but still came up empty. He hated to admit it, but that last one stung even more than the rejection of her old password. He thought of the Orwellian term "nonperson." That was what he had become. As far as the database of Culver University was concerned, Bruce Banner was a nonperson. He had simply ceased to exist, although unfortunately his lack of existence wasn't so comprehensive that the army would hesitate to shoot him on sight.

All evidence of his efforts, his experiments, his personal history, had been thoroughly expunged. For all that he had accomplished on an official level, he might as well have never lived at all.

As he sagged back in the chair, trying to figure out what to do next, an icon popped up on the screen, accompanied by a ringing sound. He looked up and saw that he was receiving a chat invite from someone calling himself or herself "Stealthwarrior229." He looked at it for a long time as the ringing continued.

He had no idea what to do, frozen by indecision. Common sense said it was impossible that they had found him here. But . . . what if they had? What if this was some sort of trick? What if he clicked on it, accepted it, and in doing so confirmed their suspicions, causing half a dozen commandos to come crashing in from all directions?

On the other hand, what if it was friend and not foe?

Feeling as if he were taking his life in his hands, he clicked "Accept." The video chat window opened to reveal a digital animation of a huge monstrous creature. Banner's eyes went wide as he watched the monstrosity smash through walls, rampaging. Whoever the hell this was, they knew. *They knew.* And they were warning him that they were coming for him, that they were going to "out" him.

He gripped the armrests, paralyzed, wanting to bolt but transfixed by the sight of the cyber beast as it continued on its rampage and then, abruptly, it found . . .

A box of pizza, whereupon the monster ate the pizza, box and all. And as Banner watched uncomprehendingly, the monster started to shrink rapidly, growling in contentment, until it transformed into an image of the grad student, Amadeus Cho.

Trying to stop his heart from racing, Banner lifted his head to look above the computer and across the rows of terminals. Cho was giving Banner a thumbs-up.

Banner didn't know whether to laugh, cry, or take the computer monitor and smash it over the kid's head. He settled for returning the gesture halfheartedly and then getting the hell out of there.

"Gone. All of it. Like it never happened."

Banner was seated in the small, spare room above the pizza place that Stan had made available to him. He was perched on the edge of the bed with a hangdog expression. He looked like someone who had just had his hopes crushed at every level. Stan, sitting opposite him, was sure that Bruce pretty much looked the way he felt. Stan was unsure what he could possibly say in this situation that would serve to make Banner feel better. He settled for providing straightforward information: "The whole building was closed for a year after the explosion. Military guards . . ."

Banner showed no interest in finding out the details. Probably it was of no consequence as far as he was concerned. It was in the past, and to hear Bruce tell it, he had been excised from the past like a cancer. What was the point in learning the specifics of what had happened?

Leaning forward, resting his chin dejectedly on his hands, Banner said, "I don't know what I was thinking. There's nothing for me here. I don't know why I came . . . I hoped . . ."

The words hung there, the things that he wasn't saying nevertheless speaking volumes. "What'll you do now?" said Stan.

Banner shrugged. His trip to his old stomping grounds had been a failure. There seemed no point in hanging around, unless he was hoping to make a go of it as a pizza delivery guy. "I'll go in the morning."

"Where?"

"It's better if I don't tell you, Stan."

With the heavy sigh of someone who felt utterly helpless, Stan said, "I'm so sorry. I wish I could . . ."

"You did help me, Stan," said Banner, patting Stan on the leg. "You've got no idea how nice it is just to see a friendly face."

From downstairs, the bell on the door tinged, indicating that a customer was entering. Banner took that as his cue and stood. "I should get going."

He started to reach for his knapsack to gather his few belongings, but Stan promptly brushed Banner's hand away. Bruce looked up at him in confusion. "You're not going anywhere," said Stan firmly. "It's about to rain like hell. I'll close up and we'll have some food." Bruce looked as if he was about to offer protest, but Stan pulled an imaginary zipper on his lip to indicate that Bruce should save his breath. Smiling in spite of himself, Bruce mimicked the gesture as Stan turned and hurried down the stairs. He was determined to usher out as quickly as possible whoever it was that had shown up downstairs. He didn't care if it cost him some business, or even some regular customers. Right now Bruce Banner was his only consideration. He called, "Folks, I'm closing up," even as he considered the fact that he knew he could do nothing to ease the soul ache the poor young guy was feeling for—

"Betty . . . ?"

He stood at the bottom of the steps that led into the main part of the small restaurant. Looking at him encouragingly was Elizabeth Ross standing next to Leonard Samson. "Come on, Stan," Betty said pleadingly, "it's Friday night!"

Stan tried to think of what to say, and nothing was readily presenting itself. He felt as if having Banner and Betty in the same building was courting disaster. "Oh, kids . . . I got nothing but a few marinaras . . ."

"Oh, I need a Mr. Pink, Stan, please! I'm dying!" It was her favorite style of pizza, a Stan original with a unique combination of plum tomatoes, shrimp, and peppers.

Samson looked at her affectionately and said in a what-can-you-do manner, "She worked through dinner again, of course."

Stan wanted to argue the point, be insistent. But it would have seemed strange and out of character. Worse, it would have aroused Betty and Samson's suspicions. He doubted Betty would make the mental leap to "Have you got Bruce stashed here somewhere?" but if they thought something was genuinely wrong, then God only knew when they would leave. Besides, she was looking at him so pleadingly, and Stan didn't see how he could just turn her down flat that way purely on a humanitarian basis. He glanced nervously toward the back room and then said gamely, "Sure. For you, sure. No problem, Betty." He said those last words particularly loudly in hopes that his voice would carry upstairs, lest Bruce walk into the middle of a very uncomfortable situation.

Bruce heard Stan talking downstairs to someone, but couldn't make out any details, although he thought he heard the name "Benny." He didn't give it any particular thought as he continued to pack his bag. It certainly wasn't going to take long to get his things together. It required two minutes and that included checking over the room three times to make certain he wasn't leaving anything behind. He knew what Stan had said about staying, but he saw no point. He associated nothing but pain with Culver University in general now, and Betty in specific. Why prolong the agony?

He glanced around the room one final time and then turned off the light.

Stan was making the pizza as quickly as he could, wishing that somehow he could change the laws of physics and make the oven bake the pizza faster than it always did. He heard movement upstairs and prayed that Bruce wasn't getting ready to go despite Stan's urging to remain where he was.

Samson was regaling Betty with a story about a patient, being careful not to mention any names. "And he's telling me that he has come to believe that he's Switzerland."

"You mean the country?"

"The whole country. His logic was pretty straightforward: Switzerland loves freedom. He loves freedom. Therefore, he is Switzerland."

Betty laughed delightedly at that. When she did so,

she made a snorting noise, which embarrassed her and caused her to laugh all the harder because of it. She turned away from Samson in an endeavor to pull herself together and she focused her attention on the pizza. "Not too spicy, Stan," she managed to say.

Putting forward an air of joviality, Stan said, "I know how you like it."

Samson came around and walked to the far wall against which there was a jukebox. He started studying the song choices.

Then Stan saw a movement at the door leading to the back room, and he heard Bruce's voice call, "Stan?"

Betty heard it as well.

Her head snapped in the direction of the speaker, and although Banner was just out of Stan's line of vision, Stan could see from her reaction that Banner had to be standing right there and she was looking straight at him.

Just in case there was any doubt in Stan's mind that Betty had spotted him, he saw her mouth Bruce's name.

At that moment Samson stepped away from the jukebox and turned to face Betty. In doing so, he came between her and her view of the back area. He saw the look on her face and he said quizzically, "Betty? What's wrong—?" An instant later the back door banged sharply. Samson turned in response to it.

Betty was on her feet and rushing past Samson, pushing him to the side so quickly that he stumbled and almost fell. He barely caught himself on the edge of the counter. "Betty?" he said again, but there was no one for him to say it to. She was gone out the back door.

Bruce dashed into the back alley and looked around desperately. He saw the Dumpster and flattened against the far side, pressing himself so firmly against it that he thought he was going to blend with the metal. Then he held his breath.

He heard the back door slam open and Betty's voice screech his name. In the distance, thunder rumbled. She shouted his name again, trying to get above the sound of the thunder. *If she comes around to this side of the Dumpster, there's nowhere for me to hide.* The one thing he had going for him was that she wasn't thinking straight. Perhaps she wasn't even completely convinced that she'd seen him. She'd only caught a glimpse of him for less than a second before Samson, with perfect timing, had blocked him from view. And the fierce wind that was whipping down the alley could have been responsible for the door banging open.

Thunder rumbled again, far closer this time, and rain began pouring. Bruce sank farther down, almost to the ground, trying to blend with the shadows. Then he heard the door fly open again. Samson was shouting, "Betty, what in God's name—?!" He heard a scuffling of feet and figured out that he had Betty by the arm and was trying to pull her back into the pizza place. This was confirmed when Samson said, "Come inside!"

He heard her feet move across the floor of the alley and the door slammed shut yet again. But it did so with such force that it rebounded and flew back open. From within he could hear Betty saying, far more loudly than she probably intended to, "Please don't lie to me. If you lie to me right now, I'll never forgive you."

"Betty, I don't . . ." he heard Stan start to say.

She cut him off. "I saw him, Stanley. Please tell me the truth."

That was all Banner had to hear. Cursing to himself, he sprinted down the alley, remaining in a crouch until he got to the far end. At that point he straightened up and started to run. He skidded on the now slick sidewalk, almost fell, righted himself at the last second, and kept going.

If he had thought that this little venture had been a

failure before, it had now hit rock bottom. Despite his best efforts to the contrary, he had inserted himself back into Betty's life, reopening old wounds and giving her needless heartache. *How much more are the people you love going to suffer because of you, Banner?*

He should never have gone there.

But now that he had . . . what the hell was he supposed to do? Leave Betty high and dry? Because he knew that Stan was going to tell Betty everything; there was no way he wouldn't. What was it going to do to her knowing that he'd been there for the better part of a week, had been watching her without making contact? He was doing her a great cruelty. He had been many things, done many things, but he had never been cruel.

Until now.

And there wasn't a damned thing he could do about it.

Except that wasn't exactly true. There was something he could do.

He just wasn't going to.

ELEVEN

The rain was coming down with full force as Samson pulled the car up into the driveway and into the garage.

He glanced toward Betty, who was seated next to him. She had been trembling for a while, but had calmed down somewhat on the trip back home. Samson was reasonably sure that she had managed to overcome the initial shock of what she had seen with her own eyes and learned from Stan. Now it was clear she was in deep thought. Samson had a fairly good idea of what she was going to say before she said it. He was, after all, an experienced psychologist, and had been with Betty for some time. That was a pretty unassailable combination when it came to predicting what she was going to say or do. It gave him the opportunity to prepare his response and mentally practice it a few times so that it would sound completely spontaneous when she had her say. In this case, he was mentally practicing the words *I think you should*. It was important that not only did it seem spontaneous but also that he meant it. Because the truth was that he thought it was quite possibly the worst notion that he had ever conceived. Unfortunately, as a psychiatrist, he had seen self-destructive behavior enough times to know that it was nearly impossible to turn someone away from such a course. They had to see for themselves the tragic ends to which such decisions could lead and then deal with the consequences. All he could do in such circumstances was offer after-the-fact guidance and hope that his patients learned from their mistakes.

Betty turned to him and said with quiet conviction, "I need to go find him."

"I think you should," he said. He saw the look of gratitude in her face and nodded. "I'll be here."

He stepped out of the car and Betty slid over into the driver's seat. She gunned the engine and pulled out of the driveway so quickly that an oncoming car had to swerve, horn blasting, to avoid getting broadsided. Samson mentally kicked himself. In being concerned over Betty's mental well-being, he had given no thought to the prospect that in her agitated state of mind and considering the weather conditions, her quest to exhume old ghosts might well conclude with her wrapping herself around a tree. He should have offered to go with her as driver. After all, he had no emotional investment in finding Bruce Banner beyond the notion of serving Betty's peace of mind.

He shouted to her, trying to call her back, but a rumble of thunder overhead drowned out his voice. By the time it subsided, she was gone.

Bruce walked slowly down the side of the highway, his jacket pulled up and over his head. Every time a car approached he would halfheartedly stick out his thumb, trying to grab a ride. Cars instead tended to speed up, as if concerned that somehow he was going to run alongside them and leap into the moving vehicle if they slowed to thirty-five miles per hour. They also tended to display impressive timing, finding puddles to zip through so that water could cascade over him in great gouts. He reminded himself that, next time he had the opportunity to scrounge through a Salvation Army box or Dumpster, he should see if he might be able to locate a discarded raincoat, or perhaps even an umbrella.

As he trudged along the highway, he tried to figure if this was the worst day of his life, or merely the second worst. Yes, the day of the misbegotten experiment when he had subjected himself to the gamma rays that had destroyed his life was probably the single worst, but this was right up there beside it. Combined with the events of the rest of the week, and he had to wonder whether—instead of trying to flag down the next car—he shouldn't just throw himself in front of it. Except there was no point in doing so, because he knew what was going to happen if he tried. *It* would emerge, that vast gray/green survival instinct incarnate, and the result would be a smashed-up car and, most likely, a dead driver.

He saw a truck approaching and redoubled his efforts to flag it down. The truck began to slow. He didn't know what it was about truckers that made them more amenable to picking up hitchers. Probably it was because they traveled coast to coast and were willing to take the risk that giving lifts to strangers entailed, just to break up the monotony. Banner could have been on the shoulder of the road wearing a hockey mask and waving a chainsaw and sooner or later some long-distance trucker would have said, "Aw, what the hell," and pulled over.

The trucker slowed and then stopped. As the rain poured down, the trucker rolled down the passenger side window and called out, "Where ya goin'?"

"On a night like this, does it matter?" Banner said, gesturing to the deluge above.

The trucker grinned widely. He had a couple of missing teeth, but Banner wasn't interested in his orthodontia; just the cab of his truck. "Good point," he said, and gestured for Bruce to climb in.

And that was when Bruce saw her.

She was still driving the same old crappy car from three years ago. She hadn't even bothered to get the dent in the right fender fixed from the time that idiot bicyclist had rammed into her while she was sitting at a traffic light.

She was going slowly, trying to watch the road, her head swiveling like a radar dish. She had not, however, spotted Bruce, since he was blocked from view by the stopped truck. She put on her signal and moved around the truck. Betty probably thought that the trucker had just pulled over to ride out the inclement weather or catch some shuteye.

All he had to do was stay where he was and she would go right on past, not having realized that the trucker was in the process of picking up the man she was looking for.

She's looking for me.

It was a startling realization for him. It was one thing to dash out into an alley shouting his name. But she had climbed into a car and, on a rotten night like this, was driving around on the off chance that she might spot him.

After all he had done to her, this was her response.

What sort of repayment for that level of selfishness was his hiding, letting her pass by, knowing that she might well be driving around for hours in a fruitless search while he was riding away into the night?

He had almost killed her three years ago, but the one element of that fiasco that he had clung to, the one thing that allowed him at least some measure of sleep at night, was that he had never meant to hurt her. There was no such excuse this time. He was deliberately hurting her, and all his convictions that he was doing it for her own good were ringing hollow.

Without even thinking about it, he walked out in front of the truck so that he was backlit by the head-lights. Betty had just moved past and was about twenty feet away, no doubt reflexively glancing in the rearview to make sure that it was safe to get back into her own lane.

The car suddenly slammed to a halt, skidded, and wound up on the shoulder. The driver's-side door flew open and Betty emerged. The rain was coming down so hard that she was soaked to the skin in a matter of seconds. She didn't appear to care.

She moved slowly at first, but then she was at a dead run, sprinting along the road to him, as if afraid that if she didn't move quickly enough he would vanish. He remained rooted to the spot. "Hey buddy, in or out?" called the trucker, and then Betty threw her arms around him and hugged him so tightly that he didn't have sufficient breath to respond. He didn't need to. He heard the trucker say, "I guess that's 'out.' Give 'er one for me, fella," and then the truck pulled out and away. Betty continued to squeeze Bruce the entire time.

His arms remained at his sides for as long as he could manage the restraint, and finally he no longer could. He reached up and around and returned the embrace, and only then did she finally speak: "Please don't go away. Please. I need to see you and talk to you."

"I want to so much," he said. "But it's not safe."

"I don't care. Please. You can't just disappear again. I couldn't take it."

How could she possibly be saying these things? Betty, of all people, who knew the risks involved in his very presence? "I don't want to make things more difficult for you. I couldn't bear that."

She had been speaking with her head pressed sideways against his chest. Now she pulled her head back and looked him full in the eyes. She spoke with a tone that indicated her mind was already made up on the subject, and now it was just a matter of making that abundantly clear to Bruce. "I want you to come with me now. He does, too."

"He?" He looked at her blankly.

"Leonard Samson. Stan said you know about us. He told me everything."

"And Leonard wants me back in your life," Banner said, unable to keep the sarcasm from his voice.

Very softly, she said, "You were never *out* of my life."

And he knew what she meant, because she had never been out of his, although thousands of miles had separated them.

He didn't need to say anything else. Instead he simply nodded. She put her arm around his and guided him to the car as if she were leading a blind man. That might not have been entirely wrong, because for three years he had been wandering in darkness, like a boat adrift with no bearings, and Betty was his lighthouse.

He just hoped that he didn't wind up crashing on rocks.

Betty's car pulled in through the driveway of her house, the garage door opening in response to the automatic door opener she had in her car. She pulled in, seemingly alone in the vehicle, and then clicked the remote once more. The door slid shut behind her, and only when it was completely closed did Banner sit up. "I think I soaked through the seat," he said apologetically.

"It'll dry." She put her fingers in his hair and wrung out some of the rainwater. "You didn't have to hide, you know."

"Habit. You never know who's watching. And if I were your father, I'd be watching you every second."

She shook her head and said, "He's not . . . really that much of a factor in my life these days."

Bruce was about to respond to that, but then realized

that it was obviously a sore subject and wisely decided to let it drop.

There was a doorway that led from the garage into a mudroom that in turn connected to the kitchen. As Banner and Betty entered, and shucked off their rain-sodden coats, Banner could hear Samson's voice coming from just beyond the kitchen. He sounded as if he were in the middle of a telephone conversation.

"Forgive me for pointing out that that contradicts everything you've told me about this situation . . . hang on a moment."

Samson stepped into the kitchen and looked at Betty and Bruce entering the kitchen from the mudroom. Water began to collect under both their feet. Samson was speaking into a cell phone, confirming Banner's guess, and Samson said, "Tilda, it'll be fine. I know it's Friday night . . . we'll pick this up in our session. Bye." He snapped the phone shut, smiled and said, "Patient."

There was a roll of paper towels on a counter near him. He picked it up and flipped it to Betty, who promptly began using it to wipe up the drips. Meantime he approached Banner and put out his hand. It was all Banner could do not to take a step backward in anticipation of Samson endeavoring to belt him. He wouldn't have blamed him. If Banner had really never been out of Betty's life, as she had claimed, then it couldn't have been easy for Samson to come face-to-face with the other man, as it were. But there was no hint of threat in Samson's bearing or manner. Instead, with what seemed sincere warmth, he said, "Leonard Samson. Welcome."

Banner shook his hand. It was quite firm. "Now," said Samson, "both of you go get out of those wet clothes. I think we all need some hot food and a number of drinks. You two are talking, I'm cooking. Now go."

He shuffled the two of them out of the kitchen. Betty steered them upstairs, where Bruce went into the spare bedroom and changed into the one extra set of clothes he had with him. It was slightly damp, since the knapsack wasn't one hundred percent waterproof, but his own body heat would dry it out. Then he went back downstairs, where Betty was in the living room, pouring them a couple glasses of wine. To allow for his perpetual sense of paranoia, she had drawn all the curtains so that no one would be able to see that he was there. He took one of the glasses of wine and she held up her own. "To old friends," he said.

"And new ones," she replied, tilting her head toward the kitchen in acknowledgment of the sounds issuing forth, courtesy of Samson preparing food.

They clinked glasses and sipped. The wine burned pleasantly going down Banner's throat. For the first time in ages he felt civilized.

"So . . . my God, Bruce, I don't know where to start. Tell me where you've been."

He started with his sojourn to Alaska, although he omitted the part about his attempted suicide. He didn't think that would be the best way to begin his travelogue, particularly with a psychiatrist nearby. And then he continued rattling off his journeys, trying to sound casual about it all. Nevertheless, Betty's eyes kept widening as he spoke of each new destination.

". . . and they just let you stay?" said Betty, when he got to the part about his time at a Tibetan monastery.

"I think it was novel at first," he said. "They don't get the spiritual tourism up there on the Northern Plateau. And I'm good at fixing things, so . . ." and he shrugged, "it was peaceful. For a long time that's all I wanted. When I heard the rug dealer down in town had gotten Internet, my brain started going and eventually I couldn't resist. That's how I got to Mr. Blue . . ."

"Mr. who?"

"A man named Sterns."

"Sterns. Samuel Sterns?"

He nodded, pleased that she'd heard of him. It would save him time, not having to go into detail about him. He wasn't surprised that she would know who he was; with the level of complexity of his work and the manner in which it overlapped with their own, Sterns would certainly have come to Betty's attention. He described to her the experimentation in which they had engaged, and watched the growing excitement in her face as she realized that he was speaking of a potential cure for his condition. Banner's own enthusiasm grew as he watched hers. It was the first time he'd actually had the opportunity to discuss these sorts of things with someone face-to-face. "And trimethodine . . . ?" she prompted when he stopped to refill the wineglass.

"I didn't think you could synthesize an inhibitor that complex, but he has been," said Banner. "I mean, three years ago . . ."

"We're all a lot further along than we were then, but Sterns is way out in front on that score," Betty admitted. "He had some kind of ethics cloud around him, but his work was so unbelievably brilliant it didn't stop him. So . . . Brazil for the corablanca?"

Banner nodded. "He's synthesizing it but I had to try to get it at the source. It took a long time just to get there. And I couldn't get a thousandth of what I'd need. If he's even right . . ."

"And now?"

"I go find him, I suppose," Banner said with a shrug. "I don't know if he's really got something, and it's a much longer shot without the data from the lab. But what choice do I have?"

She pursed her lips for a moment, then got up and went to a bookshelf with a vase on it. She reached into the vase and removed a small data flash card. It was suspended on a hook, attached to a lanyard. She went back and handed it to him. He gasped as he realized what he was looking at.

"I got in there before they carted it all away," she said. "I hoped it would tell us something someday."

Speechless, he could only manage to shake his head. "What?" Betty said.

Finally he found his voice. After nothing but setbacks, pursuit, threats, heartbreak, and disappointment, to have something like this simply handed to him . . . "Sometimes," he finally said, "there's hope . . . so quickly. Thank you." The words seemed inadequate, but they were all he could manage. Then his standard sense of paranoia reasserted itself. "Does the general know you have this?" he said with cautious concern.

"I don't think so, no."

Banner let out a sigh of relief. He saw the confused look on Betty's face and said by way of explanation, "He was there in Brazil. When they came for me. I saw him."

Betty clearly couldn't believe it. "Oh my God." Then she lowered her voice. It was as if she was concerned they were being bugged. It seemed that Banner's paranoia was starting to get to her. "He's crazier than anybody knows. I'm so sorry. How?"

"Did they find me, you mean?" She nodded. "I've twisted it around every possible way. Is there any way it could have been Sterns?"

But Betty shook her head. "I heard he's a total anarchist. Hates authority. Doesn't think he should answer to anybody. That's why he got in trouble."

"Then it certainly doesn't seem likely that he'd call in the army on me."

"Not really, no." She paused, and then said, "Bruce, why didn't you . . ."

Before she could complete the thought, Samson

stepped out of the kitchen and rubbed his hands together briskly. "I think we're all set."

He had prepared a splendid lamb stew that he served up with obvious satisfaction at the dining-room table. Banner didn't know whether to be incredibly grateful or insanely jealous, and settled for an uneasy mix of the two. As time passed, though, and convivial conversation ensued, Banner slowly came to like Samson more and more. If nothing else, he could take solace in the fact that Betty had chosen a good man who could make her happy . . . something that he, Banner, was in no position to do.

Keeping discussion light, Samson was talking about a recent patient. "And I said, Miss So-and-So," yet again cautiously omitting proper names, "I've been analyzing your condition for nearly three months and I think I can say conclusively that your issues are more caffeinated-uncaffeinated than manic-depressive."

Betty roared with laughter while Samson smiled, pleased that he had amused her. Even Banner allowed a chuckle, which was about as demonstrative as he ever permitted himself to be. He found it easier to keep himself on an even keel if he didn't allow extremes of any sort.

Adding her own interpretation to Samson's diagnosis, Betty said, "You're not so much multiple personality as spoiled brat."

Banner put in, "And your son doesn't have ADD, he's just not that bright," which caused another round of laughter.

Finally composing herself, Betty reached over and slapped Samson on the back of the hand in a mock-scolding manner. "It makes you sound cruel," she said, and then turned to Bruce and explained, "but Leonard takes a few of these to pay for all the free work he does."

"Pro whiners to pay for the pro bono," said Samson.

And something about that comment got to Banner. He started laughing, genuinely laughing without holding back as he had been before. He was laughing so hard that he had to hold his stomach as if afraid that it was going to explode. Then Banner realized that he was no longer laughing as tears started pouring down his face. Something long-held was being released and he began simply to cry. It was exactly as he had feared. By allowing himself to indulge in one extreme of emotion, it broke down the barriers to others that he managed to keep in check.

Betty and Samson lapsed into silence, bearing witness to Banner's emotional meltdown. After a few moments, Betty reached over and took his hand, lending him some of her strength until he was able to pull himself together.

"I'm so sorry," he said, feeling abashed. "It's been a long time since I felt . . . light . . . about anything."

"It's all right. You're with friends," she said, giving his hand a squeeze. She got up from the table. "Come here. I want to show you something."

She brought him into the living room while Samson cleared away the dinner dishes. There was an alcove above her office, and on a shelf—lovingly surrounded by specialized lighting—was an orchid blooming in a small trough of dirt. It was gorgeously delicate and exotic, and Banner leaned in close to look at it with growing amazement. Betty stuck her head in next to him, pleased at the smile on Banner's face.

"My God, you grew it," he said. "I knew if anybody could that you could."

"It shouldn't survive here. It took four months just to cultivate the bacteria for the soil. I almost lost it three or four times, but it's held on somehow . . . despite everything."

He studied it for a while longer. There was so much preying on his mind, so many apologies he wanted to make, and he scarcely knew where to start. "I wanted to send you something to let you know I was . . . I'm so . . ."

"I know." She rested a hand on his arm. "I . . ."

Samson chose that moment to enter the alcove. Banner felt that the psychiatrist's timing bordered on the supernatural. He smiled and said, "Ahhh, my rival for her affection." Banner was taken aback that Samson would speak that way of him before he realized that the reference was to the orchid. "Between work and this little guy I have to fight for position."

With Samson having rejoined them, the rest of the evening's chat returned to harmless subjects. It seemed simpler that way. When enough time had passed and midnight approached, it was mutually decided that a long day had been had by all, and it was, well, time to put an end to it.

Standing in front of the guest bedroom, Banner shook Samson's hand. "Good night."

"Sleep well," said Samson.

Samson headed for the room that Banner knew he shared with Betty. He realized it was a very different situation to be faced with the actuality of their being together as opposed to knowing it intellectually.

"Do you need anything?" she said.

"No. I should go early tomorrow." He hated to bring it up, but he said, "If I can borrow cash from you, I'll take the bus."

"Of course. I'll drive you out to the station."

It was hard, even awkward for her to leave him alone. He felt so tired and lonely. Finally she turned away, and really, what could he have said to her? What should he have said?

The sad truth was that, when it came to their relationship, there was nothing left to say.

* * *

Samson could hear Betty in the bathroom, crying hard. She was doing her best to stifle it, but sounds of her sobs were still getting through. He considered going to her, knocking on the door, asking her if she wanted to talk. But he restrained himself. Instead he remained in the bedroom until finally she emerged. Her eyes were red-rimmed from the crying. She stood there, not approaching him, and so he went to her because now she very much looked as if she needed him. He embraced her and softly, she said, "Thank you."

Bruce couldn't sleep.

He stared up into the darkness, thoughts of his and Betty's past running through his mind. Betty lying in a sunny room under sheets next to him . . . playing with his hand . . . biting his fingertips . . . the two of them sharing a pizza, arguing over a glass of wine about a particular esoteric point of science. He wondered if Betty was likewise awake and having similar recollections.

They were not all pleasant recollections, though. Unfortunately they all kept coming to the same tragic end: Betty lying in a coma while Banner confronted General Ross. Those two final images, the unconscious Betty and her injured father, were inextricably linked in his mind's eye.

Then he heard a noise in the living room. A distant thump. He sat up instantly, any vague sense of fatigue burned away. *Ross* was the first thing he thought as he envisioned commandos charging in.

Except if there were indeed commandos, he wouldn't have heard them. Ross's people were simply too well trained to wind up bumping around in the dark.

He tossed aside the sheets and quickly pulled his pants and shirt on, just in case. He placed an ear against the door and listened carefully before he realized what he was hearing.

Someone was putting logs into the fireplace.

That would certainly seem to eliminate any lingering possibility of it being commandos, or even burglars or some other sort of intruder. They would hardly pause in their endeavors to stop and build a cozy fire.

Still, he remained cautious as he entered the darkness of the living room. Sure enough, Samson was crouched in front of the fireplace, adding a log to a small fire he had going. That didn't surprise Banner, since he had already figured out as much. What did surprise him was that Samson had laid out a pillow and blanket on the couch for himself. He had a bottle of wine on the table nearby.

"Hey," said Banner.

He had spoken as softly as he could, but that didn't prevent him from startling Samson, who twisted about so violently that he wound up losing his balance and sitting down hard. He squinted in the dim lighting. "Good lord, you scared me."

He raised himself up and sat on the couch, gesturing for Banner to take a seat in the chair opposite him. Banner did so. Before he could ask Samson why the doctor had relocated to the living room, Samson anticipated the question and said, "It doesn't take a psychiatrist for me to see that, as Betty was lying there trying to pretend she was asleep, you were figuratively, if not literally, right there beside her. And since it was getting crowded with the three of us there, I thought it might be easier for all of us. Want some wine? I'm having a lot."

They both laughed at the absurdity of the situation. Why not? There was simply no getting around it. Samson drained the glass of wine that he had already poured, refilled it, and then gave the remainder in the bottle to Bruce. Bruce took it and clinked the bottle against the glass. They spoke in low tones so as not to disturb Betty. "You've been incredibly generous. I'm very sorry to have . . . dropped in like this."

"I think I read a Raymond Carver story about a situation like this once," said Samson, his brow furrowing in thought. "It was called 'The Cathedral.' I seem to remember thinking there was a lesson in it but it eludes me at the moment. So much for the insights of literature."

"Whatever you may think, I didn't come here to see Betty."

Slowly Samson put down the glass. "Then why did you come?" He didn't sound skeptical or hostile or judgmental. His voice was flat and neutral.

"I have a problem. I thought part of the solution might be here."

"Cryptic. But I'll take it at face value." He stared at the glass sitting on the table as if he could discern great truths reflected in it. *In vino veritas,* thought Banner as Samson said, "I'll confess something to you if you'll clear up some things for me." Banner was about to give the offer some consideration, not feeling comfortable with the prospect of conversations with Samson moving beyond the casual. Samson, however, didn't bother to wait for Banner's acquiescence, apparently assuming it as a given. "First, I confess, as a man, as Betty's lover . . . that I have always hoped you were dead. Not because I didn't like you," he added hastily as he saw Banner's deer-in-the-headlights expression, "but because I love Betty and I've known that unless you were really gone, or she believed you were, that there would always be three of us in this relationship. I've dreaded the thought of you walking through the door. But now that you're here . . ." He smiled, and to Banner's surprise, it actually seemed genuine. "I have to admit that I'm very happy about it. Because I'm also a psychiatrist. And I'm committed to putting light into dark corners, so to speak, and I'm very good at finding my way into the places people hide their secrets."

It sounded a rather pretentious self-description to Banner, and something in his attitude seemed to convey that perception, because Samson leaned forward, looking as if he desperately needed Bruce to understand. "I do it primarily because I think it helps them but also frankly because I'm interested in what people have to hide."

I'm not sure if that makes you altruistic or just a busybody with a medical degree, thought Banner, but he kept that to himself.

Samson continued, "Betty has a very dark corner that I have never found my way into, despite considerable careful effort. And the only thing I know about her dark place is that you are in it. And I'm wondering if you'll be honest enough to tell me: Why are you something that she won't talk about?"

Banner felt it would have been nice to be able to unload on Samson. Under normal circumstances Banner never unloaded on anyone, for obvious reasons. The problem was that keeping the sort of secrets with which he had to cope locked up within him, year in, year out, had hardened him to the point of becoming an emotional hermit. And, unlike average citizens, Samson's entire business in life was hearing other people's problems. Still, Banner's situation was as far removed from the type of things Samson dealt with as a human being was from an amoeba. Plus the caution that had become ingrained in Banner's personality was not as easily set aside as all that. "There are . . . aspects of my personality that I can't control," he said. "And I hurt Betty . . . in ways I will never forgive myself for."

Samson vigorously shook his head. He wasn't buying it. "You don't drop your career and fall off the face of the earth for three years because you've got an anger-management issue, Bruce. You see a shrink."

"It's a little more complicated than that, Samson," said Banner, opting for understatement. "I've been alone for a long time now. I have to be." He paused, considering his next words carefully. "The toughest part of it is that I worry about what I've done to Betty. If she's happy and you're a part of that, then that makes me very happy. Honestly. The last thing I want to do is cause any trouble for her . . . or for you. I'd kill myself before I'd hurt her again."

Samson smiled in response, but it was a sad smile, as if Banner had fulfilled his expectations. "Totally honest and yet avoiding something. Exactly like her."

They drank together in silence.

TWELVE

The thunder was still rumbling the next morning, but it was in the far distance, and the overcast clouds were beginning to roll away.

Bruce was in the guest bedroom, cinching up his belt to hold up a pair of much-too-large jeans. He tended to wear excessively large pants these days for the obvious reason—hoping for the best but expecting the worst.

He stepped out into the hallway and trotted down the stairs. When he reached the bottom, he could hear Betty and Samson in the kitchen, talking in low tones. She sounded insistent and he didn't sound pleased or particularly understanding.

". . . then I'm going to walk him there," she said.

"We'll call him a cab."

"No. I'm going with . . ."

Not wanting to see the discussion spiral into an argument, Banner chose that moment to walk into the kitchen, yawning and stretching to convey the notion that he was still just waking up and thus couldn't possibly have heard anything they were saying. Betty jumped slightly when he entered. Samson forced a smile.

"The car seems to be dead," said Betty. "I must have left the lights on. The station's only about a mile away though. You okay to walk it?"

Banner felt the smallest flicker of concern. He had developed an almost sixth sense for trouble, and now it was beginning to scratch at the back of his head. The problem was that typically he was in foreign lands, surrounded by strangers or people he was keeping distant, so it was easier to trust his impulses when his self-preservation instincts were demanding his attention. But he had broken bread with these people, loved one of them, and actually liked the other. It was tempting to just lay aside his well-honed sense of paranoia, and he tried. He really tried. "Thank you. For everything."

"Good luck," said Samson, shaking his hand.

He turned to Betty. There was an awkward silence between them. Personally, he agreed with Samson: There was no reason for Betty to accompany him, and there were half a dozen reasons why she shouldn't. But he had caught a glimpse of the look on her face when she'd been telling Samson she was going to walk Banner to the station. It was a look he knew all too well. It would have been a waste of his time trying to talk her out of it. Still, just the thought of the two of them strolling out the front door sounded so many warning bells in his head that he was almost deafened by the mental klaxons. "We shouldn't . . ." and he indicated the front door with a tilt of his head.

Betty instantly understood, even though Samson appeared a bit puzzled. "Samson can show you the back door. Remember our bench . . . by the library? I'll meet you there."

He nodded in response and slung his backpack over his shoulder. Samson walked with him to the back door and held it open for him.

Turning to face him, Banner said softly, "With any luck, you'll never have to see me again."

And Samson startled him by saying, "You'll always be welcome here, Bruce." He shook Banner's hand firmly and then stepped back. Banner walked away as the door clicked shut behind him, still wondering whether Samson truly meant it or if he was just incredibly skilled at insincerity.

Slanted light played across the quiet campus. It was early Sunday morning, and students and faculty were, for the most part, either sleeping in or at church, so Banner had picked the ideal time to make an unnoticed exit. He stepped around puddles left over from the previous evening's deluge and approached the bench that Betty had mentioned.

Mentioned in front of Samson.

Damned paranoia.

But just because you're paranoid, and so on, you know the drill . . .

And so Banner chose to take up station behind a tree and watch the bench from a safe distance. Long minutes passed and he was about to head off on his own when he saw Betty walking up the path. It was all he could do not to laugh, because Betty was straining to look casual. She was whistling aimlessly, her hands jammed into her pockets, and glancing left and right almost constantly. Everything about her screamed that she was worried about being watched. Nancy Drew, she wasn't.

He emerged from hiding behind the tree and she saw him just as she drew near to the bench. She let out a relieved sigh, clearly having been worried that Banner had decided to depart the area. He walked over to her, took her hand, and squeezed it affectionately. It didn't stop him from continuing to study their surroundings, though, and she noticed. "Is everything okay?" she said.

"I think so." But something was still bothering him, and for some reason he couldn't shake the instinct that Samson was involved somehow. Since Samson wasn't standing right there, he could ask about it. "Do you think you left the car lights on?"

"I don't remember. I must have. I was a little distracted." She tilted her head. "Why?"

Because I don't think you did. Because I could swear we were leaving the garage in darkness when we walked into the house. And that would mean that Samson did something to the car in order to take it out of commission. Or . . . it could just mean that all the rain did something to the ignition and it's just a case of a car breaking down at an inconvenient moment. Happens all the time. If it didn't, Triple A wouldn't be able to survive. He shook his head, hating that he was second-guessing himself, and then said, "Ready?"

She was.

They started to walk.

They cut across a corner of the central quad, past the trees that ran along the fringe. It remained quiet, their presence shared only with an early-morning jogger and a guy walking a girl home after what was clearly a date that had gone pretty darned well. As they walked, Banner took in his surroundings. All his ambition and expectations were rooted there. It was a symbol of everything that he had aspired to and, by extension, every place where he had fallen short.

Betty suddenly stopped him in his tracks. He looked at her in confusion, and she proceeded to pull the shirt out from the tops of the pants into which he had ineffectively tried to tuck them. He assumed that wearing the shirt out was going to make him look more stylish. He was going to have to count on Betty for that assessment since he had zero fashion sense. She then removed the Stanley's Pizza baseball cap and adjusted the strap so that it would better fit his head.

He stared at her, his thoughts tumbling.

"What is it?" she said.

"I keep trying to remember . . . what we were doing here." He indicated the campus. "I mean, what were we trying to accomplish that it was worth all this? Do you ever ask yourself that?"

"Of course I do. Sometimes it's all I think about." She paused, gathering her thoughts. "I think we were trying to understand. Advance things a little. Make a difference."

"I think that's what we told ourselves because it sounded noble to us," he said grimly. She sounded so idealistic, but the idealism had long ago been burned out of him. "At least the general was honest about what he wanted out of it. I don't think we were as honest. We were trying to show how smart we were and we broke the rules."

She shook her head so violently that it looked as if it were about to fall off. "No. You've turned this too hard on yourself. We did talk about it and we were all comfortable. The worst you can say is that you rushed it; but you took your own risks. You didn't ask anybody else to."

"Nature takes a long time to build us like we are . . . these delicate wonderfully sophisticated systems refined over billions of years. Nobody understands that better than us." He was unable to keep the bitterness from his voice. "And we come in with our big brains and think we can improve it overnight, and we monkey with it. Why are we so surprised when it blows up in our faces?"

Thunder rumbled in the distance. There was a summer storm coming. *God, not again. How much more mood-oriented bad weather do I have to endure?*

"I have to stop my mind from replaying it," she said. "It's like a bad dream. It still doesn't seem possible it's real. But it is, isn't it?"

He so much wanted to tell her that it was indeed a bad dream. He wanted to believe that himself. In a way, it was accurate, because since that day he had been existing in a sort of living nightmare from which there was no awakening.

As she had been speaking, he had continued to survey the area in the manner that had become second nature to him. On some level, he had started to scold himself for his almost relentless paranoia, suffusing every aspect of his being and ensuring that he could never, ever have peace of mind.

That was the moment that the justification for his state of mind was made startlingly clear.

He caught the movement, just beyond the far edge of a building, of a sniper moving into position.

"Oh no." Before Betty could ask what was wrong, he grabbed her by the arm, drew her close, and whispered to her, "They're here."

"What?"

He could see it in her eyes: She hadn't yet processed what was happening. He couldn't blame her. It took the average person long seconds to fully come to the realization that they were in genuine peril when they were being endangered. There was always some element of disbelief when faced with a life-threatening situation, and the time it took the brain to fully grasp the reality of impending danger could be costly. Banner, who perpetually lived with awareness that he might have to break and run at any instant, reacted immediately. "Go home. You've got to get as far away from me as you can, right now. *Go!!*" He broke and ran, leaving Betty stunned and shouting "Bruce!" to his retreating back.

When he saw the single sniper, he knew at once that the one he had spotted was only the beginning; a single operative who had gotten momentarily sloppy and enabled Bruce to realize there was an assault force present. Seeing that Banner had become aware of them, all attempts at stealth were tossed aside as he expected. Soldiers who had moved into position without being seen exploded into view from behind columns and trees, racing in pursuit.

Banner sprinted across the campus, moving right to left across the grass in the quad, throwing in the occasional erratic dodge to try to avoid anything they might shoot at him while putting as much distance between them and himself as he could. The only prayer he had was to outdistance them, stay out of range of whatever firepower they might have.

Humvees came roaring around the perimeter road that ringed the quad. Betty froze where she was, watching in astonishment as the Humvees—one of which was carrying a mounted .50-cal gun—banged aside parked cars and blasted right toward her. For an instant it seemed as if they were going to run her over with little more thought than if she were a random bush, and then they split around her and hurtled past on either side. The high-speed procession left her in the dust, and she spun and ran after it.

Banner dashed into an inner courtyard and made a hard turn down a columned walkway racing to get out of the building area and into the greenery beyond. He wondered where Ross was and suspected that he was crouched in a van somewhere.

His current predicament was a result of one of two things: Either Samson had alerted Ross to Banner's presence (thus explaining the convenient mechanical failure of the car) or else Ross had been monitoring Betty 24/7 and targeted Banner the moment that he saw contact had been made with Betty. Either way, a worst-case scenario had come to fruition.

I'm really starting to hate being right all the time.

In a command/tech support van, Ross, Sparr, and the technicians were monitoring the progress. While Sparr was calmly adjusting to the situation, overseeing the pursuit, Ross was still fuming over the fact that the trap had been blown before it could be properly sprung.

"Goddamn it!" he shouted. "We'd have had snipers on target in three more minutes. I want to know who jumped the gun. They're going to Sadr City!"

Sparr, who knew that she wasn't responsible and therefore wasn't in danger of being shipped off to the aforementioned Baghdad suburb, did the best she could to screen Ross out as she monitored the flood of reports from the pursuers. It wouldn't be appropriate for her to tell a general to shut the hell up. She was, however, starting to reach the point where that seemed a viable option.

Banner whipped through the trees in an open field, up and out of the low gorge in the field's teardrop end. He wasn't giving any thought at this point to monitoring his pulse or focusing his concentration on remaining calm. There were no rooftops for him to rebound off, no array of small buildings for him to hide in or—most important—crowds to blend in with. This wasn't going to be about how stealthy he was or how clever. This was sheer, desperate speed, fleeing his pursuers while hoping that something happened to break his way so he could elude them. For the alternative . . .

Well, there were only two alternatives. One was that they caught him before he changed.

The other was that they didn't get to him in time and he transformed into something that would annihilate them.

This was going to end either in his destruction or theirs. There was no third choice.

He cleared the trees and accelerated across the open ground. Humvees appeared in the distance behind him and continued to close the gap. No surprise there; of the two of them, only one of them was capable of moving at speeds in excess of fifty miles per hour, and it wasn't Banner. The pursuing vehicles circled the building that

Banner had raced through and closed in a pincer formation from both sides.

From behind Banner and to the right, a line of
Humvees hurtled toward him, cresting the rise and moving in fast. He caught sight of the .50-cal gun mounted
on the foremost Humvee. Wonderful. Not enough that
he was unarmed and running. They had to be sure
they could shoot him in the back with high-powered
ammo.

Off to Banner's left were two buildings linked by a
courtyard with a pedestrian overpass on the left edge.
There was a large modern art sculpture in the forward
section of the courtyard. Banner would have stopped to
admire the architecture and sculpture if it weren't for
the people who were trying to capture or kill him or
both. The buildings might well be deserted since it was
Sunday morning, but Banner had no desire to risk any
civilians who might be around. Instead he cut to the
right, across a huge open field to the tree line of a forest
beyond. It was a long way to go, but if he could make it
to tree cover, he might get away.

**Don't want to get away . . . want to smash
them . . . smash them all . . .**

Shut up, he thought desperately, and kept going.

Sparr monitored Banner's progress, aware as she hadn't
been in Brazil that they were operating under a deadline.
The longer Banner was loose, the more time he had to
get himself worked up, the more chance that they were
going to find themselves facing something that was very
much not Bruce Banner. She said briskly over the radio,
"Target on the run, heading three-five-oh. Sniper two
has the shot. Straight at your twelve, Blonsky."

Emil Blonsky had never been much for believing in a
higher power, but as Bruce Banner sprinted directly

toward his hiding place, he started to think that maybe there was a God after all.

Blonsky and his team crouched under a camouflage cloth, secreted in the brush just within the tree line that Banner obviously thought was going to be his salvation. Blonsky was cradling a .308 sniper rifle while a spotter watched Banner with the aid of binoculars. There were three other soldiers in Blonsky's squad. One had a revolving grenade launcher, and two more were wielding M4s. Blonsky didn't want to give any of them a shot at Banner, though. As far as he was concerned, this was between him and Banner, and every other grunt in the area could take a backseat.

"Got him," said Blonsky over his comm unit.

Banner was just cresting the rise, running directly at Blonsky, who had him sighted through his scope. Blonsky's spotter moved behind a tree to keep Banner in view. He made the slightest misstep, cracking a branch under foot, but Blonsky wasn't concerned. Banner was in full running panic mode. There was no way he was going to notice such a minuscule movement.

Then he heard the rustling of wings.

Banner, on the run, noticed a minuscule movement in the grove of trees just ahead of him. He thought it might be nothing, even something as insignificant as a squirrel jumping from one branch to the next. But then he saw a flock of small birds break from the trees and take wing. A squirrel or some other small animal moving around wouldn't have prompted that reaction. Men, on the other hand, would have.

Banner skidded to a halt and stared hard ahead of him. He wasn't sure, but he thought he could see the slightest glint of something that could be glass hidden in the brush ahead. The type of glass that would be typical for a sniper scope.

Thought translated into action, and Banner broke to his left. Having no choice, knowing it was bringing him closer to pursuers, he nevertheless ran back toward the buildings that he had previously steered clear of.

Blonsky was starting to think that either Bruce Banner was the luckiest son of a bitch on the planet, or else he, Blonsky, had offended a gypsy somewhere in his life and was suffering the blowback from a curse. He racked the bolt of his rifle, aimed, and shot again, only to see his shot ricochet off a sculpture.

"Shit." He keyed his microphone. "We're made," he said, stating what must have already become obvious to Sparr. "He's heading two-seven-zero for those outer buildings." He then gestured for his team to follow him, and Blonsky and his men broke cover and sprinted out onto the field.

Blonsky wasn't even paying attention to the fact that he was leaving his team far behind as he bolted across the wide-open space between the forest and the building. His legs were scissoring so quickly that they would have been a blur to any outside observer. He continued to pick up speed, accelerating ahead of them and carrying his heavy rifle in one hand as if it were a broomstick.

Banner tore around the corner of a building, up and across a stone terrace. The situation had turned and it was no longer a pure speed game of trying to outrun his pursuers. Instead he was back to trying to outthink them, and he wasn't liking the odds. They had had far too much time to survey every square foot of the area and anticipate whatever moves he might make. Which meant that he was going to have to come up with something they hadn't considered, and he was going to have to do it on the fly.

He burst through two large doors that led inside and realized belatedly it was the library.

An elderly security guard was dozing at the desk. He looked up, startled, when Banner ran in, and he started to demand to see identification. Banner saw he was unarmed, which made him unique in terms of the men Banner had encountered that morning. Banner shoved him aside, knocking him over and feeling slightly regretful over having done so, but it wasn't as if he had the time to turn around and apologize.

He dashed between the library stacks, threading his way through the narrow rows of books. He could hear the sounds of booted feet pounding in through the doors behind him. By his admittedly rough guess, there were at least a dozen soldiers pursuing him into the library. This wasn't getting any easier.

Sparr watched the monitors carefully. Banner had entered the library building and, if they surrounded it right, they would have him pinned. "We've got him boxed," Sparr told Ross. "First platoon has the building."

"Blonsky, hold where you are," said Ross. "I don't want him slipping through to those trees."

Blonsky had reached the small copse of trees just beyond the buildings. "He won't get past us," his voice came through to Ross. Ross could tell from Blonsky's tone that he wasn't at all happy about the order. Small surprise there; Blonsky had made it clear to Ross that he wanted Banner for himself, and Ross had promised to do his best to accommodate him. But he wasn't going to do so if it meant compromising the goal of the mission. In case there was any doubt in Ross's mind, he heard Blonsky say under his breath, "But I hope he tries." Blonsky waved his team into position under the cluster of trees flanking the other side of the court. "Look alive, this could get interesting," his voice came over the microphone.

Sparr continued to study the monitor screens. She watched soldiers swarming around the building, pouring out of a transport and taking up positions around the sculpture. Another squad sprinted in from the far side, and the Humvee with the .50-cal was two hundred yards out and closing fast, ETA thirty seconds at most. She also watched as two significant pieces in the offensive plan were moved into position. It was armament that was referred to as "Disco," and if Banner did wind up transforming into that creature, Disco was going to ensure they weren't caught flatfooted this time.

Then one of the van-mounted cameras spotted something heading directly toward the command vehicle.

It was a woman. Her face was a mask of fury, her fists were clenched, and she was charging straight toward the van looking prepared to rip it apart with her bare hands. She recognized the woman instantly.

"Crap," she muttered. The general was already in a foul mood; this was hardly going to improve it.

Tearing up narrow stairs in the library, Banner could hear the sounds of pursuit drawing closer. He was out of time. He ducked between two shelves, fell to his knees, and yanked the data card out of his pocket. His fingers fumbled around in removing the metal ring and lanyard. Soldiers raced up the stairs, reached the upper landing, and Banner was convinced he was done. But they sprinted right past his hiding place, giving him enough time to get the data card clear of the ring. He pulled a water bottle out of his pack, ripped the cap off, and then took the data card and shoved it into the back of his throat. With pure willpower, he forced his throat wide enough to accommodate the card, and then slugged back as much water as possible, as fast as he could. He coughed and gagged and some of the water fountained back up out of his mouth, but he managed to choke down the card.

He glanced down the narrow aisle just in time to see a soldier looking straight at him. The soldier yelled out an alert, but Banner was already up and running out the far end.

Sparr watched in dismay as Betty Ross caught up with the command vehicle and started to yell, "I know it's you! General, please!"

Sparr cast a quick glance at the radiation monitors. Everything was still normal. She could afford a few seconds to inform Ross of this latest complication. "Sir? Sir? It's your daughter."

Ross turned and saw Betty on the monitor. He switched channels on his audio just in time to hear her saying, "General, come out of there! Dad, please!"

Without hesitation, Ross threw open the door of the vehicle. There were two rangers in the van with him, and they emerged right behind him, rifles at the ready. He faced his daughter, impatient, casting glances toward the library. He had no time for a confrontation with his only child, but that was obviously what she was seeking. "Please don't do this," she said. "He needs help!"

"You can't see this clearly. Now get inside," he said, indicating the van. He moved to grab her arm and she pulled away.

Suddenly Sparr called from within the van, "Target is in the overpass! Have visual!"

This was backed up by one of the soldiers on the ground shouting, "There he is!"

Ross, Betty, the Rangers, everyone within earshot looked up. Sure enough, Banner had emerged into the pedestrian overpass between the two towering buildings. In the distance behind the overpass, black clouds were gathering, the biblical-level angry weather unrelenting.

Blonsky waved his team into position, watching Banner struggle like the trapped rat that he was. Banner was running through the pedestrian tube and skidded to a halt as he saw soldiers at the far end blocking his path. He spun, tried to retrace his path to the library, and didn't make it more than five paces before more soldiers appeared at the other end. There was nowhere for him to go.

"Damn," said Blonsky, uncaring if Ross or Sparr heard him.

Sparr did but Ross didn't. Ross, however, was still aware of the danger they faced and had no desire to send yet another snatch-and-grab off the rails. "Do not engage, repeat, do *not* engage," said Ross to Sparr.

Dutifully relaying his orders, Sparr snapped through the microphone, "Hold positions. Stand down."

"Put the special unit in the north end of the field," said Ross. "If he changes, he'll try to make for the forest and that's where we'll hit him with our little surprise."

"Those buildings will take a direct hit," said Sparr, clearly concerned. "If there's anyone in them . . ."

"*Do it!*"

Once the order had been given, it was not within Sparr's prerogative to argue with it. She checked the positioning of the two Humvees with the massive machinery mounted upon them to make sure they were where they were supposed to be and their energy levels were correct. She nodded in approval at the readings. "Disco's online," said Sparr. "Set up overlapping fields and seal off the north end."

A huge power source kicked in on the equipment mounted on the Humvees. It was a deep, bass, and very ominous humming. The ground, the very air around them, was starting to rumble. Sparr said, "Put canisters in that tube, one on either side."

Banner was reacting with clear surprise as the soldiers at either end of the open pedestrian walkway suddenly retreated into their respective buildings and slammed the doors, bolting them. He wasn't sure what was going on . . . and then he spotted two soldiers with grenade launchers coming from around the corners of the building. Before he could react, they fired gas canisters that arced through the air and burst through the windows enclosing the walkway. They clanked into the ceiling, clattered to the floor on either side of Banner, and detonated. Instantly the overpass began to fill with paralyzing gas.

Banner ripped off his work shirt and rolled it up into a ball in front of his face. Ross watched, not looking away for so much as an instant. Then Banner vanished, consumed by the smoke.

Betty was screaming his name. Ross rather uncharitably wished he had some knockout gas handy that he could use on his daughter. Then she abruptly tore away from the Rangers and sprinted across the wide stretch of grass toward the tube. "Get her back here!" said Ross, but the soldiers were already sprinting after her.

The tube was filling with white smoke. Banner's head whipped back and forth. His pulse was hammering faster and faster, and he saw Betty running across the grass toward him, soldiers in pursuit. One soldier reached her and grabbed her by the arm, but she threw an elbow at him and fought forward before the second soldier tackled her from behind. She hit the ground hard.

Banner dropped his shirt and pressed against the glass. Everything else was forgotten: his desire to survive, his fear, everything was washed away in a sea of rage. His eyes flared green, and then his body seized and he dropped into the smoke.

The radiation monitors spiked into the red. "Geiger's lighting up!" called Sparr.

Ross grinned. His real quarry was about to arrive and his moment was at hand. "Keep cameras on it!" he shouted, and to himself he said, "Now they'll see. Now they'll all see."

Lights flickered in the smoke as if Banner were a miniature generator. He was contorted in agony, his whole body seizing, his eyes glowing green, and then the color green surged from the base of his skull and flowed through his face and down his neck, under his T-shirt and through his arms. Nothing was visible to anyone on the outside because the smoke was obscuring it, but Banner was staring at his arms, watching them twist and distort into someone else . . .

. . . something else . . .

His hand slapped against the glass, clawing in agony, now greenish gray. Then the arm swelled and rippled, muscles exploding along the length of it. His hand slipped off the window and hit the floor, bracing against it, swelling and changing, and then his right foot exploded out of his brown leather boot. Banner's howls of agony echoed through the air, and then roars of fury replaced Banner's screams. And Banner himself was replaced by something else as well, something massive that rose into view, silhouetted through the smoke.

Betty . . . must help Betty . . . they threatened Betty . . . they hurt Betty . . . no one hurts Betty . . . *no one hurts Betty . . .*

* * *

Sparr watched as a gargantuan form, one that had replaced Banner's, became visible within the smoke and rose, its arms over its head. Then its arms spread wide and smashed its fists forward. Glass shattered along the length of the tube, smoke pouring out of it, revealing the head and shoulders of a titan. The creature snarled and then leaped down from above, smoke trailing off it as it fell.

It hit the ground, which trembled beneath it, and then it stood. For the first time, Sparr had a clear view of the monster that had pounded through the Brazilian factory and effortlessly annihilated the squadron of commandos.

It was human in shape only. Approaching ten feet in height, with skin that seemed almost translucent, shifting from green to gray depending how the light hit it, it was impossibly muscled and looked like something that had stepped straight from the depths of hell. Gargantuan, muscles rippling, it was a force of nature on foot.

It roared its challenge.

Sparr's jaw literally dropped. "This was not in the recruitment video," she said.

The creature took three powerful strides forward, clearing the horseshoe of the courtyard, stepping out into the open field, eyes darting around, seeking its tormentors. Its eyes spotted Betty on the ground, Ross beyond, and it flexed its muscles and roared with rage, ready to fight.

Ross had clambered back into the van, and he said into the microphone, "We're going to Bravo. Move him toward the cannons. Keep your cool and be ready to move. Alpha team, give him all of it."

Immediately a barrage of machine-gun fire pounded into the right side of the creature, beating it back from the sculpture near which it had been crouched. Six soldiers converged with assault rifles, and one was wielding an M-60 on a tripod. Rounds peppered the creature like bees, enraging it.

Noise, more noise, trying to hurt us, keep us from Betty, keep me from Betty, no one keeps me from Betty, not men, not men with weapons, not puny general, no one . . .

It raised an arm to ward off the bullets at first, but then instead of being driven back, it charged directly toward the origins of the assault. The soldier with the M-60, mounted and ready to go, opened fire. The rounds from the M-60 appeared to be hitting the creature harder, and perhaps it was even feeling some sting from them.

The creature's response was to raise its hand like a shield, the heavy rounds pounding against its palms and raking down its legs. They slowed the creature somewhat.

But they didn't stop it. Not even close.

It bounded toward the soldiers, picking up speed, and they scattered frantically to get out of its path.

"Stevens, get her out of here!" Sparr said, pointing at Betty.

The soldiers snatched Betty up and ran from the van. She shouted for her father, but he didn't respond. Ross was oblivious of anything but the monster, and the monster wasn't cooperating. Instead it was going the wrong direction: straight after Betty.

"Get that fifty on him, dammit!!! Move your asses!"

The driver floored it, heading toward the sculpture to intercept the monster. The gunner opened up with the large-caliber gun. The Humvee ran parallel to the monster, blasting with everything it had. The creature was running parallel to it, bullets rebounding. Trees whipped by as the Humvee closed on its target, and then suddenly it was no longer there.

"We've lost visual!" the gunner reported. The sculpture was directly in sight, but the creature had vanished.

And then it was suddenly there again, landing directly in front of the Humvee. Ross tried to shout a warning, but it was too late as the creature drove its fists into the engine block, jacking them up into the air like a skateboard. The creature struck again, this time driving the engine block into the ground. The driver leaped from the jeep, but the gunner clutched frantically onto his weapon, refusing to desert his post. He paid brutally for that dedication as the creature heaved the Humvee into the air and smashed it against the massive black steel plates of the twenty-foot-high sculpture over and over. The gunner was sent hurtling through the air, slung out of the vehicle as if from a catapult, and then the Humvee disintegrated in an explosion of metal and gas. The detonation scattered the remaining soldiers who were on foot.

I will not let this happen again. Not again, thought Ross as he barked over his shoulder to Sparr in the van, *"Where the hell is my gunship?"* Then he snapped the microphone to his face and said to the troops, "All right, keep your cool! If you can't push him, get him to chase you. But move him toward those cannons, dammit!"

Meantime Sparr was saying into the radio, "Base, we need that bird in the air, ASAP."

Soldiers emerged into the destroyed overpass from either side, proceeding cautiously, since the monster might well have compromised the integrity of the structure. Blonsky's team across the field reacted immediately, blasting away at the creature with assault rifles. Blonsky racked and fired his sniper rifle over and over. He was relentless, despite the fact that no matter how many rounds slammed home, they seemed to have no effect. The monster had not released its grip on the engine block. Instead it lifted the block over its head with no more effort than if it had been wielding a soccer ball, and then it lobbed the engine block at a troop carrier. Soldiers saw it coming and barely leaped clear before it struck the carrier squarely and exploded. The carrier erupted in flame, and Ross—grim-faced—watched as a number of his people went up in flames, throwing themselves to the ground and frantically rolling to try and extinguish the fire.

Leonard Samson exited the front door of his house with fear etched on his face. His concerns were justified and exacerbated as he heard the sound of small-arms fire clattering in the distance. Then there was the dull boom of something exploding, and a plume of black smoke stretched toward the skies.

Every instinct told him to run back into the house, perhaps even hide under a bed. The problem was that he knew without question that whatever the hell was happening over in the quad, Betty was smack in the middle of it.

He slammed the door behind himself and then sprinted in the direction of the conflagration, praying that he wasn't too late and wondering just what the hell he was going to do there once he arrived.

Blonsky reloaded and, as he did so, watched soldiers continue to fire away at the creature, both from above on the overpass and from nearby Blonsky himself. The monster wasn't even bothering to acknowledge them by this point as bullets smacked off its back and clanked off the steel plates of the big sculpture. It was shrugging off machine-gun fire with such ease that they might as well have been pelting it with olives. In fact, it seemed far more interested in the steel plates on the sculpture. The creature lunged against the statue, pulling loose one of the plates to the accompaniment of rivets popping and the screeching of metal as it tore away. It held up one of the metal plates as if it were a shield and appeared to like what it saw, because it reached around and started to tear loose a second metal plate.

"This is a joke," said Blonsky, deciding that someone had to come up with a better idea and he was the best candidate. "Cover me."

The soldier to his immediate right, armed with a revolving grenade launcher, stood there paralyzed with shock at what he was witnessing. Blonsky dropped his rifle and snatched the launcher from the soldier. Then he raced across the grass, heading straight toward the monster that was systematically destroying the sculpture. Blonsky crossed the courtyard and neared the creature just as the final rivets popped away and the creature pulled it loose. It now effectively had two huge steel shields, one of them with jagged edges like a circular saw blade.

Blonsky aimed low and started firing off grenades as fast as he could, aiming at the monster's knees. Anything that stood was only as good as the strength of its legs, and Blonsky reasoned that if he could at least knock the creature off its feet, that might give him some advantage. Perhaps it would be an advantage that could be ridden to ultimate triumph.

The creature staggered slightly under the repeated blasts from grenades, which buoyed Blonsky's hopes. The assault managed to get the creature's attention, and its head swiveled toward its assailant. That was just what Blonsky wanted. "Remember me?" he shouted.

Apparently it did. The monster roared and came straight at Blonsky, wielding its new metal toys as if they were scythes. Blonsky, moving in a manner that any observer would have deemed impossible, avoided the slicing plates by spring boarding off them. As he did so he continued to fire his weapons at the creature at close range. He bounded from one to the other and back again, performing feats of athleticism that were impossible by any existing measure.

Ross reacted with amazement to what he was witnessing. "By God, he's doing it!" He noticed that Sparr was looking at him in confusion and suspicion. She must have realized that something was up with Blonsky, but she didn't know what it was. This wasn't the time to bring her up to speed; there was just too much else going on. Instead, remaining focused on the problem at hand, he spoke into his microphone: "Disco's on deck. Get the hell away from those buildings."

Blonsky heard his team cheering for him, and confidence surged through him like a narcotic. He had actually managed to draw the creature's attention away from the statue and the building and focus its considerable ire entirely upon him. Some would have seen such a tactic as insanity, and perhaps even a recipe for suicide. Not Blonsky. He was thriving on the fact that this time he, not the monster, was running the table. Granted, most of Blonsky's strategy consisted of staying out of the creature's way, but that was certainly more than anyone else had been able to accomplish. And one couldn't mount a good offense unless one had defense down first.

At that moment, Blonsky was moving at a dead run and the creature was pounding hard on his heels. Yet Blonsky was actually pulling away from it somewhat. He waved frantically for his team to get the hell out of the way, since at that moment they were dead ahead of him and if they didn't move, would likely wind up genuinely dead ahead of him. They all seemed to realize at the same time that they were going to be trampled if they didn't part faster than the Red Sea, and so emulated that Exodus moment by splitting to either side as Blonsky, the modern Moses, sprinted straight through the piece of land they'd just vacated.

Blonsky was now a hundred yards away from the building (minimum safe distance where human life was concerned, or so he'd been told) and the creature still wasn't managing to gain on him. The weapons code-named "Disco" were in position just ahead of him: two Humvees, each with a massive directional speaker disk mounted upon the back, situated fifty yards apart from each other. Blonsky dashed between the two and shouted, "Hit him! Hit him now!"

There was the briefest of hesitation on the part of the soldiers, because Blonsky was not remotely far enough away from the devices to ensure his safety. But then they saw the monster pounding straight toward them, and any further thoughts of waiting were instantly set aside.

They opened fire with what appeared to be speakers, except they were not speakers at all. Not in the conventional sense. They were instead sonic cannons, unleashing a murderous cone of low-frequency sound. The effects of the cannons should not have been visible to the naked eye, yet Blonsky could actually see huge circular waves issuing forth from them, distorting the air between Blonsky and the creature that was pursuing him.

About to be trapped in the cross fire with the creature, Blonsky suddenly leaped forward, his arms outstretched like a diver. The vault carried him an impossible twenty feet into the safety zone and then he rolled, bounded to his feet, and turned to see the results of the assault.

The first of the concussive sound waves struck the monster on the right side, knocking it to its left knee. The second, coming hard on the heels of the first, pounded it from the right, catching it in a crushing cross fire. Its hands flew to its head and it staggered, roaring uncomprehendingly, like a dinosaur not understanding why the ground beneath it had suddenly transformed into tar and was sucking it down.

Noise so much noise worse than ever coming from everywhere can't escape it the air turned into noise how is that possible just everywhere pounding against us brain on fire brain going to explode that would be better if that happened yes anything better than this all the noise noise noise *noise* . . .

The monster staggered and roared yet again. Considering everything that was happening around the beast, it was phenomenal that those were the only ill effects it was displaying.

Clearly the army had underestimated the amount of impact that Disco would have on the surrounding area. Sparr had warned that the building would take a hit, but she thought the result would be some windows breaking. That projection had fallen woefully short of the actuality as, while the surrounding trees vibrated and split, the building windows didn't just break; they exploded. Glass flew everywhere as if grenades had been set off inside the buildings, blasting the windows apart with concussive force. And the windows were the least of the problems as brick and mortar shattered from cornices and ledges, blasted loose from the building face and sending showers of debris down upon the troops.

It was more punishment than the pedestrian tube overhead was able to take. It vibrated uncontrollably, huge chunks falling from beneath it as a precursor to total collapse. The soldiers who had been standing inside it scrambled frantically in either direction, trying to seek relative safety in the buildings themselves. One soldier, smack in the middle, hesitated, trying to figure out which end was closer. The hesitation cost him as the crossover gave way completely, crumbling beneath his feet and sending him screaming to the ground below.

One of Blonsky's men apparently hadn't properly distanced himself from the concussive force of the sonic cannons. Or perhaps he had tried to get a better look at the creature they were fighting. Whatever the reason was, he paid for it as the concussive force of the cannons blew him sideways. He had been wearing ear protection in anticipation of Disco's use, as they all were, but the protection was jolted loose from him. Blood poured out of his ears and mouth and he lay on the ground, shaking violently. Then the sonic cannons liquefied what was left of his internal organs and he stopped moving.

The onslaught that a mere mortal had been unable to withstand for more than a couple of seconds continued upon the creature. All things considered, it was bearing up remarkably well, but it was still feeling the ill effects. Its skin was literally rippling under the waves of sound that were wrapping around it. Had the soldiers been able to see through the creature's eyes, they would have perceived a world that was insanely distorted, viewed through an insane fun-house mirror of warped perception.

The creature fell forward onto one fist, trying to hold itself up, but unable to withstand the relentless barrage.

Betty Ross screamed at her father, "You're killing him!"

That, of course, was not Ross's intent. He knew, however, far better than his daughter did, what the creature was capable of. He also knew the capabilities of the cannons. Sparr and he had used all the available data to calculate down to the nth degree just how much punishment the creature could endure before falling unconscious, rather than just dying. Granted, there was a margin for error of plus or minus five percent, and within that margin, the creature's death was a genuine possibility. It was a risk that Ross was willing to take; after all, they could always garner useful information from an autopsy.

Betty, however, clearly was not interested in taking the risk. She tried to pull away from the soldiers who were holding her back so that she could reach the monster. Beauty, as always, was drawn irresistibly to the beast. She was not given the opportunity, though, as the soldiers effortlessly held her back despite her best efforts to obtain her freedom.

Leonard Samson, running as fast as he could, approached the crest of the field and saw a panorama of carnage spread wide before him. Soldiers were scattered about the area or half buried under rubble, moaning for help or lying eerily silent. Vehicles were overturned or burning or smoldering wrecks. Huge pieces of metal had been ripped off that abstract statue in the front courtyard.

And in the distance, the most impossible sight of all, a creature that looked as if it had wandered out of some of the most nightmarish delusions that any of his patients had conjured up.

And then he spotted Betty, standing near a black van. Not standing, actually. She was struggling mightily in the grasps of two soldiers, holding her by either arm. She was trying to pull loose from them and run toward the creature. Toward the shadowy demon that had haunted her for three years. Samson shouted her name, but either she didn't hear him or she ignored him. Instead she was calling out to the creature . . .

Calling it "Bruce."

No. Not nightmarish delusions, Samson now realized. This thing had emerged from the darkness that lay within Betty, and it was not psychological or nightmarish in nature, but rather all too real. He was staring upon the twisted, bestial face of that which his lover kept locked away within her. He understood for the first time why she had been the way she was. It wasn't that she had been refusing to open up to him. Rather she had been trying to protect him . . . from this.

Leonard Samson had never felt more proud of Betty than he did at that moment. Proud of her . . .

. . . and ashamed of himself.

Sparr emerged from the van. Watching this monstrosity over the monitor screens continued to add an air of unreality to the proceedings, as if she were simply watching a 1950s creature feature on television. She needed to see it with her own eyes. As she stepped out of the van, the general's daughter was continuing to scream "Bruce!" at the top of her lungs.

Still being pummeled by an endless barrage of noise, there was no way that the creature could possibly have heard her. It was beyond credulity; "incredible" in every sense of the word.

And yet the beast turned in response.

Even from this distance, Sparr could see its form, its mass, increasing.

"Oh my God," whispered Sparr. "The madder it gets, the stronger it gets."

Despite all that common sense would have dictated, the creature was still clutching onto the metal sheets that it had peeled off the sculpture. It had seemed the random act of a beast, to be taken no more seriously than a dog becoming obsessed with a chew toy. Now, though, the degree to which they had underestimated the creature became woefully evident as, bursting with new power, it spread its arms wide and then brought the metal plates together like cymbals.

The crash was unbelievable, creating a counter to the sonic waves that had been assailing it. It gave the creature freedom, if only for a moment, but the creature pounced on that freedom to hurl one of the plates like a massive discus. The metal plate slammed into the cannon to the creature's left, cutting the weapon in half and nearly bisecting its operator for good measure.

The second cannon refocused its sound waves upon the creature, but it was only half as effective, since it did not have the second gun to catch the monster in a cross fire. Then the creature hauled its other makeshift shield into place, holding it up so that it blocked the creature's head and upper shoulder from assault. Sound waves poured around it, bouncing off and cascading away. It allowed the monster to achieve a brief respite, and that was all it required to gain solid footing in mounting a counterattack. Slowly, inexorably, the creature began to stride toward the source of its aggravation. It was like watching a man struggle against a sustained blast from a fire hose that was being turned upon him.

This, however, was no fire hose, but a state-of-the-art piece of defense weaponry.

On the other hand, this was no man that was staggering, foot by hard-won foot, toward the sonic cannon.

Blonsky had grabbed up the nearest grenade launcher and opened fire upon it, aiming for the legs, trying to bring it down. But where the grenades had provoked at least some response from the monster earlier, now it wasn't even noticing them.

Credit the cannon operator who didn't cut and run, despite the unnerving sight of the baleful monster coming closer and closer with every stride. The metal was vibrating violently in its grasp and yet it still held on to it, maintaining a shield, until it was close enough to bring the shield slamming directly into the cannon. The impact tore apart the weapon and, for good measure, smashed the entire back end of the Humvee as neatly and as thoroughly as a junkyard car crusher. The can-

non operator had barely leaped clear in time or he
would have been a permanent part of the newly crafted
metal sculpture.

General Ross didn't know what felt worse at that moment: to see the carefully crafted devices code-named
Disco thoroughly annihilated by the monster, or the defiant look of triumph that Betty cast his way upon seeing
the army's latest failed attempt to take down her monstrous boyfriend.

"Two minutes out, Major," the voice of the approaching pilot came over the van's radio.

Ross tapped the microphone. "All positions, engage
him. Just keep him busy. Prepare to fall back on my
order."

Nobody moved.

Ross had never seen anything like it before. A direct
order had been issued, but no one was responding to
it. Instead they were standing exactly where they had
been, weapons leveled but nobody wanting to take a
shot. Nobody was engaging the thing. *Welcome to the
modern army,* Ross thought bitterly.

And then he saw that one man, at least, wasn't backing down. Predictably, it was Blonsky. His launcher
empty of grenades, Blonsky snatched up an M-4 assault
rifle from near the crushed sound cannon and raced at
the monster. He screamed invectives, coming across to
the general like the modern-day incarnation of the classic berserker warrior. Nothing—not issues of his own
safety or even common sense that would dictate he'd be
well advised to head in the other direction—deterred
him from attacking his enemy.

His enemy, for its part, simply stared at him. It was
difficult to say if the creature was confused by him, or
thought him amusing, or . . .

No. It was more than that, Ross was sure of it. The

creature recognized him. But not just in the sense that they had encountered each other earlier in Brazil. It recognized Blonsky, Ross believed, as someone who had undergone some degree of the same process that had resulted in the creature's own creation. In a twisted way, they were distant cousins, and this was a bizarre sort of family reunion.

"Closing. What's the target?" came the pilot's voice.

Ross didn't respond, so caught up was he in watching Blonsky's reckless brave assault on the creature. Sparr took up the slack, bounding back into the van and grabbing the microphone. "Two-nine-oh from my position, three hundred yards, ten feet tall and green."

There was the briefest of pauses. "Come again?"

Sparr saw no point in repeating it; it wasn't going to get any easier to explain. "You heard right. Put everything you've got on it. Take it out." She snapped the comm link to the local frequency and said, "Ground teams pull back."

Sparr's voice came over Blonsky's radio. He ignored it. His gun was out of ammo, but he felt as if power was hammering through every cell of his body. He threw the gun aside and advanced on the monster, which was towering over him, dwarfing him. Astoundingly, he was walking with a slow, confident swagger, as if he were the one with the upper hand. *"Come on, Banner! That all you got?"*

"Blonsky, fall back now!" came Ross's voice over the radio. Blonsky yanked the comm unit away from his ear and tossed it aside. Ross wasn't saying anything he was interested in hearing.

The creature's eyes narrowed, and its lips drew back revealing snarling teeth set into pale green gums. There was that look of recognition that went deeper than merely remembering Blonsky from Brazil. Blonsky's mouth twisted in a sneer of contempt that mirrored the creature's. The monster lifted its shoulder as if it meant to swing the shield it was still clutching.

"Come on," said Blonsky challengingly, "let's see what else you've g—"

He never finished the sentence. Catching Blonsky completely off guard, the monster snapped its foot forward, slamming its massive sole directly into Blonsky's gut. Six inches lower and Blonsky might well have been singing soprano for the rest of his life. As it was, there was the ungodly sound of who-knew-how-many bones shattering in Blonsky's body as the commando was sent hurtling backward. He kept soaring up, up, like a football, in an arc that reached fifty feet at its apex. Tumbling out of control, insensate, he began his plummet that ended up with his landing a good hundred yards away from where the monster's foot had connected with him. He then skidded from that point, tearing up grass and dirt before finally slowing to a halt. His legs and arms were twisted at impossible angles, a broken marionette of a man.

"Oh my God," said Sparr.

Ross said nothing. His jaw clenched; he had just seen his best ally, his best chance at reining in or at least slowing down the creature, knocked around like a rag doll. Lightning ribboned overhead, splitting the sky, and rain began to pour.

The creature turned toward Ross, except it obviously didn't give a damn about Ross. Its focus was entirely on Betty. With slow, measured strides, it started walking toward them. No reason for it to hurry; it had plenty of time.

"Fall back and find cover!" Ross called out.

The troops, who had utterly failed to obey his earlier order to continue the attack, were all too happy to do exactly as they were told this time around. They ran as quickly as their legs would carry them, determined to put as much distance as possible between themselves and the creature.

While the soldiers scrambled back across the road, and the rain continued to fall, Ross could hear the first sounds of helicopter rotors cutting through the air. He knew that it announced the arrival of an Apache gunship that would be, even now, using its targeting computer to zero in on the monster.

What Ross had failed to take into consideration was that, when he had ordered his men to depart the area, the soldiers who had been holding back Betty were just as ready to obey his orders as everyone else. Since he had said nothing about slowing themselves down by hauling along his protesting daughter, they had thought nothing of leaving her behind.

As a result, when Ross fell back along with Sparr, he didn't think to look and see where Betty was. He had just somehow assumed she would be in the company of the soldiers who had been holding her back.

Instead, liberated from her captors, she slowly moved toward the advancing creature.

The Apache gunship rose over the forest line, approaching from behind the creature. Since Betty was standing directly in front of it, the creature's body was between the Apache's targeting sights and her.

She reached up slowly, tentatively, and touched its arm. "Bruce?"

The creature stared down at her, as if she were a stray thought it was trying to recapture. Then dim recognition flickered across the creature's face.

Its mouth slowly started to open, the beginnings of a word perhaps forming upon its lips.

Ross and Sparr, meantime, hustled for cover. It was Sparr who suddenly spotted the soldiers that had been holding on to the general's daughter. When she saw that Betty was no longer in their company, she risked a fast glance behind her. To her horror, she saw Betty standing less than a foot away from the transformed Banner.

Then she realized that Ross was oblivious of his daughter's whereabouts. Instead he was barking into his handheld comm unit, "Fire, goddammit!"

Even as she heard the pilot's voice come back, "Hold on to your hats," over her portable headset, Sparr shouted, *"Hold fire!"*

Too late.

The Apache was armed with two massive rotating cannons and both of them went hot upon the general's command. They started firing at the target, tearing up the earth around Betty and her inhuman shield.

From a distance, Samson screamed, "No!" but there was no one near him to hear . . . not that it would have done a damned bit of good if there had been.

Betty instinctively pressed into the creature's body for shelter as rounds pounded into its back. Some actually managed to tear up its skin and the creature roared, taking care to keep its body between the Apache and Betty as it turned to face its latest tormentor. It roared, its clenched fists trembling with rage, while the Apache started to accelerate in order to bring the full concentration of fire upon him.

"Cease fire!" shouted Sparr, and she waved her arms desperately to try to grab the chopper's visual attention, since it didn't seem to be registering her verbal orders. Then she realized that the chopper might well be ignoring her. They had their instructions from the general; she was hardly in a position to gainsay him.

The gunship was a quarter mile away, coming in low and fast. The creature pivoted its body like a Greek discus thrower and hurled the remaining plate from the sculpture through the air. The gunship didn't see the improvised missile until it was too late. It ripped through the rotor tower, cleaving the main rotor off the ship. The aircraft went down nose-first, plowing into the ground fifty yards from the creature and Betty as the pilot and gunner leaped clear.

The Apache erupted, a massive ball of flame, and the creature grabbed Betty to its chest and wrapped its arms around her, shielding her. Ross and Sparr—and, from a distance, Samson—watched in horror as the flame engulfed Betty and her unlikely protector, while huge shards of metal tumbled around them. The concussive force knocked over everyone else in the area, and Ross was convinced that he had just witnessed the death of his daughter.

And the thing that horrified him the most was that, at that moment—and only for a moment—he was more interested in whether the creature had somehow survived.

Something within him recoiled at his priorities, and he went emotionally numb. *Betty . . . my God . . . what have I done . . . ?*

The answer, as it turned out, was nothing.

The creature emerged from the inferno, cradling an unconscious Betty Ross in its arms. Parts of its body were still smoldering, as were the tattered trousers that were dangling improbably from its waist. Then the rain came down harder, snuffing out the remaining bits of flame. The creature advanced on Ross, who was still splayed on the ground, looking up helplessly. If the creature had chosen that moment to bring its foot down on Ross's head and crush it like a melon, there wouldn't have been a damned thing he could do about it.

Instead it simply snarled down at Ross with a disdainful air that said to Ross, *Next time . . . will make this time look like a kindergarten recess.*

And then the creature began to run. Past the soldiers, past the wreckage, past Blonsky's unmoving body, and the strides lengthened with each step. It smashed into the trees at the far end of the field, knocking the foremost of them aside, and then vanished into the forest of trees. The tops of them shook violently as the creature passed through and then, after long moments, they stopped. It indicated one of two things: Either the creature had taken up residence in the forest nearby or, more likely, it had vanished from the area entirely.

Leonard Samson stood on the porch of his house, staring out into the rain, trying to process what he'd seen.

He didn't even remember walking from the edge of the field back to the house. One moment he was at one place, and the next he was back home. He was almost tempted to think that none of it had happened. That he had had a bad dream, entered a fugue state, and sleepwalked from the living room outside. Now, having awoken, he had to separate fantasy from reality. That should have been an easy chore. Certainly all the stuff with Bruce Banner transforming into a green/gray monster and running away with Betty in his arms was in the fantasy category. It hadn't happened. It could not possibly have happened. Such things . . . they didn't happen.

That's what he kept telling himself, and he was fascinated to discover that a celebrated and highly lauded psychiatrist was as fully capable of denial as anyone else.

"You did the right thing calling me."

Samson did not even bother to look to his left to see Thunderbolt Ross addressing him. The remains of Ross's platoon were parked along the street. There weren't all that many of them.

Ross drew closer and rested a hand on Samson's shoulder. His voice softened from its usual gruffness as he continued, "You're doubting it now because it went bad, but your instincts were right. You see who he is now. What he is."

"No, I don't, actually," Samson said in an almost clinical tone. "He wasn't what I thought he'd be at all. It was strange to me that she would never say what happened between them. She's one of the most honest people I know, so it bothered me. But it was this, wasn't it. And you knew about it, too . . ." Now he did look at Ross for the first time. "When you called me a year ago, you knew. And you were all a part of it?"

Ross didn't bother to answer. Obviously he had other things on his mind. "I need to know where they're going. She'll be in incredible danger as long as she's with him."

"From whom?" For the first time Samson's detached facade began to crack. "He protected her," and his voice rose, "*you* almost killed her!"

"I give you my word that her safety is my main concern at this point. Bruce's as well. I care about him more than you realize. I don't want to hurt him, I want to help him."

Samson took a step back and said with undisguised contempt, "You know, it's a point of professional pride with me that I can always tell when somebody is lying. He wasn't . . . and you are." He waited to see if Ross reacted to that, and was disappointed to see that—beyond a slight twitching around the eyes—Ross gave no visual response. "But I don't know where he was going," Samson went on. "I know that she'll help him if she can."

It had only been moments earlier that Ross had been putting forward a sympathetic air. Now, seeing that none of it had played well, he settled back into more familiar territory: United States standard-issue hard-ass.

"Then she'll be aiding a fugitive and I won't be able to help either of them."

Ross stood there for a few seconds, apparently feeling it important that that declaration sink in. It was meaningless to Samson, who knew that Ross wasn't remotely interested in helping anyone except Ross. Then the general turned and headed down the driveway toward his waiting van.

He called after Ross, "I used to wonder why she never talked about you. Now I know."

Ross walked away without looking back.

THIRTEEN

Betty awoke to a monstrous face looking down at her.

Off guard, disoriented, she reacted out of pure instinct and swung her open palm. It cracked across the creature's face, with the result being a startled grunt from the creature and a yelp of pain from Betty who nearly sprained her wrist from the impact.

"Oh, no!" she said, starting to realize what had just happened. "I'm sorry. I'm . . ."

The creature pulled its—

No. Not its. He's not a thing, not a monstrosity. He's Bruce. I can see Bruce's face, hidden in there, distorted, transformed, but he's in there.

The creature pulled his head away from her and backed up. Betty sat up and had to brace herself as the cave spun around her . . .

Cave?

Yes. That was it. They were in a cave. Betty saw that it was getting dark outside, which gave her an idea of how long she'd been out. It was still raining, but the cave was providing her a measure of shelter. He was still regarding her suspiciously. She couldn't blame him. The events of the morning were a bit patchy to her, but she remembered enough to know that he had saved her. And now he had brought her to this place and found shelter for her . . . and the first thing she had done when she had come to was smack him. Not that she had hurt him, of course. She was still trying to shake off the pain in her wrist. Still, he certainly deserved more consideration than having yet another person attack him.

He was already standing up. She looked at him more closely and realized that he was crouched because he couldn't fit under the cave ceiling fully upright. He seemed confused, disoriented. Betty huddled against the wall, feeling the cold air down to her bones. She still had her raincoat on, but it was torn and frayed. Her purse was slung across her shoulder. Sliding the bag off her shoulder, she removed the raincoat and draped it across herself like a blanket. Then she looked up at him and noticed that he was wounded, a dark green stain spread across his upper shoulder, and more cuts were on his arm. She stood and walked toward him. "You're hurt."

Brucecanyouunderstandmeareyouhurt? The words are distant and the sound of them is like acid rain sizzling, they are said with concern and the meaning is hard to discern and we sense they are well-intended but why does it hurt why does everything have to hurt why can't they stop hurting us?

Then his mind processed the words, as if he had stepped out of himself and was hearing them with another part of his brain. He began to settle down, to feel relaxed with her presence, and suddenly a white flash of lightning ripped across the sky. Betty flinched back automatically as the being that had been, and still was, Bruce Banner, let out a terrifying roar, and rage distorted his face into a fearsome sight.

Looking for the source of what he saw as an attack, the creature grabbed a mammoth rock and, as thunder rumbled after the lightning flash, strode out into the rain and heaved the rock skyward. Then he roared back at the rumbling noise cascading across the sky.

He's picking a fight with God. And if it ever came down to that, I couldn't say for sure who would win.

She stepped out into the rain and touched his arm. He turned toward her, still growling. "It's okay. We're okay," she assured him. She took his massive arm and, out of reflex, looked more closely at his arm to see if there was any sign of infection. At first she thought that the shadows were playing tricks on her, because it seemed to her that the wounds were smaller than they had appeared barely a minute before. Then she watched without looking away and saw that, no, she wasn't imagining it. The cuts were indeed dwindling. His body was visibly healing itself, with the speed of the healing increasing exponentially. The smaller the wounds got, the faster they healed. It was remarkable.

"Come here. Come on."

She pulled him out of the rain, or more correctly, he allowed himself to be pulled. She sat down and gently tugged for him to sit next to her. He inflated his cheeks and let out a grudging huff, like a gorilla, and did as she indicated. When the lightning blasted overhead again, he jumped only a little, but seemed calmed by the way she was stroking his upper arm. As the storm continued to thunder, he stopped reacting altogether. His head slumped back against the cave wall and he sighed. It was such a human sound to come from something so huge. It was like watching a lion stretch itself and see in it the basic mannerisms of a house cat.

She rested her head against his shoulder and listened to his slow, steady breathing that sounded like a train rumbling down tracks.

Betty Ross had to fight down an impulse to laugh.

My God . . . he still snores . . .

"Will he walk again?"

General Ross was standing in the intensive care unit

of the army base's hospital ward, asking questions of a doctor that he very much suspected he already knew the answers to. The doctor, an older, bearded man named Milgrom, checked the chart before he spoke. Ross noticed that he did that every single time Ross asked him a question, as if the information on the chart might somehow change from moment to moment.

"Most of the bones in his body look like crushed gravel right now," said Dr. Milgrom. "If he lives, he'll be lucky if he can lift the straw to eat his liquid meals."

They had been walking down the hallway and came to a stop at Blonsky's bed. At least, Ross assumed it was Blonsky. Between the multitude of tubes sticking out of him that made him look like he was wrestling a squid, and the fact that his face was swollen beyond the point where he still looked remotely human, Ross really had no way of knowing for sure short of running a DNA match.

"I will say this," said Milgrom, naturally looking at his chart yet again. "He's got a heart like a machine. Never seen anything like it outside a racehorse."

Ross had. And he had never thought he would see it again.

If Blonsky's body began to show the other properties associated with that machinelike heartbeat, then Ross knew that Blonsky would do far more than walk again.

Far more.

This isn't over, Banner. Not by a long shot.

It's over. Dear lord, it's over. Thank you, thank you, thank you.

Betty had not intended to fall back to sleep, but then she blinked her eyes and discovered, much to her surprise, that sunlight was flooding in and it was finally no longer raining.

Furthermore, she realized that she was curled protectively around a transformed Bruce Banner. His chest was rising and falling softly, and he still had that faint buzzing emanating from his chest, but it hardly sounded like a train anymore. More like an outboard motor from a small boat.

If she had happened to stumble over him without any knowledge of who he was or what he endured, she would have assumed he was a drug addict recovering from an overdose. He looked pale and unhealthy. When she sat up he promptly started to shiver in the chill morning air, so she lay back down next to him to provide him warmth. The shivering stopped.

It was astounding to her, the contrast between the staggering vulnerability of his current form and the indestructibility of the being he transformed into. Of course, indestructibility was all relative; she remembered the wounds he had sustained.

The recollection prompted her to check over Banner's skin, running her fingers over his shoulder, his arm, seeking some sign of the damage that had been inflicted on his other form. There was nothing. He might have been sallow, but he was whole. There was not so much as a mark on him.

Her touch stirred him to wakefulness. Slowly he raised his head and moaned softly. Then he saw her looking down at him. He seemed almost afraid to smile.

"I must still be asleep," he said.

"Why would you think that?"

"Because of all the times I've had this exact dream . . . waking up . . . seeing you . . . and . . ."

"And . . . ?"

Suddenly his upper body began to convulse. He yanked away from her, went to his hands and knees, and vomited in the corner of the cave.

She wanted to go to him, to help him or provide sympathy—something—but he waved her off, obviously not wanting her anywhere near him. When his guts stopped heaving, he said in exhaustion, "Okay . . . that was never part of the dream."

"You have no idea how relieved I am to hear that."

She went to him, helped him to his feet and said softly, "Come on. We need to find someplace where you can get warmed up."

"Betty . . . I'm sor—"

She put a finger to his lips. "Not now. Not when we're both tired and scared and cold and half naked. This isn't the time to start having deep emotional discussions. It just isn't."

He nodded in agreement and, leaning on her more than he would have liked but exactly as much as he had to, limped out of the cave and into a new day.

The town was called Trimpeville, population eight hundred and twelve, or so the sign said when they made their way past it. Trimpeville, as it turned out, was nestled in the Appalachians, and the entire source of Trimpeville's income appeared to be campers requiring supplies (available courtesy of the only superstore within a hundred-mile radius, the store being the primary employer of the town) and travelers who were making their way from one place to another and using Trimpeville as a place to take a break.

Because of that, Trimpeville actually had a small, ten-room motel, which had the inspiring name of MOTEL in a large lit sign with the "l" burnt off, leaving the word MOTE. Banner seemed to feel there was some strange bit of irony in that; Betty didn't see it, nor did she care. What she cared about was that the place didn't take credit cards, which was probably just as well. Better to live off the grid for as long as they could manage it. Fortunately the room was cheap enough that it only made a small dent in the amount of available cash she had on her. But it didn't help matters when she saw cockroaches scuttle hurriedly away the moment she entered the room and turned on the light. Still, considering everything she had just dealt with, it was actually a nice change of pace to endure something as mundane as cockroaches.

Bruce had been hiding behind the ice machine as Betty walked past with the key. There seemed little point in having Bruce accompany her to the front desk and provide something memorable for the desk clerk as a half-naked man with tattered pants and a woman's raincoat draped over his bare torso. Hell, it was bad enough that the desk clerk had looked at her oddly when he'd asked for the license number of her car and she'd had to admit that she didn't have one, a curious happenstance considering Trimpeville was within walking distance of, well, not a damned thing. So why provide further curious elements, such as a half-dressed male companion, which might be enough for him to perhaps mention to the authorities, with the possible upshot being yet another squadron of soldiers descending upon them?

She realized then that she was already thinking the same way that Bruce had been when they had first reunited. Despite the fact that she knew her father's implacable nature all too well, she had still felt as if Bruce was being needlessly overcautious. Yet here she was now, with barely twenty-four hours having passed since the events of the previous day, and she was already being every bit as paranoid as Bruce had been. *My God, what must three years of living like this have done to him?*

Bruce looked ready to pass out. She stepped over to him and helped him to half walk, half drag himself into the room. "I had a dream once . . ." he said.

"Was I in this one?"

"No one was," he said as she eased him onto the single chair in the room. "It was just me and the . . . the

other me. It. The world was over, and it was just cockroaches and us. Giant cockroaches. And they kept de-
vouring the other me, but the skin would always grow
back so they could devour me all over again."

She looked at him and shook her head. "I had forgotten how much fun you aren't in the morning. Do you
think you can stand enough to take a shower? Get yourself cleaned up?"

He nodded and made his way into the bathroom. He
pulled the door shut so that it clicked softly behind him.

What the hell have you gotten me into, Bruce? Then
she shook her head, trying to dispel that sort of thinking. He hadn't gotten her into anything. She had done it
herself, all herself . . . with a little help from her father
and his big boom-boom toys. Despite all the destruction
that he had rained down upon his tormentors, Bruce
was actually the person least to blame in all of this.

Steam rose from around Banner as he stood with his
head under the shower. It was hardly the best shower in
the world, with water leaking from the joints of the
shower head, the water pressure was lousy, and a faint
whiff of mildew hung in the air. Still, considering the circumstances, it was a small and very welcome bit of civilization.

His eyes had been closed, but then he looked up at the
water coming down . . .

**A spray of ammunition is coming at us,
fired in a steady stream by the advancing
Apache helicopter and . . .**

Banner stumbled back, banging up against the other
side of the shower. His feet nearly went out from under
him, but he caught himself at the last moment and
avoided falling.

As always, his memories of what had transpired while
he had been in his other incarnation were vague. Brief

snapshots of reality at best. He couldn't really decide if that was a good thing or a bad thing.

Then nausea swept over him once more. *Not in the tub, not in the tub.*

He stumbled out of the shower and fell forward. He broke his fall by grabbing the edge of the toilet, then opened the lid quickly and vomited into the bowl. As the waves of nausea passed, he heard the door to the hotel room click open. Betty had said she was going out; now apparently she was back.

Of course, maybe it wasn't her. Maybe it was Ross and his soldiers again. If so, Bruce was all too ready to give up. Let them slap cuffs on him; hell, let them put a bullet in his brain if they could. It was probably how he was going to wind up, sooner or later. Why wait?

He heard the rustling of shopping bags being set down in the room outside. Since it seemed unlikely that General Ross had been thoughtful enough to go to the grocery store before stopping by, the odds that it was Betty were upped considerably.

He was seized once again with more nausea. He couldn't understand it. Was it related to the transformation? He hadn't had this sort of reaction back in South America. Why—?

Then he felt something hard coming up his esophagus, and suddenly he realized. Moving as fast as his tortured body would let him, he pulled himself away from the toilet and up to the sink. He retched one final time and a small plastic card was pushed out of his mouth and clinked into the sink.

Ohhhh right. I almost forgot about you. Well . . . if it's going to come out one way or the other, I suppose this beats the alternative.

"You okay?" came Betty's voice through the door.

"Yeah, I feel better, actually," he said. He grabbed a towel and wrapped it around his middle, rather than pull back on the now-tattered rags he'd been wearing. He stepped out of the bathroom and held up the object that his body had just expelled. "Just getting this back."

"Oh! The data!" Her eyebrows arched. "You ate it?"

"Yeah. Under the circumstances I had to improvise."

"Wow." Obviously deciding she didn't want to press him on the circumstances, she instead indicated the bags. "They didn't have much selection but I got you a few options. First things first."

She tossed him a new pulse monitor. He caught it reflexively and looked at it in surprise. "You're kidding me."

"Gotta love superstores. Okay, now, it ain't Armani, but . . ."

She started showing him clothes, holding up sizes. He gave her thumbs-up on some, shaking his head on others. She held up a large pair of purple pants, pulling the waist in both directions to display how stretchy they were. She tossed them to him and he held them up to himself. He winced. "Problem with the color?" she said.

"I'm an irradiated freak, that doesn't mean I've lost my sense of style."

"Oh, as if you ever had any to lose," she laughed. "They were the stretchiest ones they had."

"I'll take my chances." He opted for some trousers that were less elastic but also, gratefully, less purple.

He went into the bathroom and changed into one of the outfits she'd obtained for him. Betty could see the edges of his body as he did so, brief flashes of skin. She looked down, wrestling with her feelings. Everything had been happening so quickly that this was the first moment she really had to step back and take stock of it all.

The thing was, she realized that stepping back was not quite as easy as all that. Her emotions were too raw, the events too recent. In the three years since she had last seen him, she had never managed to attain any sort of closure in their relationship for obvious reasons. So rather than developing scar tissue, their severed relationship had remained a big gaping wound, and seeing him here was just sticking a knife into that wound and twisting it.

And yet . . . it felt good. She was astonished to realize that. Her relationship with Leonard . . . it had been nice. Sensible. Pleasant. Comfortable. But it had lacked the fire and passion of her feelings for Bruce. She had told herself repeatedly that that was actually a good thing, a smart thing. Now, though, she was beginning to think that she had been kidding herself. Trying to convince herself that she didn't really miss it, didn't need it, much like the fox sniffing disdainfully at the grapes that were out of its reach by declaring them to be sour.

Well, here were the grapes, within ready reach, and they didn't seem the least bit sour to her. Not at all.

Banner emerged from the bathroom and she smiled at him with affection. His hair was an unkempt mess. Seeing how she was looking at it, he ran his fingers through it in a vague manner, trying to smooth it out and not coming close to succeeding.

"When was the last time anybody but you cut your hair?" she said.

He shrugged.

"Give me five minutes," she said. "Go lie down. Take it easy."

He did as he was instructed. Betty went into the bathroom and took a fast shower, anxious to wash away the last dregs of a night's sleep in a dank cave. There was a short white robe hanging on a hook mounted on the bathroom door. Betty didn't know if it was something provided complimentary by the motel—which she doubted—or, more likely, a previous guest had carelessly left it behind and the cleaning crew, presuming there was one, just left it there. She put it on, emerged from the bathroom, and found Bruce lightly dozing on the bed. He awoke as soon as she came out, and she directed him over to the chair. He straddled it, leaning on the back of it, as Betty draped a towel around his upper body. Using a pair of scissors she always carried in her purse, just because one never knew when one might need scissors, she busily and efficiently whacked his hair into shape. Suspicious, he tried to reach up and check out what she was doing to his hair, and she playfully flicked his hand away.

"I *have* done this before," she assured him.

He dropped his head forward and she rubbed his neck a little, loosening up the muscles.

Her voice softened. "How did you manage this all by yourself?"

"With clippers, usually."

She tweaked his ear. "That's not what I meant," she said.

He reached up, caught her hand and held it on his shoulder. "I know," he said so softly that she almost didn't hear him. "I thought I couldn't risk . . . this. The two of us together. That it was better to deal with it alone. I was wrong. This is . . . better." He said the last word with a sigh.

She bent over and kissed the top of his head. Reaching back, he touched the side of her face, and she bent lower and kissed his temple. As if a hole had been blown open in a dam, he twisted around in the chair and kissed her passionately. Her mind screamed a warning at her but she completely ignored it as he pushed her back toward the bed, all the hopes, fears, and frustrations of the past lonely three years washed away in hopes of a brighter future with her. He lay atop her, sliding his left hand beneath her bathrobe, and as his palm came into contact with the soft warmth she whispered encouraging words of love in his ear.

And then, to her astonishment, he said, "No, wait," in a voice so strangled that it was barely recognizable as his own. He pulled away from her, rolled off her, and he kept saying, "I'm sorry . . ."

Betty was gasping for breath. Her body was trembling like a car that had just had its gears stripped. "*What?*"

"We can't."

"It's okay," she assured him, reaching for him, "I want to."

"No. I can't. I can't get too excited."

He held up the pulse monitor on his right wrist. It had been flashing at one hundred, and now was starting to drop, slowly but steadily.

"Oh God." Then, with hope in her voice, she said, "Not even a *little* excited?"

He smiled ruefully and shook his head. She moaned softly, knowing he was right, hating him for being so. She flopped back onto the bed and looked up at him. He was sitting right there but he might as well have been looking at her from across the Grand Canyon. She gazed longingly into his eyes and then spotted a scar under one of them. It was small, scarcely noticeable. She reached up and touched it gently. "All the other ones are gone."

"That's mine. His heal. Mine don't."

"Yes, they do. They leave a mark but they stop hurting."

She hesitated, and then moved her bangs aside. He leaned forward, looking confused, and then he spotted what she was showing him: a white scar just behind her right temple. Mortified, he turned away with a pained expression.

"No, look at me," she insisted. She took his chin in her hand and turned his face so that he was looking at her. "That pain didn't last. Not knowing was so much worse. It took me two years not to look for you in crowds. I stopped looking but I never stopped hoping. I never stopped."

There was clearly so much that he wanted to say. The great thing was that, now that they were together, none of it needed to be said. Words were unnecessary when a touch of his hand to her face was all that was needed. He kissed her tenderly and held her gently to himself as she gazed balefully at the heart monitor. *Nuts*, she thought.

Thunderbolt Ross sat alone at a desk in the Strategic Operations Command Center of the base. Since there were no strategic operations in progress at the moment that the base was overseeing, the place was empty at this late hour.

Ross's attention was split. Part of it was on the phone call he was engaged in, the receiver pressed against his ear. The other was on news footage, being broadcast on a monitor screen, that he very much wished hadn't existed. He had thought that he had gotten off lightly insofar as press coverage was concerned, because the invasion of the campus had happened early enough and quickly enough that they were gone before news crews were aware that anything was transpiring.

Unfortunately in this day and age, it was impossible to keep anything under wraps.

The footage that he was watching was grainy and from a sufficient distance that details were impossible to discern, thank God. Apparently some damned news copter had caught sight of the scene while delivering routine traffic updates. Traffic! Who the hell was driving anyplace on a Sunday morning that they needed to know where jam-ups were, anyway? Why weren't they either in church or sleeping in?

The result was background footage that hinted at

what had gone on, and now a reporter was moving through the aftermath of the battle, surveying the rubble from the fallen pedestrian overpass, the mutilated sculpture, and assorted other debris. "Rumors continue to swirl about a violent clash between the forces of the U.S. military and an unknown adversary on the campus of Culver University earlier today. But we do know that authorities have renewed the long-cold hunt for fugitive scientist Robert Bruce Banner."

Banner's picture filled the screen.

How the hell did they know that? Who the blazes blabbed? Whose ass can I put in a sling for letting word of that leak out?

All those questions ran unanswered through his mind as Ross spoke hurriedly on the phone to Joe Greller on the other end. "For God's sake, Joe, the National Guard can't get tents to hurricane zones in time, and you're telling me I've got to liase with part-timers?"

"It's domestic on paper, so Guard and FBI have to be involved," said Greller, speaking from his office in the Pentagon.

"FBI!" Ross had the feeling that if he had undergone the treatment instead of Banner, his fists would be shattering the receiver to pieces right about now. "Did the chiefs get a look at those tapes? Do they think that was a video game?" Every second of their encounter with Banner and his monstrous alter ego had been recorded via the visual and audio feed in the control van, and all of it had been dutifully forwarded to Greller.

"They saw them," Greller said flatly. "Nobody's doubting anymore."

"What's the FBI going to do? Pull out badges? Do a profile? Why don't we get ATF while we're at it?"

"Believe me, if I thought alcohol and tobacco could get the job done where the firearms are failing—as your own video shows—I'd bring in the ATF in a heartbeat.

Look, use the FBI for intel and equipment and then tell
'em to back off." Clearly believing the subject was
closed, Greller turned to other matters. "What about
Blonsky?"

"Not looking good." He paused. Wouldn't be any
harm in tossing a bit of flattery Greller's way. "He was
everything you said, though. He made it happen. You
saw the tape."

"I did. And I saw the way he was moving before he
got hit." There was a hesitation in Greller's voice, and
Ross correctly read volumes into that hesitation. "Reminded me an awful lot of something I think we'd both
like to forget."

Ross should have known he couldn't slip anything
past Greller. The man was just too damned sharp. "Are
you asking me a question, Joe?" said Ross carefully. "Or
would you like me to put the lid back on this thing?"

Greller didn't respond immediately. That didn't surprise Ross. Greller was not one to take a precipitous action or speak without considering all the ramifications.
Finally Greller, noncommittal, said, "Make your list and
get back to me."

Before Ross could say anything else, Greller hung up.
No reason for him not to, Ross reasoned. Everything
that needed to be said had been. He hung up just in time
to see the television reporter standing next to two college kids, slackers, both of whom looked stoned out of
their minds. Apparently in today's journalism, that was
what passed for sources.

"Very few outside the military got a firsthand look at
who . . . or what . . . the soldiers were fighting," said the
reporter. Indicating the two students next to him, he
continued, "Sophomores Jack McGee and Jim Wilson
were coming home from a hike and witnessed some of
the battle. McGee, who happens to be a reporter for the
campus paper, captured this on his cell phone."

As the voices of the reporter and the idiot boys continued, pixellated images of the beast taking on the army, and kicking their collective asses, played across the screen. Ross grimaced as he saw them.

"Can you describe what you saw?" came the reporter's voice.

"Dude, it was like a huge and green . . . *huge* . . . I mean, like, the way Steve Nash looks standing next to Shaq? Shaq would look like that standing next to this."

"Dude, it was so big," said the other young fool. "It was like this huge . . . *hulk*. And home was stompin', yo."

"Home was stompin', yo"? What the hell was wrong with this country, that people couldn't even speak proper English anymore.

The camera switched back to the newscaster, who said, "Further search for the mysterious 'Hulk' was delayed by powerful thunderstorms—"

The mysterious Hulk. Trust the media, always trying to name everything they know nothing about. Thank God "Hulk" has no chance of sticking . . .

Ross was interrupted in his musings by Sparr, who burst in and said grimly, "It's Blonsky."

Without a word Ross followed her out of the command center. They went straight to the hospital ward, hustling down the hall, through the door of the ICU. Certain of what he was going to see, Ross said, "Has anybody found out if he has next of kin or family?"

"You can ask him yourself."

He fired her a confused look. Her face remained immobile as nurses and doctors grouped around Blonsky's bed stood aside upon the general's approach. Blonsky was sitting up, talking and laughing with the medical staff.

Ross couldn't believe it. He was responsible for it, and yet the actuality of it was breathtaking. Blonsky didn't have a mark on him. Not only that, but his body had healed into a more muscular shape than before; not absurdly so, but still, he looked tanned, healthier, better than he had before.

The general now understood why Sparr had looked at him the way she had. Her grimness had made him think that Blonsky was dead. Had that been the case, Sparr would have been much more matter-of-fact. But Sparr was no fool. She knew that this miraculous recovery had to be more than it seemed, and it was equally obvious to her that Ross was responsible for it in some manner. Her expression now said it all: *More secrets, General? More things you're keeping from me? How large a body count are we going to have to pile up before you act as if you and I are on the same side?*

He said nothing to her. At this point there was nothing *to* say.

Blonsky spotted him and immediately got to his feet. He was wearing a hospital gown but he looked so authoritative that he might well have been sporting his dress uniform. He saluted and Ross returned it. "Good to see you on your feet, soldier. How do you feel?"

Blonsky smiled lopsidedly. "Pissed off and ready for round three."

FOURTEEN

Bruce Banner studied the array of things on the bed that Betty had been carrying in her purse: a phone, a credit card, bank card, driver's license, some cash, some makeup, her university ID, a small camera and—most curiously, considering it was not something that she typically carried around—her passport. He picked up the passport and looked at it questioningly.

Betty tucked in her blouse and looked momentarily embarrassed. Then she said gamely, "I thought if you asked me to go, I ought to be ready," she said. When she saw his startled expression, she continued, but her voice was huskier and more full of emotion than even she expected. "I didn't know if I was going to be able to let you go on that bus. I thought I'd better be ready."

He took that in, moved by the sentiment, and saddened that he could not provide anything in response save for wistfulness. There was so much he wanted to say at that point, but nothing seemed either appropriate or adequate. Instead he kept himself focused on business. "Can't use any of it but the cash. Don't even turn the phone on, they can track it."

"My lipstick? Can they track that?"

He smiled. "No, you can keep that."

"We're not going to get where we're going on seventy bucks."

"Not quickly enough," he admitted.

She did not even hesitate as she reached up, undid a

small chain around her throat, and pulled it loose. A solid gold pendant dangled from the end of the gold chain. She held it up without a word.

Banner shook his head forcefully. "No. It's the only thing of hers that you have. No," he said.

Gently but deliberately, Betty took his hand and placed her mother's pendant gently into his palm. She curled his fingers around it and said with complete conviction, "We'll get it back."

He had no idea if that was true. The odds were that she didn't either. But he had to hope that she was right, because he knew they had no other choice. They had to get out of the area, had to get as far away as possible, because he had no doubt that, even now, General Ross was doing everything he could to find them.

The Strategic Operations Command Center was now bustling with activity. At least two dozen people made up Ross's team—expert technicians in intel gathering, in law enforcement, in every discipline that would be required to round up and neutralize the threat that Bruce Banner presented. As photos of Betty Ross and Bruce Banner filled the monitor screens, the assembled team was listening carefully to Sparr's briefing.

Ross had to credit Sparr: Whatever irritation she might have felt with Ross, whatever sense of betrayal she was experiencing because he had been repeatedly less than forthcoming, it wasn't affecting her ability to do her job. All business, she was saying, "Federal is already monitoring phone, plastic, and Dr. Ross's Web accounts, and local PDs have been put on alert. They'll pop up somewhere, and when they do, it comes straight to us."

As much as he was loath to contradict Sparr at this point, Ross had to clarify something. "They won't just pop up," he said, immediately attracting all attention in the room. "He made it three years and got across borders without making a mistake and he won't use a damn credit card now." He paused, and then said meaningfully, "If he were trying to escape, he'd be long gone. He's not trying to escape this time. He's looking for help. And that's how we're going to get him. We don't know where they're going but we know what they're after and we know he's been talking to somebody. You've all got copies of that correspondence. There are only a few hundred people in the world who have what he needs. Figure out who they are. He's going to one of them."

One agent tentatively raised his hand and Ross nodded toward him. "I'm unclear," said the agent. "Are we calling Dr. Ross his hostage or an accomplice?"

Sparr stepped in quickly before Ross could answer. "We have no information on her condition or anything that leads us to believe she's helped him in any way."

Ross appreciated what Sparr was trying to do. She was attempting to cover for him, make it so that he didn't have to acknowledge hard truths. There was no point. He had already come to terms with the reality of the situation. "If she's alive and she's with him, then she's helping him," said Ross. Sparr fired him a look but said nothing. His voice flat and even, he continued, "He'd never hold her. It's her choice."

Slowly she nodded, taking note of the severity of his assessment. She kept her gaze locked on him as she said to the assembled staff, "Under no circumstance whatsoever are your people to engage these subjects directly. Apprehension will be handled exclusively from this office. Call it in and we'll tell you what to do."

All of which sounded exactly right to Ross. The only problem was—and Sparr knew it as well as Ross—that telling them what to do could be a serious problem considering that they had yet to come up with any strategy that worked. Hard to tell others what to do when you yourself did not know.

Banner tried not to let his guilt overwhelm him as he leaned against the outside of the storefront proclaiming itself to be MANTLO & WEIN'S PAWNSHOP. A guy walked past him carrying a television, heading inside. He barely glanced in Banner's direction, which was pretty much how Banner preferred it.

He knew he should have been the one who was in there doing what needed to be done. He had tried. He had made it to the front door, was about to enter, and then wound up turning back to Betty and trying to convince her that there had to be another way. With a sigh of impatience she had taken the pendant from him, told him to wait right where he was, and that she would take care of hocking the pendant.

She had worn that locket every day that Banner had known her. "You can't," Banner had said insistently. "It means the world to you."

"No. *It* doesn't," she said, and left unspoken in the way she had said it just what there was that *did* mean the world to her. It was obvious that she was, in fact, looking right at it, so obvious that she didn't even have to say it. She had patted him once on the face and then turned and headed into the store.

For a moment, it left Banner envious of his towering, rampaging alter ego. Strong where Banner was weak, confident where Banner was uncertain. He almost felt jealous of it.

A bell attached to the door jingled and Bruce looked up. Betty had emerged from the pawnshop and was walking around the corner to meet up with him. She held up the cash that she had gotten for it. It was not an insignificant amount.

"We'll get it back," Bruce said, echoing her earlier comments.

"Yes," said Betty with confidence. "We'll get it back."

He wondered if she truly believed it or if she was just putting on an act. It was difficult for him to say, because he wasn't entirely sure where he stood on the likelihood of their recovering it. He knew for certain that he would try. But life was too uncertain; Bruce Banner making a promise was like trying to walk uphill on a sheet of ice while wearing roller skates.

That didn't mean that he wouldn't do everything he could to try.

Their next stop was a service station down the road. They had spotted a beaten-up pickup truck parked at curbside with a FOR SALE sign on it. They walked into the office, where a young guy named Dennis who couldn't keep his eyes off Betty, confirmed that, yeah, it was for sale, all right.

"Why don't you go out and take a look with him, dear," Banner said. "I know so little about cars; I'll just be in the way."

Betty turned to him with obvious confusion. Dennis was still staring at her so fixedly that he didn't notice Bruce subtly inclining his head toward the computer that was sitting just to the young man's right. Betty, however, did see it, and understood immediately.

"Yes, by all means, honey, you stay here," she said to Banner, and focused a megawatt smile upon the counter man. "I'm sure this young man will be easily able to handle my . . . needs. Won't you?"

He vaulted over the counter, displaying a rather annoying athleticism. Dennis glanced disdainfully at Banner, who smiled grimly in return. *Yes, well . . . I could pick up one of the cars you have around here and throw it half a mile, if I'm in the right mood. How do you like them apples?*

Naturally he kept that comment to himself. It would have run contrary to Banner's main interest, which consisted of making sure that Dennis remained totally and utterly focused upon Betty. Dennis cooperated; he followed Betty out like an eager puppy dog and paid no attention whatsoever as Banner walked behind the counter.

He was in luck. Dennis had his e-mail account open. Betty had told him a private e-mail account of hers that he could use if necessary, which he was prepared to do. It was not, however, his first choice, because he didn't rule out the possibility that Betty's father had his people all over it, and using it might well serve as a beacon for those who were pursuing them. But nobody in the government was going to be monitoring the e-mail account of some guy in a service station in the middle of nowhere. He typed the covering memo: *What you requested is attached. Maybe it's time to meet. Green.* Then he plugged the data card into the computer and hit Send. The computer drive whirred for a few seconds and then the e-mail was off into the ether. It was a matter of a few more moments to delete any trace of the message from the e-mail account's send log. Then he smiled, pleased with himself. The mighty Dr. Bruce Banner had just managed to outwit a pimply teenager who would probably never see the inside of a college. *Take two gold stars out of petty cash, smart guy.*

Minutes later, Betty was removing the FOR SALE sign from the rear passenger window of their newly purchased vehicle. Bruce was climbing into the passenger side, not desirous to drive. God forbid they should get pulled over for some minor infraction, they'd be truly cooked when Bruce proved unable to produce a valid American driver's license.

"Hey," Betty said from behind him. He turned and

saw that she had her little camera out. He gave her a quizzical look.

"It's been worse than this before, right?" she said.

"Yes. Much worse," he said, unsure of where she was going with this.

"And you're not just running now, we're on the way to something better. So smile . . ."

The most he could manage was a sad, uncertain grimace that bordered on a smile. She looked as if she were about to try to get better from him, but then just shrugged and snapped the picture.

Then she came around to the driver's side and started up the truck. It coughed slightly in protest, as if it were annoyed that someone was waking it up after an extended nap. It almost stalled out but Betty convinced it otherwise and then it roared to life with enough strength that Banner thought, *Wow. Maybe it will get us to our destination at that.*

Betty climbed in and soon they were heading due east.

They chatted for a while about inconsequential matters. Now that they were together, it still felt as if there were a sizable wall between them that couldn't be breached through mere discussion. Finally Bruce lapsed into silence, a darker, more thoughtful mood falling upon him. Betty glanced at him after a time and prompted him with the tried and true conversation starter of, "Penny for your thoughts?"

He hesitated, reluctant to bring it up, but not seeing a way around it. "How long have you known Samson?"

He saw that the question clearly surprised Betty. Not so much that she threw wide her arms and said *"Whaaaaat?"* and lost control of the car. But she did raise an eyebrow. "About a year and a half. I met him when I took some time off. When I came back he arranged a visiting fellowship to come with me, and then he stayed."

"Do you trust him?"

"Yes, I do." She started to sound concerned. She obviously had no idea why Banner was asking, and her worries were all over the place. She probably thought that this was somehow related to what had nearly happened in the motel. That perhaps she didn't trust Samson to be faithful to her and therefore had no trouble being unfaithful to him with Bruce. Something like that, when the fact was that such aspects of their relationship were of no relevance to him right then. She started to say, "Bruce, you know that I . . ."

He put up a hand, interrupting her. "You don't have to explain anything to me. Ever. He seems like a good man and he treats you well and that makes me happy."

"He does." She paused, and then said, "But I never trusted him with this. With what happened to you, and with you, and the . . . I guess 'trust' isn't the right word. I didn't test his faith in me by asking him to believe something impossible."

So she did know that Banner was concerned about something other than their romantic relationship. That was good to know. They might not have been quite on the same page, but at least they were somewhere in the same chapter. "Who could? Sometimes I even convince myself that it's not real."

He was about to press her gently on the possibility that Samson might have been the one who brought Ross and this strike force crashing down upon them, but she switched topics before he could. "What's it like . . . when it happens? What do you experience?"

Banner tried to figure out the best way to describe it. "Remember those clinical experiments we volunteered for at Harvard? The induced hallucinations? It's like that, amplified by a thousand. It feels like someone is pouring a liter of acid into my brain. The sound is the worst."

"Sound?"

"Everything is amplified. It's like I'm under constant aural assault."

"Do you remember anything?"

"Fragments. Nothing I can derive anything from."

"But then it's still you . . . inside it."

He shook his head. "It's not me."

Betty obviously wasn't prepared to accept that answer. "In the cave, I felt that you knew . . . that *it* knew me. That *he* did. Maybe your mind is in there. It's just . . . overcharged . . . can't process what's happening."

They drove for a while longer, but Betty's mind never left its train of thought. "You know," she said a half hour later, as if they had never broken off the conversation, "Samson works with people on 'conscious dreaming,' helping them direct themselves out of their nightmares even though the conscious brain seems asleep. Maybe . . ."

"I don't want to control it," Bruce sat flatly. "I want to get rid of it."

He looked out the window, tormented, and said once more—as much to himself as to her—"I want to get rid of it," and then he lapsed back into silence.

Thaddeus Ross sat in his office that was just off the main planning room. He was savoring the taste of the cigar in his mouth, looking with morbid amusement at the NO SMOKING sign attached to the wall. He puckered his mouth in an "O" and puffed out a few rings that bounded off the warning sign, displaying his contempt for it. The army might well have been his life, and there was a chain of command that he respected beyond measure. But no dad-blamed sign stuck up on the wall by some unknown fool was going to tell Thunderbolt Ross what to do.

A small desk lamp provided the only illumination in

the room. Ross idly watched the smoke from his cigar curl upward and dance dangerously close to the smoke detector. There was a brisk knock at the door and Sparr entered, causing light from the main room to flood into the smaller office. She laid a fax on his desk.

"From Quantico. The academic language in the published stuff could be three dozen off our list. And we haven't even got samples from three dozen more."

Ross nodded, his back remaining to the desk. He heard Sparr turn to leave, but she didn't. Obviously she had something on her mind, and Ross had a few guesses as to what it might be.

"You keep seeing it in your mind, don't you," said Ross without turning.

She hesitated. "Yes."

"Did it shake you up?"

She didn't answer and now he turned to look at her. She appeared to want to lie, to refrain from admitting just how thrown she had been by the creature that the media had dubbed "Hulk." Rather than lie, she just stood there.

"Damn right it did," he said, answering for her. "It shook *me* up."

"It was . . . outside my training," she said. "An enemy has an agenda and we fight to block it. That . . . had no agenda. It was just . . ." She hesitated.

"Major," he said brusquely, "you're not going to be any damned good to me if you're afraid to speak your mind. Words aren't bullets, and even if they were, I've taken my share in my time and I'm still here. So stop hemming and hawing and just say what you're thinking."

It came out all in a rush: "If he wants to eliminate that, who are we to be trying to stop him?"

He did not answer immediately. He had to admit to

himself that, at least to Sparr, it was a valid question. The answer was not an easy one, and he puffed on his cigar a couple of times as he thought of the best way to frame it. "Major," he said finally, "a great writer once said, 'There are clefts in the Rock where we see the back part of God and tremble.' "

"Maybe somebody else reworded it, but it's based in the Bible," Sparr said immediately. "From Exodus. God placed Moses in a cleft in a rock and passed by, and Moses saw the back of God departing, but not his face."

"Very good," said Ross. "Major, there is no training for what you saw out there because it's not an enemy that confronts us. It's a new power let loose through a crack in the cliff of Nature's mystery. And how many times do you think that's happened? In all of human history?" He ticked them off on his fingers. "Fire . . . the splitting of the atom." He couldn't come up with any others, and Sparr didn't appear to have any further suggestions. Clearly she understood what he was talking about. He leaned forward, tapped out some ashes from his cigar into the trashcan at his feet and set the cigar down carefully on the desk blotter. Then he folded his hands and said intensely, "The universe unveils a secret and people recoil, cowering in fear and awe. But then comes the person who stops trembling and steps forward to face the flame and seizes the burning stick and says, 'This I will master and use.' And civilization's history has been written by those men. We've glimpsed the back part of God, Major." He leaned back in the chair, and he was scarcely able to keep the sense of wonder from his voice. "And for our nation and for our way of life, I intend to put a harness around it. And history will say that here, at this moment, we overcame our fear again and claimed the future."

Sparr stared at him. It seemed to Ross that she still appeared uncertain, as if trying to determine whether she was dealing with a man of vision or a megalomaniac, or maybe both.

He picked up his cigar and pointed it at her. "You're a good soldier, Kathleen. If you want to go back up the rabbit hole, you'll go with nothing but my thanks."

She considered it for perhaps two seconds, and then shrugged. "I'd just end up staring out the window, wondering who was screwing up in my place."

"All right, then."

"One other thing, General."

He waited.

"I was thinking that we obviously don't have the manpower to cover the entire country. But we don't have to. If the DOD bumps up the terror alert . . ."

"Then that will automatically put more eyes on more cars," Ross said, a slow smile spreading across his face. "If they get near any major cities, heightened security at checkpoints could spot them for us. Good thinking, Major. I'll make a few calls."

"Thank you, sir." She saluted. He returned it and she turned on her heel, her shoulders squared, and exited the room. As he reached for the phone to give Greller a buzz, he wondered why in the world he couldn't have a daughter like that. The only children he felt as if he could take real pride in were surrogates such as Sparr . . . and Blonsky.

Blonsky sat on a table in the med lab while two medical technicians were prepping the syringes that had been used to deliver the first dose of the Super Soldier serum. As they prepared to give him a second treatment, Ross stood nearby, arms folded. He had left the cigar behind in his office. Even he wasn't going to be obsessive enough about his stogie to try to smoke in a hospital wing.

"You ready?" said Ross.

Blonsky smiled. "Let's even the game a little."

"Absolutely, son," Ross said to him, and nodded to the technicians for the procedure to begin. He looked on and thought that no father could have been prouder.

FIFTEEN

In the course of their sojourn, Banner had come to the conclusion that if Betty Ross was forced to leave her chosen profession—which might very well be the case considering her activities of the past week—she might want to consider a future in long-distance trucking. The woman had a cast-iron constitution.

Betty had made it clear from the outset that she was determined to try to cover as much distance as possible, as quickly as possible. "We're on borrowed time," she said to Banner. "You just know my father is busy mobilizing the whole damned country. The longer we stay in one place, the more chance we have that we'll be spotted. So we need to keep moving." Banner was hard-pressed to say that her simple logic was flawed in any way. She had learned the lessons of reasonable paranoia very quickly. Experience was a good teacher.

And so they had been in constant motion. They made sure to stop every few hours to stretch their legs at Betty's insistence, pointing out that sitting for too long in one position could cause deep vein thrombosis. They certainly didn't need to have one of them wind up in a hospital with a blood clot. They confined their meals to drive through windows at fast-food places.

The longer they were together, and the closer they drew to their destination, the lighter Banner's mood became. They would listen to talk radio stations and shout their annoyance at the various pundits who pontificated about this, that, and the other thing. Or the radio would wind up tuned to a music station and Betty and Bruce would sing along. They tended to favor easy listening and oldies stations, although Betty took a heretofore unknown delight in screeching along to heavy metal. During those times Bruce would just grin at her enthusiasm, if not her inability to stay on key while belting out Aerosmith.

In all these years when she had been this idealized presence in his head, he had forgotten how wonderfully fun and down-to-earth she could be. When he put his mind to it, he was able to push away from his thoughts the circumstances that had brought them to this situation, and think of them simply as a couple who enjoyed each other's company.

The time flew past.

At one point, Banner awoke feeling disoriented and startled. He sat up abruptly and looked around, and then recollection flooded him. He wasn't entirely sure how long he had been asleep, and then the radio informed him that it was 3:10, with a traffic update to come in sixty seconds. He rubbed the sleep from his eyes and saw that Betty had tuned the radio to 1010, which he quickly discerned was a news station.

Betty noticed him stirring. "I thought I should let you sleep."

"Where are we?"

"Stuck in traffic, but getting close. I put on the radio to see if I could get a bead on why. Maybe an accident or something."

That was when he realized belatedly that they weren't moving. Traffic had completely locked up. If his own eyes hadn't told him that, the radio confirmed it moments later.

"And you're looking at a solid hour backup on the inbound Holland Tunnel, and an hour and a quarter on

the Lincoln," said the traffic reporter. "All this report-
edly due to heightened security alerts."

Betty and Bruce exchanged looks and then he stepped
out of the car. A couple of vehicles around him honked
at him in irritation, but he suspected it was directed
more at the situation than at him. Certainly he wasn't
causing any sort of hazard by getting out of the car;
nothing around him was moving, and when it did, it
didn't go much more than an inch at a time.

Slamming the door behind him, he passed quickly between cars, down the unmoving rows of traffic, getting
closer to the tollbooths. He hadn't thought to ask her
which tunnel she was at, but the signs saying HOLLAND
TUNNEL, HALF A MILE answered that question.

Then he saw it and his heart sank. The radio an-
nouncer had been absolutely right. There were soldiers
in the distance, and they appeared to be doing random
searches, looking into cars, checking trunks, and asking
for identification.

He didn't know whether this was a genuine security
elevation, or if Ross was somehow behind it. Either way
he didn't dare take the chance.

Banner sprinted back to the truck and came over to
the driver's side. "Let's go," said Banner.

She blinked in confusion. "Go where?"

"We've got to get out."

"Right *here*? I mean, *now*?"

"Yes, right here. Let's go."

She looked ready to argue further, but saw the look in
his eyes and quickly realized that not only was there no
point in arguing with him, but he was very likely right.
He had, after all, managed to elude capture for three
years, so following his instincts was simply the smart
way to go. Betty opened her door, grabbed her bag, and
slid out. The two of them darted through traffic on foot,
and if Bruce's exit had garnered a few irritated honks,

the both of them abandoning their vehicle—guaranteeing that the traffic jam would be further aggravated—resulted in a cacophony of horns blasting and irritated drivers howling obscenities at them. But none of that slowed them in the least and, minutes later, they were gone.

Soon they were wandering around an industrial section of Jersey City. They approached the docks, and Banner looked across the river toward the Manhattan skyline. Never had the phrase "so near and yet so far" had such personal resonance to him.

"Hell of a view, isn't it?" came a voice.

Banner glanced toward the speaker. It was an older man, rail thin, with gray hair and sunglasses. He was mooring a small outboard motorboat with fishing tackle in the back. The boat's name—*Excelsior*—adorned the side.

"It sure is," said Betty. "You going out fishing?"

"Coming back in, actually," said the fisherman. "Just not biting. Pretty much a waste of a day."

"How would you like it to be a bit less of a waste?" Bruce said abruptly. Betty looked at him in confusion, and then she realized.

"What've you got in mind?" said the fisherman.

They were running low on funds: They had some money left over from the purchase of the truck, and fortunately Betty had charmed Dennis into throwing in a couple of containers of gasoline, so that had helped them along the way. But refueling had been draining their reserves, and even though they'd been eating as cheaply as they could—they'd been subsisting on candy bars since Pennsylvania—they were nearly tapped out. But they were still able to find an amount to make it worth the fisherman's while . . . and Banner half suspected that the elderly gentleman was not averse to spending some extended time in Betty's company. He was starting to regret that he hadn't had her along with him for the past three years. Her astounding ability to charm the male of the species, young and old, could have made getting around a lot more bearable.

Soon they were racing across the Hudson River in the bow of the small outboard motorboat as the fisherman opened up the throttle and urged more speed out of the good ship *Excelsior*. He hadn't once asked them why they needed a ride into Manhattan. Considering the way he kept sneaking glances at Betty, Banner suspected he didn't much care, thus reinforcing Banner's earlier theories. He smiled to himself. Aside from the fact that his life was in perpetual turmoil, he was one of the luckiest men in the world when one considered the company he was keeping.

It was getting late in the afternoon by the time that Bruce and Betty found themselves in Battery Park, studying a map mounted on a kiosk. Betty tapped their destination and said, "Long way uptown. Subway's quicker."

"Me in a tight metal tube underground with hundreds of other people in the most aggressive city in the world?"

Betty checked their low financial reserves and made a face, but conceded Banner's point. "Right. Let's get a cab."

If avoiding stress was their goal, it turned out to be not the best plan they could have pursued.

The cab they flagged was moving normally when they hailed it. But the moment they were inside, the driver transformed into the human equivalent of Goofy from those old Disney cartoons about traffic safety. He blasted up the Avenue of the Americas, slashing across lanes without signaling, or at least apparently thinking that blaring one's horn was an acceptable substitute for signaling. While Bruce and Betty were tossed around like rag dolls, the driver accelerated with the aggressiveness of an F1 racer. He sent a bike messenger crashing into a line of parked cars in a desperate swerve to avoid calamity, raced through yellow lights that were turning while he was still a block away, and the entire time he had his radio blaring and was chattering away on a hands-free cell phone.

Banner's pulse monitor jumped to ninety-nine. At the rate things were going, Banner started to think that he should make love to Betty in the backseat. If he was going to have his pulse go out of control, it might as well be while doing something fun. But Betty hardly looked in the mood, white knuckling the ride and appearing to be fighting back the urge to vomit up the Three Musketeers bar she'd devoured in Trenton. So he closed his eyes and breathed slowly, endeavoring to reverse his body's pulse rate.

Finally Betty couldn't take it anymore. She leaned forward and banged on the security partition between them and the driver. *"Let us out! Now!"*

"We're not there yet!" the cabbie said.

"I know that! Now! Pull over now, you lunatic!"

The cab obediently screeched to a halt by the entrance to Central Park near Columbus Circle. The door flying open, Betty and Banner piled out. Banner staggered and grabbed a lamppost for support, resisting the urge to kiss the ground as being too melodramatic. Betty flung some crumpled bills through the passenger-side window.

With more fury than he had ever seen her express, Betty embarked on a tirade against the cabbie. *"God forbid you should give a shit about the living, breathing people in the back of your office-on-wheels-with-no-shocks . . ."*

The driver didn't seem especially concerned. "What's the matter, baby?" he said with a grin. "You no like a good ride?" He blew a kiss and the cab roared away with a screech of tires. Betty took the opportunity to kick the rear fender as it blew past. "*Asshole!*" she screamed.

Banner noticed the bumper sticker that read, HOW'S MY DRIVING? CALL 1-800-BITE-ME. *Too bad we didn't see that before we got in; it probably would have tipped us off.* Betty, meantime, was still fuming, and he said in what he thought was a helpful manner, "You know, I can show you some techniques to help you manage that rage a little better . . ."

"Zip it," she snapped at him. "We're walking." She stormed across the street against the red light without bothering to look. Cars screeched to a halt. One of them honked. She flipped the driver an obscene gesture. Banner ran after her, mouthing *Sorry!* to the irritated driver.

They headed into Central Park on the last leg of their destination, a mere sixty blocks away.

Please don't let us get mugged, thought Banner. He was starting to think that if it came to deciding between dealing with the army and dealing with the day-to-day realities of Manhattan, the army was starting to look better in comparison.

Major Sparr sat in a glassed-in office full of desks and computer terminals. She set aside a stack of papers she'd been going through and rubbed her eyes. It didn't help. Raw information, names and places and all manner of intel, floated in front of her even when she had her eyes closed. *He could be anywhere,* she realized bleakly. *He could be hiding in a cave with bin Laden, for all we know.*

Just to add to her aggravation, an intelligence officer walked in with a stack of brand new files. She moaned when she saw them. He didn't look unsympathetic as he set them down on the desk. "These are the ones Quantico says could fit the profile in Scandinavia."

Sparr sighed and nodded. As the intelligence officer walked out, she rubbed her temples and stared at the computer. This was getting her absolutely nowhere. She needed to find a different approach instead of just sifting through reams and reams of data.

What the hell have I got to lose? Sparr thought, and she booted up Google. When it came up, she entered under the search function, *"Mr. Blue cellular biology."*

To her surprise she got 180,000 hits. *This could take a while,* she thought, but she quickly discerned that that was not the case. Most of the first several pages were dead ends, either offering up ebooks about system modeling in cellular biology, or random combinations of words such as an article about blue nuclei. On the third page, however, she found a link to a YouTube video. She clicked on it and it brought her to a video of a press conference with what appeared to be some scientist demonstrating—according to the printed description—a "breakthrough in medical science." The scientist's name was Samuel Sterns. Sparr leaned forward, curious as to the relevance of "Mr. Blue" in the proceedings.

". . . full cell saturation," Sterns was saying, "a method of moving desired compounds into every cell in the body which will revolutionize medical therapies."

Sparr took one look at Sterns and he instantly gave her the creeps. He had an unusually long, almost oblong head, brown hair in a buzz cut, and an air of smug superiority that sounded alarms in her brain. In the video he was busy placing an inert blue dye into a bizarre-looking machine that was, in turn, hooked up to what appeared to be a young graduate student. The student said apprehensively, "Are you sure about this?"

"Science is never about being sure. It's about discovery," said Sterns blithely.

The machine functioned for long seconds, and Sterns's eyes were focused with nearly insane fervor upon the readouts. Then there was an audible gasp from audience members, and the camera—which had been on Sterns— shifted to the student. His skin was in the process of turning a bright, royal blue. He looked like an oversized Smurf. People laughed and clapped at the demonstration.

"What's his name?" asked a student.

"Who, Mr. Blue, here?" said Sterns cheerily.

Sparr bolted forward, eyes wide. There was more to the video, but she could always come back to it. She returned to Google and, her fingers practically flying across the keyboard, she typed in, "Samuel Sterns cellular biology."

This time she clicked on the very first link and hit pay dirt: It brought her directly to the website for Empire State University. Seconds later she was staring at a photo of Sterns, listed as faculty at ESU and unquestionably the same man on YouTube.

She jumped to her feet and sprinted down the hallway, thinking, *It fits, it fits, it all fits.* She burst in through Ross's office doorway. He had been on the phone and looked up at her with undisguised surprise, since this was not exactly what could be termed her usual method of entering a room. Sparr didn't care as she threw wide her arms and shouted, as if having just uncovered the secrets of the universe, *"They're going to New York!"*

"Well then," said Ross with a wolfish grin, "so are we."

SIXTEEN

Samuel Sterns emerged from the ESU science building, checking his wristwatch and shaking his head. He almost managed to get himself run over by a couple of kids on rollerblades who blasted past him without slowing down. Sterns barely avoided the collision, but didn't bother to shout after the rollerbladers. He just shook his head as if they were some great disappointment to him.

"Excuse me, Dr. Sterns?"

He glanced to his left and saw a vaguely familiar-looking woman approaching him. "Yes?"

"Sorry to bother you. I'm Elizabeth Ross."

The name suddenly clicked together with the image. He'd seen her photo accompanying some very scholarly writing. "Dr. Ross, my goodness," he said, shaking her hand fervently. "I devoured your paper on synthesizing myostatin. To what do I owe the pleasure?"

She pushed some of her hair out of her face and it was only then that he noticed that she looked rather disheveled, as if she had walked a great distance. He was going to ask her about it, but before he could she said, "There's someone who would very much like to meet you."

A man stepped around from behind her. He didn't put out his hand. Instead he simply stood there, looking at Sterns as if he could scarcely believe it. Then, very softly, he said, "It's Mr. Blue, isn't it?"

The words took a moment for Sterns to process, and then his eyes widened even as his voice dropped to a stunned whisper. "Mr. Green?"

"The name's Banner," he said. "Bruce Banner. And this has been a long time in coming."

"It has, my boy, it very much has." Now he came forward and shook Banner's hand, but then said, "Quickly, quickly," and gestured for them to follow as he glanced right and left. "We shouldn't be standing around out here. Can't be too careful, you know."

"Believe me," said Banner, "I know."

Banner looked around Sterns's lab with a mix of awe and revulsion. He knew, in the staggering clutter that consumed every square inch of the place, that he was seeing evidence of a great mind at work. But it seemed undisciplined, even scattershot. That worried Banner, the notion that Sterns had trouble remaining focused.

At the moment, though, Sterns didn't appear to be having any focusing issues. He was zeroed in on Banner's situation with laserlike accuracy, showing Banner and Betty the results of his research, shoving a small mountain of folders at them. Banner scarcely knew where to start. Sterns kept moving, like a hummingbird on crack, barely stopping to draw breath as he spoke at high speed. "It took some work, let me tell you. We've never tried to concentrate the trimethodine a tenth of what your peak exposure correlates with. That you survived an event like that to stand here and discuss this . . . it has something to do with Dr. Ross's myostatin primer capacitating a hypertrophy of the cells of course, but it's beyond my reckoning. We could study it for years."

"But you think you've got the concentration right?" said Betty.

"Well yes, on paper anyway. And my cell saturation

will make sure we don't miss any spots . . . but . . ." For the first time he slowed in his rapid-fire delivery and turned to Banner. "Even if this goes perfect . . . if we induce an episode and deliver exactly the same dose . . . I still can't promise this will cure you. It might only be an antidote to suppress the specific flare-up." He tilted his head and gave Banner a curious look. "When you have one of these 'spikes,' is the experience extreme?"

Banner cleared his throat. "You might say that," he said mildly.

"Well, I can't wait to see it."

Betty made a slight choking noise and then exchanged a look with Banner that said more than any words might have.

Sterns continued meantime, oblivious of the silent exchange. "You know, I must say . . . I wondered if you were real. And if you were, I wondered what it would look like . . . a person with that much power lurking in him. Nothing could have surprised me more," he said with a chuckle, "than this unassuming young man shaking my hand." Then he grew serious again. "I'd be remiss, however, if I didn't point out if we overshoot by even a small integer, these concentrations carry extraordinary levels of toxicity."

"You mean it could kill him," said Betty.

His head bobbed. "Well, yes, most definitely."

Betty gave Banner a worried look. He didn't blame her. They'd come a long way just to have her watch him die. "There's a flip side to that," said Banner. "If we miss on the low side, if we induce me and it fails, it will be very dangerous for you."

"I've always been more curious than cautious," said Sterns, which Banner could readily believe. "It's served me well so far, but if that's what kills this cat in the end . . . well, at least I'll have peeked around a few corners."

Sterns's enthusiasm had to make Banner smile in spite of himself. The man had no idea that he might be hurtling headlong to disaster. But it seemed as if, even if he was, he didn't especially care. For Banner, whose heart and soul had been so heavy for the last three years, it was entertaining to see a scientist who was so utterly gung ho about the concept of discovery. Sterns clapped his hands together briskly and said, "So then we're all agreed? Into the glorious unknown!"

General Ross's forces were mobilizing at the army base. A Sikorsky was winding up its jets on the runway . . .

And Emil Blonsky heard it.

He was nowhere near it. Instead he was in the locker room some distance away, staring at himself in the mirror, studying his face and naked upper body. He heard the jets revving and made a mental note of it without registering the fact that he really should not have been able to hear it at all. His senses were beginning to expand, and he was unaware of it, for his attention was elsewhere.

Something's different, he thought.

His shoulders and neck seemed to have massively grown. He didn't mind it; it appeared to be solid muscle. By his reckoning, he would have had to pump iron five hours a day, every day, for a year in order to obtain this sort of additional mass under ordinary circumstances. He flexed it and grinned as he saw muscles stretch and then grow taut. It was as if he had steel cables under his skin.

What Blonsky was unable to see on his naked back was that something truly bizarre was occurring with the bones of his spine. They had become enlarged, protruding from between his enlarged muscle in a disturbing way. The metamorphosis had literally just happened; the medical technicians had not had the opportunity to see it. If they had, they likely would have informed General Ross that Blonsky wasn't going anywhere. It was fortunate for them that such a scenario had not occurred, because Blonsky would not have taken well to being grounded, especially when a mission to take down Bruce Banner was being mounted. It was what Blonsky had been working toward, what he had been waiting for. It was what he had been willing to risk his body, his health, his very life for, and he wasn't about to let a few doctors stand in the way of a showdown between himself and . . .

. . . what was that name that the media had called Banner's monstrous counterpart? Oh, right . . .

The Hulk.

Blonsky pulled on his shirt, finished dressing, and headed out to the Sikorsky. He climbed in and there were already other Special Forces soldiers in place: three two-man sniper teams with special thermal scopes and rifles against one wall. Blonsky sat against the wall and saw a familiar face, a soldier who had been in his platoon during the campus battle. Johnson, Blonsky thought his name was. That was it. Tommy Johnson. He nodded in acknowledgment. Johnson shook his head, clearly amazed. "Great to see you, Captain," said Johnson. "Don't take this wrong, but I thought you were a goner."

Blonsky made a dismissive noise. "Takes more than that to put me down."

"How you feeling, man?"

"Like a monster," grinned Blonsky. In imitation of the creature they had fought, he grunted aggressively and flexed his arm. His bicep actually split the seam on his sleeve a little. Johnson blinked, not quite believing what he had just seen.

Sparr and Ross came back to the rear of the craft in order to brief the team. She had copies of blueprints of the layouts of the target building, which was apparently on the New York City campus of ESU. *God, what is it with this guy and colleges?* Blonsky thought. Out loud he said cheerily to Sparr, "Back on the Hulk hunt, Major?"

Sparr made a face that indicated she wasn't thrilled with the "Hulk" moniker that the creature had picked up. Ross didn't appear to appreciate it any more than she did as he said, "*Banner* is the target, Captain."

"Snipers have the point," said Sparr, all business. "Delta in backup." She traced the attack path with her finger on the blueprints. "If we get there before they move again, we'll have two tries. If we can't take him inside, we'll try for a shot as he exits. If we can't hit him unaware before he makes the street, then plainclothes will try to follow him and we stand down. Under no circumstance is Banner to be engaged directly."

"And if he goes nuclear?" said Blonsky.

Ross leaned forward and said, "Then we'll have failed to learn from our mistakes, won't we?" Blonsky frowned, not liking the sound of that. Ross had been preparing him for just such a confrontation; he didn't want to see the possibility shut down before it even began. Ross continued, "He's never turned unless he was cornered or hurt. If we can't take him out from long-range or if he makes us and he runs, we fall back and let him go. Any other questions?"

Yeah. What the hell do you need me for, shot up with Super Soldier serum, if not to take him down no matter what? It seemed to Blonsky that Ross was hedging his bets. He kept talking about restraint, but he had been preparing Blonsky for a scenario that promised exactly the opposite. "Not much of a rematch," said Blonsky.

"One point five million people within a five mile radius," said Sparr, indicating a map of the ESU area. "You want to fight that thing here?"

I'm good with it.

Blonsky said nothing, but Sparr cast a suspicious glance at him as if she knew what was going through his mind. Then she moved toward the front of the plane and sat close in toward Ross. "You sure about your boy?" she said in a low voice.

"I need a dog in the hunt that's not going to run from the bear if it shows up," Ross told her. "If we do this right, I'll never have to let him off the leash."

Blonsky leaned back and grinned. He had heard every word. He'd been exactly right: Ross was indeed hedging his bets. There was only one thing he was underestimating. This dog wanted the bear to show up. Indeed, the hunt simply wouldn't be complete without it.

The engines roared to full throttle and Blonsky winced. "Why do they have to make these things so damned noisy?" he grumbled to Johnson. Johnson, who didn't seem at all bothered by the noise, gave him an odd look but didn't reply.

Bruce Banner stepped out from the small, cramped bathroom with his clothes draped over his arm, stripped down to his stretchable Lycra shorts. Sterns was busy making the final adjustments on the device that was intended to administer the cure, but he did a double take when he saw Banner. "Daring fashion choice," he said with a raised eyebrow. "I had no idea you were a middle-aged woman. *Ow!*" That last came because Betty had just slugged him, not ungently, in the upper arm.

"Think of all the money I'll save on wardrobe if this works," said Banner. Then he looked at the table that Sterns had set up. It bore far too much of a resemblance to the sort of table condemned prisoners lay upon just before they were administered a lethal injection. The look of the table couldn't help but send his mind down some rather morbid directions. "If this starts to go bad, promise me you won't stay and try to help me."

"Bruce . . ."

"It's the worst when it starts. You have to promise me you'll run or I can't do this."

Betty nodded. Banner suspected she was being less than candid; that she had no intention of going anywhere. But he couldn't just stand there arguing and calling her a liar, especially not after everything she had done to get them there. Sterns indicated the nylon medical restraints. "If you have a strong reaction, these will keep you from hurting yourself."

Sterns still wasn't getting it. Banner supposed he couldn't blame him. It was impossible for Sterns to imagine what would be facing him if something went wrong with the procedure since it was so completely out of the realm of normal human experience. Telling him really couldn't convey it. He had to see it. The problem was, if he saw it, then it was going to be far too late. "If I have a strong reaction, you're not going to need to worry about me."

Banner climbed onto the table and lay down. Sterns tilted it back so that Banner was at a slight angle and strapped him in. Then Sterns inserted an IV into each of Banner's arms and legs linked to the cell saturation machine. Sterns primed the machine while giving Banner a thumbs-up as if Banner were in the cockpit of a Sopwith Camel about to launch itself into the sky. Banner studied the machine because he had nowhere else to look. It was pretty simple, really: a canister with the antidote and a high-tech plunger designed to send it through his body. As he looked it over, trying to see if there was any design flaw that could possibly—oh—result in him turning into a ten-foot rampaging behemoth, Sterns attached contact pads connected to electrical wires on Banner's temples.

Finally he held up a plastic bite-suppressor to Banner's mouth, but Banner shook it off. No point. If he transformed, he'd bite right through it.

Sterns shrugged at the rebuff and put it aside. He took a deep breath and let it out as if he were the one about to undergo the procedure. "Ready?"

No.

Banner nodded.

Sterns flipped a switch, and Banner's world went white.

Betty had been having the same thought as Banner, namely that Sterns may have believed he was prepared for what was about to happen, and what could happen as a result, but he really wasn't. To be fair, though, if someone had tried to tell Betty about the possibilities when she and Bruce were working on the project, would she have believed it or even been capable of understanding it? Not likely.

She knew what was coming, but even so she jumped at the same time that the electricity jolted through Bruce's body. He spasmed, every muscle in his body straining against the restraints. She stifled a cry. Bruce wasn't wearing his pulse monitor, but she didn't need to see readouts to know that his pulse was through the roof.

Sterns watched, his face impassive.

Then Banner's eyes snapped open, and she saw green light glowing in his eyes. A pulse of green energy erupted from the base of his skull, sending gamma radiation shooting through his entire body.

For the first time, Sterns looked startled, as if he had been operating on the assumption that nothing could surprise him and was only just now getting an inkling of how much he didn't know. "My God," he said.

It was Betty's turn to become dispassionate after her initial reaction to Bruce's painful jolt. "There's more. Wait for it."

Banner's body began to swell, stretch, and harden. Sterns was visibly staggered. He stumbled back as if someone had just punched him in the chest, but he didn't look away. He didn't even blink. For Betty it was the equivalent of watching the man she loved being tortured in front of her—a torture in which she was complicit. Banner howled in agony, and it was all Betty could do not to shut down the entire procedure.

Sterns took several steps toward Banner, staring at the changes that his body was undergoing. Betty noticed too late. She tried to grab Sterns, to pull him back, but that moment the restraints popped like rubber bands and one of them struck Sterns right in the face. It was like being hit in the face with a two-by-four, and Sterns was knocked back, dazed.

Bruce had not yet hit his full transformed growth, but he was already over six feet and growing fast. The only thing that stopped him from leaping clear of the table and destroying the lab was that he was still writhing in the throes of the electricity. Within seconds, though, the voltage would lose the power to hurt him. There wouldn't be enough electricity in the world to hurt him.

"*Now! Do it!*" said Betty.

The table began to buckle under the weight of Bruce's changing body as he continued to grow. He raised his head and his faced twisted in a snarl.

Betty yanked the wires clear of Bruce's head. The flow of electricity ceased, but that didn't stop the change from progressing. He was too far gone for that. Taking the only gamble she could, she jumped onto the table over him, leaning over his massive torso, looking into his eyes.

"*Bruce, stay with me!*"

He howled from the agony of the transformation, but there was a fierce desperation in his eyes, which Betty saw as a determination to hold on to what shreds of his own personality might still be there. She turned and shouted to Sterns, "Do it now!"

Sterns hit the button and the antidote started to flow into him. Betty's gaze remained fixed on Bruce's eyes. She knew that if the cure was going to take, it would be reflected there first.

What she saw in there was something totally unexpected. It wasn't Bruce's eyes that were looking out at her, not Bruce's personality. It was . . . *its*. It was *his*. The being that she'd heard the radio news referring to, in their reportage of the battle at Culver, as the Hulk. The Hulk was looking out at her through Bruce's eyes, and it was angry, yes, but it was also scared, if such a thing was possible, pleading not to be rejected, not to be consigned to whatever oblivion it existed in when it wasn't wreaking havoc in the real world.

And then the Hulk began to recede from Bruce's eyes as if it were being pulled down into a whirlpool. Slowly, painfully, the process started to reverse. The fluid of the antidote moved through the massive veins and found its way into every corner, calming the radiation fire in his blood. He began to shrink, the poisonous green color in his skin receding. Within seconds Bruce was back, lying on the table, which had bent nearly in half from the increased weight of the Hulk. Betty stroked Bruce's forehead, wiping away some of the sweat that covered it. He was as wrung out as any runner having just completed a marathon.

"It's all right," she whispered. "You're all right. It's over."

The night sky above Central Park's Great Lawn was alive with the noise of whirring helicopter blades. As it

descended, Blonsky and his team hit the ground running. Sparr and Ross moved in with the mobile communications team right behind. All of them sprinted toward
waiting unmarked vans.

Contrary to Betty Ross's opinion, it was not over. It
was just beginning.

SEVENTEEN

"The pulse came from the amygdalae," said Sterns. He had been video-recording the entire process and was pointing to a screen capture of the exact moment that a burst of green had erupted from the base of Banner's skull. "At least that's my theory. It wouldn't be possible to say for sure unless we were running a CAT scan during the procedure. But it certainly seemed that it was emanating from the medial temporal lobes in your brain."

"That would be my guess," said Betty.

Sterns seemed pleased that she agreed. "I think Dr. Ross's primer lets the cells absorb the energy temporarily and then it abates. That's why you didn't die of radiation sickness years ago. Now maybe we've neutralized those cells permanently or," and he raised a cautioning finger, "maybe we just suppressed that event. I'm inclined to think the latter but it's hard to know because none of our test subjects survived. But of course they were getting gamma in much lower doses externally each time. But you!" and the rather odd excitement he'd been displaying earlier began to resurface. He certainly bounced back from trauma very quickly. "It's like you've got a turbo booster in your brain. It's one of the most wonderful things I've ever seen!"

Banner had just finished buttoning his shirt. As he placed the pulse monitor back on his arm, he was starting to feel extremely uncomfortable with Sterns's level of enthusiasm. Obviously Betty shared that concern. "It's not wonderful for Bruce," Betty pointed out.

"In a medical science sense, of course. You're miraculous."

"So how did you know it would work?" she said, clearly trying to pull Sterns away from his unnerving enthusiasm over Banner's condition.

"I didn't," said Sterns. "But now that we have the data on Bruce's initial . . ."

"Wait," said Banner, bringing Sterns to a halt, which was something of an accomplishment in and of itself. "You said 'test subjects.' What test subjects?"

Sterns grinned like a child about to show a parent some carefully constructed arts and crafts project and gestured for them to follow.

Sniper teams were taking roof positions around the lab building. Each team included two shooters one of whom was armed with a thermal scanner. The scanners came on line, and thermal images of three people appeared. Bruce Banner, Betty Ross, and their newfound ally, one Samuel Sterns, were sighted.

Sparr's voice came over Blonsky's earpiece as he and his team moved into position in the ESU science building lobby. "Target is the tallest one in the middle." Blonsky muttered profanities to himself. If some damned sniper dispatched Banner before Blonsky had a chance at him, he was not going to be a happy camper.

A sputtering and useless ESU security guard was being hustled out of the building by an NYPD SWAT team member. Blonsky fired him an annoyed look and considered the option of shooting him, just for target practice. He reluctantly discarded the notion as he moved toward the stairwell, operating on the notion that the guard wasn't worth a bullet when ammo might well end up being at a premium.

* * *

Bruce Banner stared around at a nightmare.

The room looked as if there had been an explosion in a baby factory. Oversized jars everywhere, everywhere, with floating human fetuses. Each of them looked different, but they were all equally monstrous . . . and they were all equally him.

"Oh my God, what have you been doing?" said Banner. Betty was standing next to him, all the blood drained from her face.

Sterns seemed unaware of the horror that they were feeling. "Well, you didn't send me much of yourself to work with," he said as if Banner had been inconsiderate of his needs, "and I couldn't risk blowing the opportunity, so we concentrated it and grew more. The same thing you were trying to do with the calandras. You were my flower, see? We haven't had any survivors yet of course, and we're still trying to figure out which is more toxic, your blood or the gamma, but . . ."

"We've got to destroy all of it," said Banner.

Sterns blinked owlishly. "Sorry, what . . . ?"

"All of it. Right now." He stood in the middle of the lab, turning in a slow circle. "Is this your whole supply?"

"You must be joking." Sterns wasn't kidding; he genuinely thought that Banner wasn't serious and was attempting some sort of jest at his expense. "We'll share a Nobel for this, the three of us. Think of the applications!"

Banner tried to keep calm. Fortunately he had a good deal of practice doing exactly that. "It doesn't matter if it can't be controlled," he said patiently. "You don't know the power of what we're dealing with here."

"But we've got the antidote now! I mean it, Bruce! A Nobel Prize! I think we've really got a shot!"

* * *

"At your discretion, shooter, when you have a shot," said Sparr.

She stood in front of a panel of video monitors observing the soldier camera feeds. Ross stood directly behind her. On the thermal imager, Banner had moved into a window zone, but Betty had unwittingly stepped in, blocking a clean shot. Sparr heard Ross grunt, but she couldn't tell if he was concerned that his daughter might accidentally get hit, or if he was just pissed off that she was presenting an obstruction.

"Almost," came the sniper's voice.

A long pause, and then Banner's image moved away from the window completely.

"No shot," said the sniper.

Sparr mentally shrugged. This was annoying, but hardly a major problem. This time everyone was in position and Banner was blocked in from all directions without even being aware of it. This time nothing was going to go—

"Blonsky's going in! He's going in!" It was Johnson, shouting an alarmed warning.

On the one hand, Sparr couldn't believe it. On the other, she easily could. It would be just like Blonsky to get impatient and decide to seize control of the situation. Ross grabbed the microphone and shouted, "Blonsky, stand down!"

Sparr wasn't expecting Blonsky to stand down. She was expecting him to make matters worse. But this was no time to tell the general "I told you so." Actually, it was hard to envision that there would ever be such a time. Instead she said into the mike, "Shooter, be advised."

"Almost," said the shooter, still focusing on his mission.

It was nice to know someone had his priorities in order.

* * *

Blonsky heard Ross's voice coming over his headset. He ignored it. Ross's wishes were of no relevance to him at this point, if ever again. Blonsky's priorities were no longer Ross's. He was seeing the world differently. Different things mattered to him.

No. That wasn't true.

Only one thing mattered to him, and that thing was twenty stories up.

He drew closer with impossible speed, not running up the stairwell so much as jumping. He covered eight stories in a matter of seconds and kept going.

Banner wanted to take Sterns and shake him. "They don't want the antidote! They want a weapon. They want it to fight for them and if they get it then we lose control of it!"

Apparently Sterns hadn't learned from the experience, only minutes old, of underestimating things when it came to Bruce Banner. "Oh, look, I hate the government, too, but you're being a little paranoid, don't you think . . . ?"

Suddenly the windowpane shattered. Banner felt something pinch his neck, like a bee sting. He reached around for it and felt something sticking out.

A tranq dart.

He heard a scream. It wasn't Betty. It was Sterns.

What a girl, thought Banner.

"Target is hit," said the shooter. "Dart on board."

Sparr let out a sigh of relief. Despite her confidence that they had things under control, she'd been haunted by visions of what New York City would wind up looking like if things went wrong. It would have made 9/11 look like a Boy Scout jamboree.

But now it was all over except for the shouting.

* * *

"Get out now!" shouted Banner. His knees started to buckle and Betty rushed over to catch him. Through bleary eyes, he saw his pulse monitor dropping from one hundred twenty-five to one hundred fifteen.

The door exploded inward. Betty jumped up protectively, turning her back to Bruce and facing whoever was charging in. It was a soldier. Just one. As his brain became muddled, Banner thought that odd. Usually they traveled in packs, didn't they?

The soldier didn't slow. He shoved Betty aside. Banner's mind was scattered, and he found himself analyzing the amount of force the gesture seemed to require as opposed to the result, the result being that Betty flew five feet through the air before crashing into the far wall. If the wall hadn't been there, she would doubtless have kept going.

She slid to the ground, landing on her arm, and crying out in pain.

Betty . . .

Something within him roared, but it was muted and frustrated and so, so helpless . . .

Blonsky hadn't expected Betty Ross to go flying as far as she had. Clearly he was going to have to work at adjusting to the amount of strength he possessed. He was not, however, the least bit concerned about injuring Betty. She had taken up with a known threat to national security. If all she wound up with was a broken arm, then she should consider herself fortunate.

Banner's eyes were livid but hazy. He was struggling to focus as Blonsky punched him to the floor, then seized his shirt and yanked him up. His eyes bored into Banner's, searching for what was truly important. *"Come on! Come on! Where is it?!"* He slapped Banner once, twice. Banner's head lolled back. Blonsky let Banner slide to the floor, then drew back his rifle butt with the intention of slamming it against Banner's head.

"*Blonsky!*" It was Johnson.

"*Show it to me!*" screamed Blonsky, and he cracked Banner in the side of the head. Banner's eyes rolled up and he lapsed into unconsciousness.

"*Stand down, Blonsky! Now! General's orders!*"

Blonsky whirled and Johnson stood there with his gun pointed straight at Blonsky and the trigger cocked meaningfully. It was at that moment that Blonsky realized something with a pure certainty: If Johnson shot him at point-blank range, it wouldn't stop him.

Drawing strength from that knowledge, Blonsky stepped back, holding his hands up, palms out.

"Target is secured," Johnson's voice came over the microphone.

Sparr sagged back in her seat, relief flooding over her. Then she swiveled in the chair and faced Ross.

"Good," was all Ross said. He didn't ask how his daughter was.

Sadly, Sparr wasn't surprised.

"Bruce . . ."

Slowly Bruce opened his eyes and looked up at her. "Oh thank God," she whispered. "You're awake. It's going to be all right, Bruce, all of it, I swear . . ."

"Where . . . ?" His voice was thick and confused. He looked up and clearly realized that they were outside.

"We're on 120th Street. The police have blocked everything off." The world around them was bathed in red, courtesy of the massive collection of spinning lights atop surrounding police cars. "You're on a gurney. They're wheeling you to . . ." She paused but continued to move alongside him. "To wherever."

"You okay . . . ?" His gaze fell upon her arm, which had a splint on it. "My head's cold . . ."

"You have an ice pack against it. That soldier, Blonsky, hit you pretty hard."

"Got a hard head. No worries."

He tried to reach up toward her, and it was only at that point that he realized he had enormous wrist shackles keeping his arms immobilized. Soldiers walking alongside him glanced at him suspiciously, as if they were expecting him to suddenly break loose and start throwing them around like poker chips.

Suddenly the soldiers stopped moving. It happened so abruptly that Betty almost went right past them. She had been looking at Bruce and so wasn't paying attention to anything in front of them. She turned and saw that her father was standing directly in front of them.

The general leaned in toward Bruce and whispered something. Betty couldn't quite hear it and before she could get close enough, Ross stepped back and waved the gurney on. Then he turned his attention to her. "Betty," he started to say.

She turned away from him and walked off, following Banner. Not a word passed between them.

Ross watched in a detached manner as his daughter stalked away from him, her body stiff with suppressed rage. She didn't understand. She never had. She never would. He had become resigned to that, or at least thought he had.

Sparr was standing just at his elbow. "Never seen anyone come round from a tranq dose like that," she said. "Why the hell aren't we keeping him under?"

"You want to be the one to stick a needle in his arm that he doesn't want?" said the general. He nodded toward Betty's departing form. "She's our best insurance. Keep her right next to him. He knows if he pops off it's her that gets hurt."

"What do you want to do with Sterns?"

He considered it briefly. "I want him pinned in that lab with you," he said. "Don't let him leave the room to piss until he's identified every bottle, every box, every machine in the place. Then package it up and get it back home. Then get aiding and abetting charges and get him turned over to us. If Banner won't give us answers maybe we can get him to."

Sparr nodded and headed into the building. Ross watched her go, then headed off after Betty.

The Sikorsky was sitting on the Central Park Great Lawn, right where they had left it. Banner, still in shackles, was being brought up the rear ramp of the ship, with Betty following slowly. Ross caught up to her and put a hand on her arm.

"Betty," he said again.

She pulled her arm away from him. Her face was a mask of cold fury. It was a look Ross knew all too well; he'd seen it far too many times from Betty's mother. "I will never forgive what you have done to him. And to me."

"He is a fugitive," said Ross. "He made choices and I have a responsibility."

"You made him a fugitive!" she said, her voice rising. "To cover your failures and save your career. He told me what you said to him after the accident, before I woke up . . . what you proposed. That's why he ran and gave up."

"His work . . . his blood . . . is the property of the United States Army and my duty supersedes my personal feelings in this matter."

She stepped in close to him and said, "Don't speak to me as if I'm your daughter. Not ever again." She moved up the ramp.

"It's only because you're my daughter that you're not in handcuffs, too," he called after her.

She stopped at the top of the ramp, turned back to him, and said, "What did you say to Bruce? When you stopped him as they were wheeling him away just before?"

"Ask him."

"I'm asking you."

I said, "If you took it from me, I'm going to put you in a hole for the rest of your life."

"I told him to have a nice day."

Betty stared at him, and then shook her head and walked away from him into the ship.

She had her mother's walk, too.

Samuel Sterns felt that he could do business with this Major Sparr individual. Granted, she was part of the vast military-industrial complex, but at least she was proving interested in his research. "Mr. Green" had been something of a disappointment. He lacked vision. Major Sparr had vision.

An Army Ranger was standing sentry outside the door while Sterns sat in a chair, his legs comfortably crossed at the knees. Sparr was leaning against a lab table and was saying, "Are you telling me you can make more like him?"

"Not yet, no," he admitted. "We've sorted out some of the pieces but I don't think I could put together the same Humpty Dumpty just yet, if you follow me. Anyway, what happened to him was a freak accident. The goal is to do it even better."

"But Banner's the only one we've got to worry about for the . . ."

She didn't complete the sentence. Instead she jerked forward a little, her eyes rolling back, and Sterns thought in confusion, *What an odd time for her to get sleepy,* right before she slumped forward and hit the floor.

It was at that point that he saw the Ranger who had been acting as sentry sprawled on the floor. And stepping out from the shadows was that same lunatic commando who had been smacking Banner around and saying things that made no sense at all. He had pistol-whipped Sparr into unconsciousness, and—by all reasonable logical deduction—had disposed of the sentry as well. He had a small plastic tag on his uniform shirt that said BLONSKY, E. on it.

"Jeez, what is it with you hitting people all the ti—" Sterns began to say, and then he suddenly found himself staring down the barrel end of Blonsky's pistol. The trigger was cocked. Trying to keep his composure in the face of possible demise, Sterns uncrossed his legs and then recrossed them in the opposite direction. Fighting to keep his voice from cracking, he said with forced casualness, "What could I have possibly done to deserve such aggression?"

"It's not what you've done. It's what you're going to do."

He smiled. "Well, I like your use of future tense in that sentence anyway."

Blonsky uncocked his gun and holstered it. "I want what you got out of Banner."

Surveying Blonsky's extremely exaggerated pectorals, Sterns said, "You look like you've got a little something extra in you already, don't you."

"I want more. You saw what he becomes?"

"I did. It's beautiful," he said wistfully. "Godlike."

"Make me that."

Sterns shook his head. He had never been one for caution, except when he was busy throwing it to the winds. Still, even he had reasonable concerns from time to time.

"But I don't know what's already in you. The mixture could be . . . an abomination."

Blonsky grabbed Sterns by the front of his jacket with one hand, lifting him easily. He yanked the gun back out of its holster and placed it under Sterns's chin.

Seeing the definite need to clarify his position, particularly since his feet were dangling above the floor, Sterns said, "I'm not unwilling. I just need informed consent. And you've given it!"

EIGHTEEN

As the Sikorsky cut through the air above the Hudson River, Bruce and Betty sat across from each other toward the rear of the ship. Armed soldiers flanked them on either side. He was still cuffed, but they had unstrapped him from the gurney. Ross was up toward the front with communications officers and a bank of monitors.

There was so much that Banner wanted to say to her. But this was neither the time nor the place. The real tragedy was that the proper time and place might never come.

She reached over to him and took his hand in hers.

He mouthed to her, *I'm sorry.*

She smiled, shook her head, and responded in equal silence, *Don't be.*

Blonsky was lying on the same table that Banner had been earlier. Sterns had hooked up his cell saturation machine and was busy clicking the "Mr. Green" blood canister into the infusion port. Then he rolled the gamma projector that he had developed over into place. He had had plenty of time to discuss the specifics of such devices with Betty Ross while Banner had been preparing for his attempt at a cure. He had been pleased to discover that the projector he had developed, while not identical to the one that had resulted in Bruce Banner's accident, was sufficiently similar in its specs that it could reasonably be used to duplicate the circumstances of the Hulk's birth.

The birth of a god.

When he had heard about that, Sterns had desperately wished that he could have been there. Fate had been good to him; he was being given a second chance. How often in life did people receive a genuine second chance?

He aimed the white crosshairs over Blonsky's forehead. "Brace yourself now," said Sterns, "because this is probably going to hurt like hell. Then again," he added philosophically, "birth usually does."

For Stoller and Robertson, two experienced commandos, this had been a very puzzling mission.

The target, Banner, didn't appear to be much of a threat. "Schwarzenegger, he ain't," Stoller had said, and Robertson had been hard pressed to disagree. Moreover the entire concept of the general's daughter being involved in this business made it even more suspicious. Robertson was busy theorizing that the truth behind this whole business was that Ross's daughter had run off with this skinny scientist that Ross disapproved of, and he had just utilized a million or so of taxpayer money to mount a military operation designed to chase down his wayward kid, when he and Stoller heard a scream.

They had been standing in the stairwell of the science building, left on station there just in case—so they had been told—this Sterns guy tried to make a break for it. Didn't make a lot of sense; Sterns would have to have gotten past both Sparr and Johnson, not to mention that odd duck Blonsky, before he got anywhere near the stairs. That didn't seem especially likely. But Ross had insisted that underestimating "these people" resulted in nothing but regrets, and therefore he wasn't going to take any chances.

From the sound of that shriek—a man's voice—Ross might well have been right to be cautious.

The two commandos sprinted up the steps, their weapons drawn, and burst into the corridor, looking around for some sign of the threat. They found it immediately: Johnson lying on the ground in front of the lab door, the lab where Banner and the general's daughter had been captured. There was another howl that seemed to Robertson to be mingled with a roar of demented triumph. It was coming from the lab.

Stoller took point and kicked open the door. Robertson was right behind him.

It was the last action they ever took.

Outside the ESU science building, two Delta Force soldiers, Jeffries and Sterling, were watching a couple of New York's finest—a policeman and policewoman—half a block away, chasing off curious passersby who came up to the police barricades and wanted to know what was going on. Jeffries was lean and athletic, and often referred to Sterling as "Pretty Boy," since Sterling had never met a reflective surface that he didn't like and tended to study his own rugged features with unabashed pleasure. At that moment, Jeffries was feeling frustrated, because the show was clearly over. He and Sterling had been instructed to work with the cops to keep the block locked down until further notice, but it was hardly a challenging detail. What made it particularly irritating was that Jeffries was insisting on talking about stuff that he'd heard secondhand about the battle at Culver University and acting as if it were fact instead of tall tales.

"Ten feet and green," Jeffries repeated what Sterling had just told him, his voice dripping with sarcasm. "You're getting your news off *Inside Edition*. 'The Hulk.' Gimme a break."

"I'm telling you," said Sterling, glancing toward a

store window and smiling in approval at what he saw. "Whatever went down, it shook Tommy up. He said we should be heads up on this one."

"Only action we're gonna see is those blue shirts bringing each other coffee," said Jeffries, indicating the police officers.

The sudden shattering of glass from overhead brought Sterling and Jeffries to immediate attention, unslinging their rifles within a split second. They looked up and then scrambled back when they saw an enormous piece of some sort of equipment plummeting from overhead. The gaping hole in the side of the building was enough to make clear that the equipment had been thrown right through a window, sending a mass of brick and glass cascading to the street below. But the debris was a distant second in terms of danger compared with the equipment itself, which arced through the air and rebounded off the wall of the opposite building before crashing to the alleyway below. The police officers sprinted to avoid getting hit, ducking into an alcove halfway down the alley. The equipment hit the ground, rolled end over end, and came to a halt in the middle of the street.

Jeffries and Sterling stepped out into the street, their weapons at the ready, trying to get a fix on what the hell had just happened. Suddenly they started for cover as they heard machine-gun fire coming from above where the fallen equipment had originated.

"What the hell—?" began Jeffries.

He didn't get through the sentence as the machine-gun fire abruptly ceased, making him believe that the threat—whatever it had been—was neutralized. He thought that right up until two soldiers came hurtling through the hole and spiraled to bone-crunching deaths on the street below.

Jeffries instantly toggled his wireless as Sterling

looked on, goggle-eyed. "Delta Four to leader! Something big just went off down here!"

"This is Ross," the general's voice came back over the comm unit. "What went off?"

"Something just took out Stoller and Robertson! Blonsky and the major are still up there!"

"Come on!' said Sterling, snapping from his paralysis. He was moving toward the fallen bodies of Stoller and Robertson, and Jeffries followed him. The cops hadn't budged from their alcove in the alleyway, apparently content to let the Delta Force soldiers sort out what the hell was going on.

Then all of them heard something that would have been impossible for any of them to miss. It sounded like a battering ram, crashing out the back side of the science building, several stories up, facing out onto 120th Street. Before the commandos or the cops could get over there to see what was going on, there was another huge noise that sounded as if a falling satellite had landed on top of a parked car. The immediate screeching of a car alarm verified that a car had indeed been hit hard by something, but the nature of whatever it was that had done the damage was still unknown.

The alleyway ran along the side of the science building and opened out onto 120th Street, but before the Delta Force commandos could sprint down it and get to the adjacent street to see what had happened, they heard something that made them automatically flatten against the wall. It was an unbelievable roar of rage. Jeffries, always a fanciful individual, thought for a second that a T. rex had burst out of the building and was about to rampage through the streets of Manhattan.

Then, at the far end of the alleyway, Jeffries saw something surge past them. It was massive beyond anything he had ever seen, at least fourteen feet tall. And then it was gone before he could get a clear look at it. He turned to Sterling, looking for confirmation that the commando had seen the same thing that he, Jeffries, had. Sterling nodded, unable to speak, his face deathly pale. Then, without a word, Jeffries was running for the far end of the alley, with Sterling right behind him. He heard the pounding of other feet and realized that the cops were following them. *Props to the cops; I'd have bet they'd run the other way.*

They emerged onto the street and stood there, staring at the car that was howling its car alarm as if bellowing its dying scream. Sounding an alarm was the only thing the car was still capable of doing; it had been smashed flat, lending additional credence to the T. rex theory if Jeffries hadn't already caught a glimpse of the creature that had done this.

"Look!" shouted Sterling.

Jeffries's head snapped around just in time to see the massive greenish-brown back of something disappearing to the right around the corner at the end of the block. It was heading up Broadway, and the sounds of more cars crashing, and the screams of people, filled the air.

"What in God's name was that?" said a cop.

Jeffries couldn't believe he was about to confirm everything that he had scoffed at Sterling for claiming, but he could not deny the evidence of his own eyes. He said into the microphone, "The Hulk's in the street," and didn't add the four words that, as far as he was concerned, should follow: *God help us all.*

In the Sikorsky that was rapidly cutting across the night skies above New York, Ross was reacting quickly to what he had just been told by his commandos. He was radioing to Sparr and saying, "Get our guard support teams moving back there and get PD special units out . . ." Then he heard the shocking report that the Hulk was in the street.

As if sensing that they were confused and incredulous, the soldier whom Ross believed was Jeffries said, "Repeat, the Hulk is in the street. Where the hell are we?" That question was more directed to someone who was on the ground with Jeffries. "120th and Broadway. Heading up Broadway!"

Ross looked at Banner, who was staring at him from the opposite end of the Sikorsky. Banner looked confused, apparently able to sense that something was going on but not having any idea what it might be. Bruce Banner might have had many talents, most of them destructive, but Ross was sure that being in two places at once still remained beyond even Banner's abilities. "That's impossible," he said into the comm unit. "Now hold it together, soldier. Have any of you got a live feed?"

"Yeah."

"Then stay with it and get me a visual. We've got help on the way. Now get moving." He leaned forward to the pilot and said, "Turn us around."

He didn't bother to tell Banner and his daughter what was happening, mostly because he wasn't sure what it was. But he could hear Banner's voice carry from the rear of the chopper, saying to Betty, "We're going back."

For one moment Ross actually wondered if this all had been some sort of monumental misunderstanding. That his belief that Banner was the one transforming into the Hulk had always been off base somehow. But that didn't make any sense. He had seen it himself . . . or had he?

Don't doubt yourself. You have no room in your life for doubt. Doubt gets people killed.

Jeffries activated his mini helmet battle camera and shouted, "C'mon!" He sprinted toward a parked open-top Humvee, Sterling right behind him. As he got there, he saw to his astonishment that the policewoman had not only followed them, but had clambered into the driver's seat. "Can you drive this thing?" he said, trying not to keep the skepticism out of his voice.

"Marines, eight years," said the cop. She was square-jawed and had a pugnacious jaw outthrust. "Let's go." Her partner was climbing into the passenger seat and gave Jeffries a look that said, *I wouldn't argue if I were you.*

Despite the situation, Jeffries found himself liking her. He took note that her name, according to her badge, was Stockwell, and nodded to Sterling. Sterling and Jeffries climbed into the rear behind the other cop, who was younger and baby-faced, but no less determined, and named Hayes, and they peeled out to the right. Stockwell made a quick right up Amsterdam and set off after the creature they believed to be the Hulk.

The lab of Samuel Sterns was a study in destruction.

Flames were flickering and smoke was hanging in the air. The canister of blood that was labeled "Mr. Green," the blood sample belonging to Bruce Banner, sat in the saturation machine, broken and dripping onto the floor.

Except it wasn't actually making it to the floor.

Sterns was lying unmoving directly beneath it, a hideous gash open on his forehead, the sample dripping into it. His face was frozen in an expression of horror and amazement. It would have seemed to any observer that his obsession with curiosity had, as it typically did to the cat, dispatched him.

Sparr lay nearby, unmoving. Her radio was on the floor next to her. It had gone active automatically when the emergency channel was activated by Jeffries, and he could be heard calling out his position: *"121st Street moving north! What is that thing?"*

And as Sterns lay there, underneath his scalp, there

was a single pulse of green energy, causing the skin to ripple, as if his brain had momentarily swelled . . .

The Humvee blasted up Amsterdam Avenue, hugging the left side. Stockwell handled the wheel deftly, steering around huge potholes in the street that Jeffries very much suspected hadn't been there before the Hulk had begun his rampage. Jeffries and Sterling were standing up in the back of the Humvee, their assault rifles at the ready. Jeffries was keeping his view trained on the cross streets as they whipped by. He kept getting only glimpses of the creature's flank as they moved up parallel streets. It was smashing cars, hurling people as it went. He couldn't even begin to imagine what the thing's screaming victims must be thinking of this refugee from a horror movie showing up out of nowhere and rampaging through the streets.

He heard Ross's angry voice through the headset, shouting, "Goddammit, I said get me eyes on that thing!" The remark wasn't directed to him; he was doing the best he could. Ross was trying to get other soldiers into position so he could have a clearer view of what the Hulk was up to . . .

Except . . . wasn't Banner supposed to *be* the Hulk? That was what Sterling had said Johnson had been claiming. Swore that Banner had transformed into the monster right before his eyes, which didn't make a lick of sense to Jeffries. Jeffries had been inclined to dismiss the entire notion out of hand, although obviously his opinion was radically changing with the latest developments. But if the things that Johnson had said were correct, then what was the Hulk doing here when Banner had been carted away in the Sikorsky?

The Humvee reached 125th Street, the heart of Harlem. Stockwell ripped the wheel to the left and slammed on the brakes. For the first time, they had a

clear view of the massive gray creature that was causing
untold destruction. Pedestrians were fleeing in panic,
cars skidding and trying to turn around.

"Sir, are you seeing this?" said Jeffries, trying to turn
his minicamera to give Ross a clear view through the
monitors on the Sikorsky. "What the hell is that? Is that
Banner?" Perhaps Banner had escaped. That had to be
it . . .

"No, it's not Banner! Hold position!"

Banner and Betty had moved to the front of the Sikorsky, pushing in next to Ross. Banner felt physically ill.
He had known the destruction that he had caused as the
Hulk (*Great, now* you're *calling yourself that. Damned
media*), but had only ever "seen" it through his twisted
and warped perceptions. He had never had the opportunity to experience it with his full senses, live and as it
was happening.

Except the Hulk wasn't the cause of this.

"No, it's not Banner, dammit! Hold position," Ross
was saying. He turned to Banner. "Sterns?"

The answer came crackling through the radio seconds
later. It was the voice of Kathleen Sparr. "General, it's
Blonsky. Sterns is dead," said the major, and from her
voice she sounded half dead herself. "It's Blonsky."

Blonsky. The name resonated with Banner. He remembered that commando with the twisted expression
who stood over him, shouting at him, demanding to see
the monster that dwelt within him. Banner had been
barely conscious and so hadn't fully trusted his perceptions of Blonsky at the time, but it had seemed to him
that the man was damned near insane, a monster in
human form.

What he was seeing now, courtesy of the soldier's
camera, was Blonsky's inner monster given substance,
and Banner's worst fears come to life. Fourteen feet tall,

gray, as heavily muscled as Hulk but with strange bones protruding like spurs at its ankles and wrists, a horrible snarling face, twisted and looking straight into the monitor. And General Ross looked struck by the thunderbolt that was his namesake as he gasped, "*Blonsky?* Blonsky is that . . . that *abomination*?" Then, his long years of experience enabling him to recover instantly from his initial shock, Ross said over the microphone, "Listen to me, soldier. Hit it with whatever you've got and then run like hell. Try to draw it after you and get it to the river. We'll send reinforcements."

There aren't enough reinforcements in the world, thought Banner.

The Abomination, as Ross had inadvertently dubbed him, was having a field day on 125th Street, reveling in destruction. Sterling dropped to the floor of the Humvee, prying open a large compartment. "What are you doing?" said Jeffries.

"You think a rifle's gonna hurt *that*? Blonsky told me he put in some real ordnance." Sterling came up with a rocket propelled grenade launcher. "That's what I'm talking about!" He spun, flipped the sight up, flipped off the safety, and threw it on his shoulder. "Now say good night, Gracie."

He fired. The Abomination turned as the RPG hurtled down the street, trailing smoke, barreling straight toward his head. Without, it seemed, the slightest effort, the Abomination plucked the missile out of the air, studied it for a moment, and then crushed it against his head as if it were a beer can. The missile exploded and, when the smoke dissipated, there was no sign of any damage.

The distorted but still recognizable face of Emil Blonsky snarled out at them from the Abomination.

Jeffries gulped and then, fighting to keep his voice calm, announced, "Time to go."

Stockwell hit reverse and floored it as Jeffries and Hayes opened fire, Jeffries with his rifle and Hayes with his service revolver. Sterling dropped the rocket launcher and scrambled to find his previous weapon.

They maintained a sustained barrage as the Abomination charged straight at them, laughing off their bullets as if he were strolling through a light summer rain. He closed the distance between them with no apparent effort and caught up with them. Pounding his fist through the hood, he heaved it up. The Humvee was yanked into the air, and the occupants were thrown about with no option save to hang on desperately. He twisted it sideways and smashed it into the ground over and over. Metal, helmets, and bodies flew in every direction.

Jeffries had lost track of the others, had even lost track of feelings in his own body. He lay on the ground, staring upward, unable to move, unable to feel anything below the neck because he had landed heavily and wrong and was cursing himself for doing such a crap job of falling properly.

He stared straight up because there was nowhere else for him to look, and then the Abomination was leering down at him, raising his clawed fist high, about to bring it slamming down.

Jeffries tried to tell him that he should perform a reflexive sex act upon himself, but the words died in his throat.

Seconds later, so did everything else in his throat.

The monitor that had provided Jeffries's point of view to Ross fizzed out, replaced with static. There was silence in the Sikorsky that Banner saw as . . . what? Shocked? Respectful? Stunned? A man had just died before their eyes, and the only thing Banner knew for certain was that the soldier was going to have a lot of company on that score.

The comm officer turned to Ross and said, "General, NYPD wants to know what to use against it. SAC has that A-10 in the air and ready. What do you want me to tell them? Sir?"

Banner heard something then that he had never heard in the presence of Thunderbolt Ross: silence. He had never known the general to be at a loss for words, for orders, for opinions.

Now Ross simply stared at the monitor, saying nothing.

"Sir?" the comm officer prompted.

"Tell them . . ." Ross paused, then cleared his throat and started again. "Tell them to bring everything they've got and head for Harlem," said Ross. Then, softly, more to himself than anyone else, he added, "And God help them."

Then he turned and looked at Banner, his face grim. And suddenly, instantly, Banner knew. He knew that Ross was somehow directly responsible for the aptly named Abomination. Ross hadn't said anything, but he didn't have to say it. He'd come to know the general only too well.

And more . . . when Blonsky had been leaning over him, shouting at him in a crazed manner . . . well, Banner hated to admit it, but there was much that was familiar in that look. Blonsky had been begging for Banner to "show" him a creature capable of destroying Blonsky where he stood. It had been an insanely risky proposition, but Blonsky hadn't cared. In a dark, twisted and even sick way, Blonsky was not dissimilar from Banner, because Banner had likewise been willing to take tremendous risks in the pursuit of knowledge. The difference was that Banner had taken those risks for the betterment of mankind, whereas Blonsky was interested in doing so purely for self-gratification. He wanted

power for power's sake. For his own sake. In that respect, Blonsky wasn't all that different from Ross.

*Am I? Am I all that different? Am I just as power-
hungry as Ross and Blonsky, deep down, and I keep
telling myself that I'm somehow superior because I had
altruistic motives? Is altruism ever really the motive in
seeking power? Or is it just the excuse?*

*Face it, Bruce—you're just as responsible for what
Blonsky has become as Ross is. That's how you're able
to recognize in Ross's face that he had his hand in this.
You see yourself in that expression. And you can tell
yourself that you're the victim in all this, and that you
never intended for any of this to happen, none of that
matters a damn to the people down there who are suffering for it.*

"The sound waves stopped it at the campus," Betty
was saying. "They stopped Bruce."

Ross shook his head. "They need an open field of fire.
There's too much down there to absorb them. Too many
places to hide. Besides, you saw the impact the sound
waves had on the surrounding buildings. If Blonsky
doesn't bring skyscrapers crashing down, the sonic cannons would."

"You can't stop it," said Banner. "You have to take
me back there."

"No," said Ross, looking astounded that Banner
would even suggest such a thing.

"It's the only thing that can stop it," said Banner. "I'm
the only thing that can stop it."

Ross knew that Banner was right. He had to know.
But he was resistant to the idea in spite of himself, realizing only now the downsides to such a move. "Forget
it," said Ross. "If I put you down there you won't fight,
you'll run."

Banner leaned forward, his voice intense. There was

no time to pussyfoot around. He had to confront Ross with the truth they both knew and only Banner was willing to say. "We made that thing, you and I. There are people getting killed down there now. We've got to try *something*."

"You think you can control it?" said Betty.

"No, but maybe I can aim it. I think you were right." He looked at her hopefully. "I'm in there. I heard you on the table calling to me and I held on . . ."

"What if you just double my problem?" said Ross.

Banner hated to admit it, but it wasn't an unreasonable concern. He was staking a hell of a lot to beliefs, theories, and gut feelings. Nothing concrete. For a scientist who depended on charts, graphs, and measurable results upon which to base his next move, leaps of faith were not exactly his weapon of choice. But if Ross could ask reasonable questions, well, so could Bruce, and his was: "Have you got a better idea?"

Ross's mouth opened automatically, but then closed. He had no ready response and obviously he realized that it didn't matter how long he thought about it, he wasn't going to come up with anything better. Instead he turned to the pilot and the escort guard and called over the roar of the Sikorsky's engines, "Put us near it. Get those cuffs off him."

"No, stay high," said Banner. "And open the door. *Do it!*" He shouted that last when he saw Ross's confused expression.

Ross nodded and a soldier hit the release button. The huge rear ramp of the chopper started to hinge open, cool night air rushing in. Bruce moved toward the back, still in his wrist shackles. "Put me over it! Go higher!"

They surged upward, climbing, the city dropping away. Bruce looked out the open exit, the city sprawling three thousand feet below him.

It was only at that point that it seemed to dawn on Betty just what he had in mind. Perhaps it took so long because it was so unthinkable that she needed that amount of time to wrap herself around it. The moment she did, she was on her feet and running to him, pulling at his arm. "Oh my God, no, what are you doing? You don't even know if you'll turn!"

In all the time they'd spent together in the last days, it was the one thing that he hadn't been able to bring himself to tell her, wrapped up as it was in massive amounts of guilt. Guilt over what he had done to her, and guilt over the act of trying to commit suicide. "I tried to do this a long time ago, when I thought I'd killed you," said Bruce. "It wouldn't let me."

He saw the look on her face, the shock that he would do such a thing, that she would be the cause of it. It was a hell of an emotional bombshell to drop on her and then leave her side seconds later, but he had no choice.

He neared the ramp, precariously sloped. Betty seized some cargo netting with one hand to brace herself and grabbed him by the shackles that were still on his hands. He wasn't bothering to ask that he be released from them. There had never been any point to them; for Banner they were far too much, and for the Hulk they wouldn't be remotely enough. "This is too risky!" she cried out over the deafening rush of air that was combining with the racket of the craft's engines. "It's insane!"

He was hard put to disagree. "I know, but I have to try. I'm sorry." Never had those two words seemed quite as woefully inadequate to address a sea of emotions, but it was all he had. He took a deep breath, kissed her, pulled her hand off him, and fell backward out the ramp.

As he fell, his eyes squeezed tight. Air rushed past him and he waited, and he remembered belatedly the fact that one's body tends to flop around in free fall if one isn't, say, a trained parachutist, which he wasn't. He could snap his spine while waiting for the Hulk to make his triumphant appearance.

Plus there was the little matter of Sterns's treatment, designed to suppress the change. That, of course, was intended to work under ordinary circumstances. Plunging over half a mile was hardly ordinary.

Besides, Sterns's endeavors had been merely science. The Hulk, when you came right down to it, was a manifestation of Banner's survival instinct, hardwired into him through countless generations of human development. It made sense that the Hulk came across like something that had wandered the forest primeval; when man's ancient ancestors were first developing their will to endure in a savage and hostile environment, they were every bit as bestial as the Hulk. The Hulk, in the final analysis, was in everyone in some measure.

How very comforting. As gravity continued to exert its hold on him, and as the Hulk continued to present no interest in resurfacing, he thought bleakly, *Leap of faith, indeed.*

Betty had screamed at first as he fell. It was purely involuntary.

The only way she could deal with the next moments was to shut down all her emotional responses. She did just that, instead observing with the detachment of any scientist, even as her emotions howled within her for release.

She knew the height that the Sikorsky was hovering at. She knew that objects fell at thirty-two feet per second until they reached terminal velocity, the point at which (*Bruce, oh my God*) his body would cease to accelerate and reach its maximum speed. In Bruce's case, the rate at which terminal velocity would be attained would vary depending upon his body position (*Bruce, oh my God, dear God, please, Bruce*), tucked in as opposed to spread-eagled, and based on that she was counting down the seconds before he hit (*please, please, please*) and his form dwindled with horrifying rapidity until she could scarcely see him, and her internal countdown was approaching zero too quickly, much too quickly (*he's not going to make it, he's not going to*), and then she saw it, a small blur of green. He had transformed.

She sagged against the cargo netting and let out a choked sob, the detached scientist giving way to the relief that flooded through her.

It was only at that point that she gave consideration to the fact that Bruce's demise might only have been delayed by seconds, considering what he was about to confront. If God was indeed looking down and holding sway over all that was happening, had He only given Bruce a temporary reprieve? It seemed needless and cruel. Then again, sometimes she had to think that the only reason the Hulk existed was because God was endeavoring to punish Bruce for engaging in scientific arrogance.

If that's the case, God, and if you're listening, then lesson learned, okay? So how about you get behind the first, best chance that the people down there have for survival?

NINETEEN

What has Banner gotten us into now?

**People, stupid people, running, scream-
ing, so loud, so terrified for their own little
lives that mean nothing, make them all shut
up or we will shut them up . . .**

People were trying to get as far away from the bizarre
creature that was tearing through Manhattan with no
seeming priority other than to create destruction. No
one was paying attention to anyone else; it was the classic example of every man for himself.

Jimmy Ferguson was one of the people fleeing the
scene.

Little Jimmy hadn't been having a particularly good
few weeks.

His brother, Timmy, had been airlifted from their
Wisconsin home to a hospital in New York with a
strange name. It had taken Jimmy a while to be able to
remember "Sloan-Kettering." As Jimmy's mother had
explained it, Timmy had to be brought there because
something had gotten into his blood and was making his
blood sick, and this hospital was filled with doctors who
were really good at curing that type of illness.

The entire family had come out because there had
been no one to leave Jimmy with, and besides, his
mother had been determined that the family should stick
together. The hospital had been working hard on Jim-

my's older brother, and just this afternoon good news had been delivered by the doctors. They said that Timmy was in someplace that was apparently a good place to be, someplace called "Remission." Jimmy's mother had wept and thanked God, and Jimmy had as well, because the truth was that Jimmy had been feeling pretty guilty about the whole thing. Jimmy had been wishing that his tormenting brother would just go away and leave him alone forever right before he'd gotten sick, and so had felt a large measure of responsibility for Timmy's subsequent plight. Thus, when word had been received that Timmy was going to be just fine, Jimmy had been mightily relieved. He was off the hook.

But Jimmy's world had now gone insane when explosions had started being heard mere blocks from the run-down apartment of his aunt and uncle where he and his mom had been staying. They'd fled the building and Jimmy had become separated from them in the crowd. He had been running around, seemingly in a circle, trying to find a familiar face, and hadn't been looking in front of him when a thunderous crash had occurred that had brought him to a halt. He gazed in wonderment at a huge crater that hadn't been there moments earlier. It was akin to something that one would see on the surface of the moon.

He stared down into the crater and could have sworn that something was moving down there.

Suddenly a pair of arms grabbed him up. He twisted around and saw that it was a police officer. He tried to bring the cop's attention to whatever it was that was in the hole, but the cop seemed intent on hauling Jimmy out of there. This he managed to do, but as he did so—just as Jimmy was carted around a corner and away from the scene—he spotted a huge green fist and arm emerging from the crater, illuminated by sweeping police spotlights.

And there was a huge green body attached, coming up right behind it.

Lights, bright lights from everywhere, and sirens, everyone and everything screaming, have to make them stop, find why it's happening, what's making it happen, and smash it . . .

The Hulk let out a roar that thundered up and down the street, and the Abomination responded in kind, his eyes flaring in recognition upon confronting the ultimate object of his desire.

They charged toward each other like gamma-irradiated rhinos, accelerating with each second until they hit with the velocity of locomotives. The collision emitted a sound like a thunderclap and the sheer force of it blew out the glass and lights of the Apollo Theater's marquee, not to mention all the surrounding storefronts. The Hulk staggered backward, although only slightly, but the Abomination seized the opportunity to swing his arm in a clothesline move that knocked the Hulk flat.

The Hulk roared his fury and the Abomination crashed into him, lifting him off his feet. The Hulk pounded on the Abomination's back, the Abomination's hide quivering and shaking beneath each blow but otherwise not showing any effect.

Bringing his feet crashing down, the Hulk halted the Abomination's power drive at the intersection of Broadway and 122nd Street. The Abomination knocked the Hulk off his feet, but the Hulk dragged him down with him. They rolled, pounding on each other, snarling and bellowing mutual defiance, beating each other savagely.

The jagged bone that protruded from the Abomination's elbow slashed the Hulk's skin. The Hulk scarcely felt it, caught up as he was in the throes of battle, and his thunderous punches rattled off the Abomination's shell-like exterior. The Abomination grunted under each impact, but the Hulk's knuckles shredded every time he came into contact with the sharp edges of the Abomination's body.

Their out-of-control skid carried them right through a large truck that had been abandoned by its driver. The impact momentarily dazed the Abomination enough for the Hulk to throw his enemy off himself. The Hulk scrambled to his feet, just in time for a moving car—driven by a motorist who was trying to flee the area and failing spectacularly in the endeavor—to crash into the Hulk's legs. The car sustained major damage, the Hulk none at all. The Hulk and the Abomination charged each other once more, the Abomination throwing a huge roundhouse swing and the Hulk ducking under it. He was learning quickly, although he would not have been able to articulate how he was doing it. He was, as always, a creature of instinct.

The Hulk came in tight and pounded the Abomination in the ribs, but the Abomination swung a huge backhand blow that sliced the Hulk's chest with an elbow spike, hitting him so hard that it spun him around. The Abomination, pouncing on the opportunity, grabbed the Hulk by the back of his skull and smashed him facedown into the hood of a car. Lashing out with his foot, the Hulk got lucky, catching the Abomination square in the side and sending him flying. The Hulk tore his face off the car hood, leaving an imprint of his profile.

The Sikorsky dipped low over Harlem.

There was a camera mounted under the Sikorsky that was standard issue for observational purposes. Typically it was used to eye the ground for possible hostile fire from surface-to-air missiles, or for spying upon enemy encampments. Now the pilot was basically trying to monitor a running fight, and he was finding it somewhat challenging.

General Ross watched on the monitors. He called to Betty to join him, but she didn't come anywhere near him. Instead she was lying flat near the still-open ramp, her foot looped through the cargo net to anchor her, and watching out the back.

She saw the Hulk pounce on the Abomination, their arms locked and spread wide, each jockeying for leverage and trying to overpower the other. Then the Hulk drew his head back and head-butted the Abomination, staggering him. The Abomination fell backward onto the street, shattering asphalt beneath him.

Kneeling over him, the Hulk seized his enemy's protruding chest bones with his left hand, hauled him upward and smashed him fiercely in the face three times with his right fist. The Abomination yanked himself backward, hitting the street. Thinking he had the Abomination on the ropes, the Hulk lunged forward. It was a tactical mistake; the Abomination clearly had hoped to draw him in, and it worked. Curling up his legs, the Abomination got his feet up and under the Hulk's chest just as the Hulk landed on him, and then thrust upward. The Hulk was sent flying, waving his arms angrily and roaring his fury.

Betty gasped. The Hulk was hurtling through the air, up and across the roof of an apartment building. He clipped the corner of what appeared to be the shaft housing of an elevator, continued on his arc, then started to descend. He slammed into a fire escape, flattening it against the side of a building, and then tumbled away, leaving a wall that looked like an elephant had been shot into it with a cannon.

In the alleyway below, a Dumpster was flattened

when the Hulk landed hard on it. Then Betty watched as the Hulk got to his feet. She couldn't believe it. A human being would have had every bone in his body shattered from the impact. The Hulk just looked pissed off.

Then she shifted her attention to Blonsky. The Abomination was running down the street, clearly unsure of where the Hulk had landed. Perhaps to get some elevation so he could survey the area better, the Abomination sprang toward an apartment building and sank his hands into the brick wall. He started to climb, his fists digging in and creating makeshift handholds.

Ross ran to the gunnery officer. "Use that thing, dammit!" Ross said, indicating the officer's weaponry array. "Give him some help!"

The confused gunner's sights, aided by the Sikorsky's mounted camera, shifted from one oversized target to the other. "Which one?"

"That big son of a bitch climbing the wall, which one do you think? Now cut him apart!"

The huge gunship cannon started blasting, tracer fire streaking through the darkness and pounding into the side of the building around the Abomination.

Major Sparr, battered and shaken, limped out of the ESU science building, scarcely able to credit what had happened.

When she had been struck from behind, she had barely had time to register—as she lay on her back—that Blonsky was standing over her with his gun in hand and his gun butt smeared with her blood. Then she had lapsed into unconsciousness. When she awoke she had discovered nothing but body after body—Sterns, then her own soldiers, but no sign of Blonsky. Upon learning that there was a monstrosity stampeding around the vicinity, she had managed to figure out pretty quickly who it was and informed the general of such.

Now she discovered that the Humvee was gone, and she had no means of transportation. Wondering where the hell she should go next, she was about to try to raise the general when she stopped and heard the sound of rotors and cannon fire—both unquestionably originating from the Sikorsky.

It was hard to be certain exactly where they were coming from, because the city was a canyon of steel and glass and noises tended to echo. She made her best guess and started moving.

Betty watched as the Abomination climbed over the edge of the roof while cannon rounds streaked at him. Many of them hit home, staggering him, wounding him. Some glanced off the bones like plates that covered him, but others ripped into his flesh and caused purplish blood to seep into view. He sprinted across the roof, the Sikorsky tracking with him.

A water tower sat on the roof a short distance away and the Abomination was heading straight for it. Betty, prone on the ramp, saw the Abomination's goal and instantly understood the danger. She craned her neck around and shouted for the Sikorsky to get some elevation, to back off. But between the roar of the rotors and the thundering of the cannon, her voice was lost.

The Hulk, meantime, shook himself off like a dog shedding water and then started bouncing up the sides of both buildings, gaining altitude.

Rebounding off the remains of the fire escape and crushing a cornice as he went, the Hulk pulled himself up over the lip of the building. Betty saw him looking up, watching the bullets rebounding off the Abomination, who was standing a distance away.

Suddenly the Abomination was at the water tower,

ripping a steel girder out from beneath it. Bullets clanged into the girder as he heaved it up, balancing it like a javelin. The Hulk looked up toward the chopper and it was entirely possible that he wouldn't have given a damn what happened to it. But then Betty saw the Hulk spot her, saw the muddled but intact mind of Bruce Banner noticing her in imminent danger, and instantly he was sprinting across the roof toward the Abomination.

Just as the Abomination hurled his makeshift missile, the Hulk hit him broadside with an impact that any NFL tackle would have envied. It was enough to throw the Abomination's aim off slightly, and the launched girder missed the main rotor of the chopper by inches. Had he succeeded, it likely would have caused the vehicle to explode. As it was, it clipped one of the blades of the tail rotor. The chopper immediately started to whip out of control.

"I can't hold it!" shouted the pilot. "I gotta put it down! *Hang on!*"

Betty was hurled across the tail ramp, her prescient anchoring of herself to the cargo netting being the only thing that prevented her from tumbling headlong out of the chopper.

The impact of the Hulk into the Abomination had sent the both of them flying, hurtling in an arc that just barely caused them to miss the underside of the plunging helicopter. She had a glimpse of them crashing to the ground in a plaza below, built with a neoclassical design, and then she lost sight of them as the helicopter barely cleared one building, clipped the side of a large university hall, and then crashed into the very same plaza that the Hulk and Abomination had landed in.

The impact ripped the cargo netting from the wall, sending Betty hurtling toward the front of the cabin. The timing could not have been more fortuitous; as the tail rotor sheared off against the side of the building, the rear ramp was smashed like a crushed can.

Betty where is Betty stupid monster stopping us from getting to Betty smashing us against wall must stop him kill him smash him . . .

The Abomination pounded the Hulk against a marble wall, like a boxer hammering his opponent against the ropes.

The Hulk tried to shove himself away from the wall. When he wasn't able to, he did the next best thing; he dragged the Abomination toward him, hauling him into a furious clinch, their faces inches from each other, teeth bared with the strain. The Abomination's massive right forearm was pinned against Hulk's throat, his elbow spike driving down into the flesh of the Hulk's chest above his heart. The wall cracked behind Hulk's head as the Hulk thrust out with his left hand, gripping the Abomination's head and trying to pull him back, while his right arm strained against the Abomination's left.

Betty was disoriented, and realized that the shattered helicopter had rolled onto its side. She twisted around, looking toward the front, and saw that the pilots had been crushed. The gunner was slumped, unconscious, the cannon bent at a right angle. The comm major had been flattened by a monitor that had exploded out from the wall upon impact.

Battered and bruised, but thankful that she was at least alive, Betty picked herself up and then saw her father pinned under a bent chair, struggling to free himself. Immediately she moved to him in order to try to pull it loose.

He waved her off. "I'm all right! Find a way out! Go! *Go!*" he said when she hesitated.

She tried to see some sort of means of escape, and the only one she could spot was the small door out of which the gunner had been firing his cannon. She moved toward it.

Then she heard what sounded like a series of small explosions and realized that it was coming from the shattered tail assembly. Sparks were bursting in cascades from it. As Betty shoved up against the unconscious gunner, trying to get out the exit, she saw sparks from the demolished rotor flying closer and closer to the huge side gas tanks, torn open and with gasoline dripping from them.

Stuck between the bent gun and the door frame, Betty saw the Hulk and Abomination struggling against the far wall. With an explosion imminent, she screamed, *"Bruce!"*

Betty needs us calling us stupid bone man is stopping us we will stop him for good forever . . .

Betty saw additional size and strength surge into existence before her eyes. The Hulk seized the Abomination's wrists and slowly spread Blonsky's arms wide. Confusion and shock registered on the Abomination's face, not understanding how one second he had had the Hulk more or less on the ropes and the next the tide of battle had inexorably shifted.

The Hulk drove a knee up into his enemy's ribs, doubling the Abomination over, and then seized his back spines and drove him headfirst into the wall. As the Abomination sagged against it, the Hulk turned and left him there, vaulting toward the downed chopper.

He was still a few feet away when the sparks hit the gas tank, and it was at that moment, when the chopper's eruption was now inevitable, that Betty came to the surprising realization that—even if she could get clear, which she now would not be able to do—she couldn't live with the knowledge that she had abandoned her father. *That's a hell of a thing to learn.*

And then, just as the flames roared up from the gas tank, literally in mid-explosion, the Hulk slammed his hands with thunderous force, blowing Betty's hair back, and then just as quickly yanked his hands apart. Betty was suddenly gasping, unable to breathe, and she realized immediately why—by bringing his hands together and then pulling them apart just as quickly, and with such power, he had created a localized vacuum. The initial burst of flame was snuffed out before it could fully roar to life, and before it could reignite, the Hulk had reached it and yanked away the sparking tail rotor, sending it flying. A few flames started to burn around the gas tank, but the Hulk blew them out with no more force than a child would have required to snuff out a birthday cake candle.

Then Betty gasped as nature, abhorring a vacuum as it traditionally did, caused air to flood back into the area. She breathed deeply, gratefully, and the first words out of her mouth to the Hulk were, "Wow. Thanks."

The Hulk glowered at her for a moment, as if having to remind himself who she was and what she meant to him.

Bruce Banner's smile played along the Hulk's lips.

"Watch out!" Betty suddenly screamed, but it was too late.

The Hulk took a tremendous blow to the side of the head, knocking him off his feet. He tried to rise, looking dazed, and saw that the Abomination had ripped away a length of chain that had hung suspended between two marble posts, symbolizing the link of one academic generation to another or some damned stupid thing that some sculptor had put in there because he thought it would be clever, never allowing for the notion that some demented monster might use it as a weapon against the man she loved. *Some people never think ahead,* Betty mused before realizing just how insane that sounded, even to her.

The Abomination had used the chain as a club, having caught the Hulk off guard once and now endeavoring to press his advantage. His eyes glinted, sensing victory. The Hulk tried to rise, battered, on one knee.

"Betty! Go!" It was Ross, having freed himself from his brief imprisonment by a chair, and he was now pulling aside the bent gun so that Betty could get herself clear of the door. Betty popped out of the ship like a champagne cork from a bottle, and then turned and helped her father clamber out. Even as she helped her father, she turned to see what was happening.

The Abomination wound up for a final blow as the Hulk, crouched, raised his fists high above his head and drove them into the ground, generating a concussion so powerful that it blew a crevice right through the middle of the plaza. The violent force knocked the Abomination off balance. He staggered and his foot sank into the newly created fissure in the ground. Even as he fell, he still tried to lash out with his makeshift bludgeon at the Hulk, but the chain arced over the Hulk's head, missing clean. The Hulk snatched the chain out of the Abomination's grasp, dove and rolled past his enemy's flailing arm, and came up behind him. The Abomination tried to move around to get at him, but his leg was still stuck in the fissure. Given a few moments, he could have gotten the leverage to yank it free, but the Hulk didn't provide them. Instead he wrapped the chain around the Abomination's neck once, twice, and then heaved back on it. The Hulk twisted him against his trapped leg, applying an horrendous amount of torque upon the twisted and mutated body of Emil Blonsky. The Abomination tried to resist, and even looked to Betty as if he might succeed.

People who had fled the area were now slowly making their way back, watching with horror at this struggle between behemoths. "Which one's the Hulk?" one person shouted, and Betty—to her shock—heard her father call back, "The one who's winning! The one who's here to save your asses!"

The Abomination's hand flailed behind him, tearing at the Hulk's face and shoulders, cutting flesh, gouging at the Hulk's eyes. The Hulk didn't flinch. Instead he looped the chain around so that both ends were held tightly in his left hand. With his right, he grabbed hold of one of the elbow spikes, snapped it clean off, and drove the point deep into the Abomination's chest.

The creature that had been Emil Blonsky made choking, gurgling noises. He reeled, and the Hulk chose that moment to lift one foot and plant it squarely between the Abomination's shoulders. He pressed out with his leg, rearing back and up on the chain with his shoulders and arms. He howled, every vein bursting.

The Abomination's eyes rolled up into his head. He slumped, went limp, and Betty knew that he could have been faking it, but she didn't believe that to be the case. He didn't seem much the type for subterfuge. The Hulk had cut off his air, and no matter how powerful he might have been, he still needed to breathe.

But the Hulk was still applying pressure, unknowing or even worse, uncaring that the Abomination had nothing left. He was going to kill him, that much was certain.

Despite everything she had seen the Abomination do, despite however much he might have deserved the fate that the Hulk obviously intended for him, she couldn't stand by and allow it to happen. "Bruce!" she cried out, and again, "Bruce!"

It caught the Hulk's attention, and he turned and looked at her balefully. The Abomination hung there, like a mouse from the jaws of a cat.

"Don't do it," she said. "It will be his actions . . . the Hulk's actions . . . but on your conscience. Please, I'm begging you, for both your sakes: don't kill him. Don't erase the difference between the two of you, or you really will be a monster. Please . . ."

She was positive that she was wasting her time, but something in the Hulk's eyes seemed to glimmer for just a moment. Then he relaxed his hold on the Abomination. The creature that had once been Emil Blonsky slid from the Hulk's grasp, fell to the street, and lay there motionless.

Then the Hulk turned his head slowly, fiercely, scanning the faces of the people watching him for any new threat, mutely challenging anyone else to come at him.

There was a long moment of awestruck silence.

And then one person shouted, "Hulk!" and then "Hulk! Hulk!" over and over again.

The chant was picked up, resounding throughout the audience, and people were clapping and shouting and applauding. Betty saw the Hulk wince from the noise, but he must have somehow sensed that it wasn't intended as threatening and so endured it. Soldiers and police officers who had arrived upon the scene, weapons at the ready—as if those would have done a bit of good—put them away, and they joined in the cheers and ovations from all around.

The Hulk remained right where he was for a few moments. Betty surveyed the damage he had sustained, the wounds and gouges in his body, the rivulets of dark green blood. But they were already beginning to heal. Then the Hulk slowly began to approach her. A soldier standing near General Ross started to raise his gun but Ross quickly waved him down. "Don't even think about it," her father said.

Betty stepped forward to meet the Hulk's advance. There was no trace of fear within her. "Shhh. It's over. It's over."

And then, to her astonishment, in a voice barely above a whisper—a voice that stood in staggering contrast to the brutish body it inhabited—the Hulk said, "Betty."

She gasped when she heard it. A tear rolled down her cheek, the precursor of many tears to come, and the Hulk caught the wetness on a huge outstretched finger. His eyes were almost drooping. He looked exhausted.

Out of nowhere, there was the beating of rotors. It was a police helicopter, with blazing light beating down from a spotlight.

The Hulk flinched, shielded his eyes, and roared. The very presence of the noisy chopper, the intensity of the lights, were probably more painful to him than the beating he had sustained at the Abomination's hands.

The Hulk ran, trying to distance himself from the oncoming chopper.

Sparr heard the applause, the shouts, and as crazy as it seemed, the word "Hulk!" being shouted over and over again. *Whole city is insane,* she thought. Then she saw a police helicopter pass overhead, heading toward the source of the shouting. She felt safer the instant she saw it.

She limped around a corner just in time to see the Hulk barreling straight toward her.

"You gotta be kidding me," moaned Sparr, and then frantically hit the deck as the Hulk hurdled right over her.

Tired of fighting tired always more trying to fight us coming after us alone alone why can't they just *leave us alone*.

The Hulk's eyes were set straight forward, focused, determined. A new level of power surged through him as he ran, building up speed, the city flying past him as he moved, his massive arms and legs pumping.

He exploded out of the side streets into Riverside Park, the police helicopter continuing to pursue him. He charged through the trees, pushing them aside, trunks snapping like toothpicks as he passed. He vaulted onto the West Side Highway and continued to run, snarling and pushing himself even harder. The Hudson River lay to his right, and then with a final burst of speed he springboarded off the highway and leaped, soaring away into the dark.

The helicopter banked in pursuit, and the pilot of the helicopter relayed back to headquarters a communication that would become immortalized in the newspapers the next morning: *"The bastard's trying to jump over the Hudson! And he might just make it!"*

He didn't.

The leap from his powerful legs was sufficient to carry him about half a mile through the air, but then his altitude began to deteriorate and—well short of the Jersey shore—the Hulk plunged into the water.

The police chopper circled his point of entry, the searchlight bathing the area in light. Once the water ceased surging, the only thing that remained to give any indication of the Hulk's presence was a column of bubbles rising up from the inky blackness of the river. Slowly, even those dissipated. The chopper continued to circle the area for an hour, waiting for some sign of the Hulk resurfacing.

None came. The Hulk was gone.

EPILOGUE

General Ross sat on a bar stool at the military base, thinking over all that had happened in the past weeks.

The arrival of Tony Stark in the aftermath of the fight—which the press had dubbed "The Battlin' in Manhattan"—could not have been more timely. He had shown up in a high-powered chopper, equipped with containment shackles the likes of which Ross had never seen. Stark had coolly claimed to have thrown them together after the news reports of the debacle at Culver, "just in case." His foresight had been fortuitous, and thanks to Stark, the Abomination was now safely ensconced in a high-tech holding facility that Stark had nicknamed "the Vault." Stark had said grimly, "Trust me . . . the way things have been going lately, you're going to have more use for this facility than you could possibly believe."

Ross had the uncomfortable feeling that Stark was absolutely correct.

Congress had announced committee hearings that were going to be launched to investigate every aspect of what had happened. Ross's involvement was probably going to wind up being center stage, the main ring in the media circus.

He found himself oddly uncaring.

He lifted his drink to his lips and stared at his reflection in a mirror behind the bar. Slowly he lowered the glass and stared at it.

He had aided in the creation of Banner's creature accidentally. He had participated in the creation of Blonsky's creature knowingly . . . happily . . . eagerly.

Thaddeus Ross stopped wondering what sort of monsters he had created, and instead pondered what type of monster he himself was to have created them. He regarded his reflection thoughtfully and tried to see his own creature within peering out at him.

He didn't see anything. But he suspected that if he looked long enough, he might catch a glimpse of it.

Leonard Samson sat on the front steps of his house.

Their house.

No . . . *his* house. He had a feeling that it was now simply his house.

That hadn't stopped him from calling steadily, day in, day out. He had left so many voice mail messages that her voice mailbox was full and accepting no more. So now he was reduced to just calling and hoping and praying.

He hit the Redial button. There was a pause and then it rang. It reached the fourth ring and he was prepared to disconnect and try again, just as he had countless times before, and then he heard something entirely unexpected.

"Hi."

He paused, confused, having forgotten for a moment that the whole purpose of a telephone was to have a conversation.

"Oh thank God," he said "You're all right! When I couldn't reach you . . ."

"I'm not hurt. A lot of people were, though."

"I know, it's been all over the TV. It doesn't seem real."

There was a pause on the other end. Finally she said, "It was real."

"Come home. Just come home."

Another pause. Longer. She was struggling to say something and he was about to switch into psychiatrist mode, to probe her feelings, and then her voice—broken slightly by static—said, "Samson, did you call somebody the night Bruce was at our home? Is that why they came for him?"

Lie to her. Tell her no. Tell her anything it takes to get her home and save the truth for when she's in front of you.

He was about to do it. About to tell her that he had no clue what she was talking about. But he couldn't.

Instead he said, "I was frightened. Forgive me."

She surprised him when she said, "I do." *Now who's lying?* Then she continued, "But I'm not coming home yet."

"Where are you going?"

"I have no idea. But I'll let you know when I do. I promise."

She hung up.

Leonard Samson stared at the phone. The wallpaper that he kept on it returned with the call concluded. It was a photo of Betty smiling out at him.

The phone slipped from his suddenly numb fingers, and he covered his face with his hands and began to sob softly.

Betty closed her cell phone and figured that that would be the last she heard from Leonard Samson for a while.

Bruce had known. He had known that Samson had betrayed them. It had just taken her a while to read between the lines of his cautious inquiries. And yet, Bruce had respected the relationship that Betty had with Samson to such a degree that he had refrained from pushing too much. That showed the kind of man he was.

Is. Man he is.

Betty had not lied outright to Samson; she had just exaggerated a bit. She had not forgiven him, but she hoped that, in time, she would be able to.

But not now. Not yet. Not for a while.

She was standing in Battery Park, leaning on a railing that was overlooking the river and the New York harbor. A ferry tugged out toward the Statue of Liberty. Tall. Massive. Green.

She tore open the envelope that had been waiting for her at the front desk of the cheap hotel she'd been staying at. She had a feeling she knew what was in it, and she turned out to be correct.

Her mother's locket fell into her open palm.

"Incredible," she murmured. Then she looked back out at the harbor, trying to imagine where he was, and wondering if he was thinking of her.

Somehow she had no doubt that he was.

A bull moose was standing knee-high in the marsh grasses along a lake, deep in the Canadian woods.

Bruce Banner stood at the end of an old, rotted deck and regarded the moose with considerably less curiosity than the moose that was looking at him. He waved to the moose. The moose did not wave back.

Banner then turned and walked back into the abandoned cabin where he had taken up residence. He wondered, not for the first time, what had happened to the owner or owners. Had they died? Had it been used for illegal purposes and the owners were in jail? So many possibilities, but ultimately what it came down to was— decrepit and rotting as it may have been—it was at least a roof over his head. A roof with holes in it, granted, but a roof.

He figured that Betty must have received the locket by now. It hadn't been all that difficult to find her: she had used her credit card to check in at a hotel in New York. That had enabled Banner to track her down, call the hotel, make certain she was still registered, and overnight the locket to her.

It had not been easy, making his way back to that pawn shop, picking up money along the way where he could through fair means and foul, before being able to liberate the necklace from the pawnbroker.

It was odd: In three years of wandering, the notion of reuniting with Betty had seemed a pipe dream. The only hope presented to him was that of a cure held out by Mr. Blue. Now Mr. Blue was gone. All hope should have been gone. And yet, just the knowledge that after three years, and after everything they had been through, Betty still loved him . . .

That was hope enough.

Later . . .

He sat in a lotus position, meditating, wearing black pants and no shirt. The cabin was no longer around him, at least in his mind's eye. Instead he saw himself seated on a beach, with the ocean slowly rolling toward him in great waves.

For so long now, he had been working on controlling himself as Bruce Banner. On remaining calm. Because he had felt that it was only as Bruce Banner that he *could* maintain control. But his experience in New York had made him realize otherwise, because he had studied the film footage, read the copious accounts of all that had transpired, which had been readily available courtesy of governmental hearings.

And he had come to a realization:

The Hulk was an unreasoning beast that believed only in smashing. But he had snuffed out a flame by creating a vacuum. That required scientific knowledge the Hulk simply did not possess.

And he had not slain the Abomination because Betty had appealed, not to the monster, but to the man within.

For those two instances, for however fleeting a time it might have been, Bruce Banner had been in control, somewhere in the deep recesses of the Hulk's mind.

If he could be in control of the beast for a few seconds . . . why not a few minutes? Or hours?

It would mean that he could stop living in fear.

And some part of him chimed in and said, *Yes. Make the puny humans live in fear instead.*

Once, such a notion would have repulsed him.

Now, as his pulse ticked along at a sedate forty-two, it sounded . . .

. . . attractive.

His pulse began to speed up. Within seconds it had raced to over two hundred. His eyes snapped open, glowing green, and he smiled someone else's smile . . .